Okay, she es[timated good] looks and charm. *Big deal.* Was she expected to swoon? Maybe the old Katrice would have remained silent and slightly mesmerized, but the new Katrice reached deep inside and forced herself to speak her mind. She lifted her chin slightly and replied in a voice that didn't sound as solid as she might have liked. "Listen, I'm not sure what you have in mind, but I'm not some country bumpkin who gets weak in the knees at the sight of a handsome face nor am I a shrinking violet incapable of taking care of business all by myself. What I am is a busy woman who has a lot to accomplish in a very short period of time. So, if you don't mind . . ."

Lee smiled and Katrice noticed a fain dimple appear in one cheek. Katrice sighted every so slightly a swallowed the rising lump in her throat.

Handsome had just clicked up a notch to *absolutely gorgeous.*

A PLACE LIKE HOME

ALICIA WIGGINS

Genesis Press, Inc.

INDIGO LOVE STORIES

An imprint of Genesis Press, Inc.
Publishing Company

Genesis Press, Inc.
P.O. Box 101
Columbus, MS 39703

Copyright © 2009 by Alicia Wiggins

ISBN: 13 DIGIT : 978-1-58571-336-3
ISBN: 10 DIGIT : 1-58571-336-8
Manufactured in the United States of America

First Edition

Visit us at www.genesis-press.com
or call at 1-888-Indigo-1-4-0

DEDICATION

As always I want to thank my sibs, aunts, uncles, nieces, nephews, and cousins for your support, encouragement, and inspiration.

Brantley, Elliot and Alexandria, I am so proud of the three of you and I think it's cool that you're proud of me, too.

Thanks Cousin Debbie for your input and keen eye.

Vickie Cordle, thanks for introducing me to the "wormy smell."

Burch, after all these years you're still one of the very best friends and I've accepted the fact that you think I'm weird (the good weird not the crazy weird).

Last, but not least, thanks to the readers and booksellers who continue to support my work!

CHAPTER 1

"Can't sleep?"

The sound of his father's voice drew Lee away from his wandering thoughts.

"Just a little restless, that's all. Probably just having a hard time getting used to all the peace and quiet around here. I know Columbus, Ohio, doesn't quite measure up to the likes of Chicago or New York, but there has been quite a bit of development near us and the traffic and noise have increased accordingly." Lee closed the magazine he'd been flipping through but not really reading.

"Funny, I thought the whole point of your coming here for the summer was so that you could relax and unwind. That stuff isn't going to help you do that," he said, nodding at his son's third cup of coffee.

"Trust me, I am trying to relax. I think the problem is that my body is in vacation mode, but my mind hasn't caught up just yet. Coffee is just one of many bad habits that I need to kick this summer."

Unsure of what was bothering his son, Sam didn't force the issue because he knew from experience an explanation would be forthcoming. He poured himself a cup of coffee and joined Lee at the kitchen table.

Lee looked from his father to the cup of coffee he'd just poured.

Sam shrugged. "I figure one cup won't hurt."

Father and son sat quietly, both wanting to speak but not quite sure what to say. The clock above the stove seemed to be ticking in synch with the low hum of the refrigerator's motor. The loud chirping of crickets could be heard through the open kitchen window.

In the continuing quiet, Sam sipped his coffee while Lee pretended to read his magazine, eventually pushing away from the table and going over to the sink. His head slightly bent, his shoulders drooping, he stared out the window into the darkness.

"The drive here today reminded me of how much I miss Paulette."

Sam knew all too well the expression Lee wore, even without the benefit of seeing his face. In the three years since the death of his son's wife, he had seen it in one form or another many times.

"Lee, there will always be memories. There's no getting around that. You lost someone you loved deeply, and that kind of love doesn't just go away. Take comfort in the fact that you and Paulette had thirteen wonderful years together. And don't forget you have a beautiful daughter, even if she does try your patience every chance she gets."

Now leaning with his back against the counter, Lee sighed. "I know that, Dad. I remind myself of that all the time, and it does give me comfort."

Sam just listened, giving his son room to be as open as he wanted to be.

"But?"

Lee smiled. As always, his father had looked beyond his words, forcing him to reveal what was in his heart.

"How can I explain this? I've had kind of a revelation over the past week or so."

"What kind of revelation?"

"There's not going to be another Paulette for me," he announced matter-of-factly.

Sam said nothing for a moment and then asked, "Would you answer one question for me?"

Lee nodded yes, even as he considered whether or not to tell his father about his latest failed attempt at a relationship. At least he would have a better understanding of why he had come to such a conclusion. On the other hand, the experience had lasted less than two weeks and hardly seemed worth mentioning.

"Are you looking for another Paulette?"

The question didn't surprise Lee, but he thought carefully about his answer before replying. "I guess if I had to be truthful, I'd say no. But, if I really thought about it and was honest with myself, my answer might be a strong maybe."

"I take it you haven't been very successful in your search."

Lee made a sound that only slightly resembled a laugh. "That's an understatement."

"So what does that tell you?"

"I know. You don't have to say it. I'm a fool."

"No, I wouldn't necessarily say that. But I do think you're setting yourself up for disappointment, not to mention placing anyone you might be serious about at a disadvantage if she has to compete with a memory."

"Believe it or not, I've told myself that already. But I can't help subconsciously comparing other women to Paulette. Most of the time I don't even know I'm doing it."

"Give it time, Lee. If it's meant for you to be in a meaningful relationship, it'll happen. Don't try to force it."

His hands raised in protest, Lee quickly replied, "Wait, Dad. I'm not looking to settle down or anything like that. It would just be nice to have a little adult companionship from time to time. I miss that more than I ever thought I would."

"Sounds like a bad case of loneliness."

"More than anything, I think I'm just in a rut. Every day I get up, send Ky off to school, go to work, we come home and the next day do it all over again. I go from one task to another like a robot. It's becoming increasingly more difficult to separate one day from the next. My job has turned into just a job, nothing more. My days, and most weekends, are spent working on a steady stream of mundane cases. I don't even find comfort in relaxing at home anymore. It has become a place where Kyra and I eat, sleep, and keep our belongings. For the first time in years I have accumulated so much vacation time that my boss ordered me to use it or lose it. How sad is that? I think I'm forgetting how to relax and just enjoy life."

"Why is that?"

Lee shrugged. "I guess I've been spending a lot of time at work, for one. My boss increased my caseload a few months ago. Two attorneys and a paralegal quit around that same time."

Sam nodded. "Kyra mentioned something about that."

"She did?"

"The part about your spending a lot of time at work. She also said that she's not very happy that she has had to spend so much time with a babysitter."

That surprised Lee. He thought Kyra loved Mrs. Carter. She was an older woman he had hired as their housekeeper and part-time babysitter after Paulette died. The woman was an outstanding cook, a meticulous housekeeper, and looked after Kyra as if she were her own flesh and blood.

Then understanding dawned.

"That's probably one of the reasons our relationship has been so prickly lately. Since the teenaged drama queen and I don't have normal conversations anymore, this is all news to me."

Lee sighed and continued. "Some kind of father I've turned out to be, huh? My own daughter can't, or won't, talk to me about things that bother her. We've developed quite a routine, though: Kyra snaps at me; I snap back. She does something to irritate me, on purpose. I confine her to her room. No real conversation or meaningful interaction, just angry words. Instead of living together as father and daughter, we seem to be existing as two people who can barely tolerate each other. But the thing I hate most about our lives now is that Kyra is growing up without her mother. This is the time when she needs her the most and, quite frankly, I'm not what mothers are made of."

Nodding in agreement, Sam said, "That's true, but only up to a point. You're forgetting something very important. She needs her father, too. Don't discount all that you have to offer that child. I know it's tough that she doesn't have a mother, but she has one heck of a father."

"Is that your opinion or Kyra's?"

"You already know I'm proud of you and think that you're a wonderful father. And as far as Kyra is concerned, I'm sure our opinions are very similar."

"Thanks, Dad. Sometimes I need a little encouragement."

"Hey, that's what I'm here for. I can appreciate that things are a bit strained for you and Kyra right now, but you're going to be just fine."

Returning to the table, Lee joked, "Did you look into your crystal ball and see that?"

"Didn't need to. With age comes wisdom, or so I'm told. Just believe me when I say that you're a lot closer than you think to bringing about calm and a new sense of normalcy in your life. In fact, I sense you are at a crossroad."

"I don't understand. What kind of crossroad? I can't handle any major changes in my life right now and I don't think Kyra can, either."

"Lee, I think there is a part of you that is ready to move on to another phase of your life. At the same time, there's a part that is struggling to hold on to the past. Afraid to let go, maybe."

"Move on to what?"

"Your house, for instance. Do you remember why you bought it?"

"Of course. Paulette fell in love with it. She said it was the perfect house for us as a family and that it would be filled with lots of kids, laughter, and love. Wait. Are you suggesting that I sell our house because it reminds me of Paulette?"

"Hmm, I notice you didn't say *home*. Didn't you just say a few minutes ago that it doesn't feel like home anymore?"

Lee nodded reluctantly.

"Just an observation. Think you can handle a little more advice from your old man?"

"Anything to help me get a sense of direction."

"You have a beautiful daughter who, despite her desire to drive you crazy, loves you with all her heart. Keep loving her back and let her know that she's special. Despite your concerns, Kyra is a lot stronger than you give her credit for. If it's change that is needed in your lives, I truly believe she can handle it." Sam walked over to the sink and rinsed out his coffee cup. He had said all he needed to say for now, but offered a final thought before leaving, "One more thing, Lee. You're a good man, a great father, and were a pretty good husband to Paulette. I don't want to see you spend the rest of your life alone because you're afraid to let go of the past."

CHAPTER 2

The aromas of bacon and cinnamon wafted upstairs and into Lee's room, gently rousing him from what had been the most peaceful night's rest he'd had in months. Used to rising before the sun, he was a little surprised to see the bright sunlight streaming into the room. Checking the clock on the nightstand, he smiled when the digital readout showed ten-sixteen.

After washing his face and brushing his teeth, Lee went downstairs to see what was smelling so good. His stomach growling in anticipation, he walked into the kitchen and was surprised to see Kyra at the stove wearing an apron and sporting a pair of oven mitts. *Could she actually be cooking? She never helped him cook or showed any interest in learning.*

Hearing his footsteps, Sam looked up from the newspaper. "Vonda, look who finally decided to join the living."

Emerging from the pantry with a jar of homemade strawberry jam, Lavonda Griggs immediately wrapped Lee in a warm hug. Vonda had always been referred to as Sam's friend, even though Lee and his brothers speculated that their relationship had long since surpassed mere friendship. Whatever the case, Lee knew that Vonda was good to his dad and good for him.

"I swear, Sam, if this boy gets any more handsome, I might have to marry him myself."

Kyra rolled her eyes and made a gagging sound.

Grinning lopsidedly, Lee bent down and kissed Vonda's cheek.

"It's good to see you, Miss Vonda. I was wondering when you would get by to see us. I kind of expected you to come by last night. Dad grilled up quite a feast."

"I wanted to, but I had to close at the shop last night. Seems like it took forever before I could leave."

"Don't worry, there'll be more than one occasion to fire up that grill this summer," Sam offered.

After helping Kyra spread icing on a pan of freshly baked cinnamon rolls and pouring Lee a cup of coffee, Vonda filled him in on life in Benton Lake and the goings-on in her own family. "Bacon and eggs?" she asked over her shoulder.

Lee looked at his dad, who said, "Not me. She's talking to you. We had breakfast already. I'm just sitting here waiting for those cinnamon rolls Vonda and Kyra made."

"Bacon and eggs sounds good. Need any help?"

Vonda steered Lee to the table and ordered him to sit down and drink his coffee. "We got this," she said, winking at Kyra.

Vonda handed Kyra a glass bowl and showed her how to carefully crack the eggs to avoid getting pieces of shell in the bowl.

Lee watched as Kyra listened attentively to Vonda, following her every direction. If he had tried to show her how to make scrambled eggs an argument would have ensued, ending with all shell and no egg in the bowl and Kyra stomping off in a huff.

"When did the Greens sell their land for that new housing development I saw coming into town?"

Vonda turned from the stove and answered before Sam had a chance to. "They're semi-retired and spend most of their time in Florida now. Mr. Green has gotten on in years and can't handle the harsh winters here. The youngest son decided he didn't want to farm all that land and sold off a large part of it to some developers from Cleveland. It's a shame if you ask me. That land has been in their family for over a hundred years, I've heard."

"What about the bakery? How long has it been closed?"

"It has been closed for a long time but hadn't been placed on the market until the end of last year. I think it was only for sale about a month or two before someone bought it," Sam explained.

"A young woman bought it," Vonda added. "I think she's turning it into some kind of coffeehouse."

"Might be a little too fancy for Benton Lake if you ask me," Sam offered. "We may be a small town, but I don't think anyone is going to get too excited about buying overpriced, fancy coffee that takes five minutes to pronounce."

Kyra placed a plate of scrambled eggs, toast, and bacon in front of her father. "Tell me how you like the eggs, Dad."

Lee smiled up at his daughter and felt his heart melt. Did she actually care what he thought? He speared a forkful of eggs, chewed slowly, and then looked back up at Kyra, who was eagerly awaiting his verdict.

"These have got to be the best eggs I've ever eaten in my life." He was slightly exaggerating, but the eggs really were pretty good, not too dry or runny.

Kyra turned to Vonda and smiled. For a few minutes she had transformed into the sweet daughter with the quick smile and an eagerness to please.

"Miss Vonda showed me how to use that wiry thing to whip the eggs, and she told me to wait until they started to cook a little before adding the cheese. We put a dash of pepper in them, too."

"Looks like I'm going to have to enroll you in Miss Vonda's school of cooking so we'll have at least one person in the house who can make meals fit to eat."

Pleased with herself, Kyra went to the sink to help Vonda clean up. "Dad, can we go to the mall in Fairlawn today?"

"For what?"

"I accidentally left some of my stuff at home."

Lee was about to take a bite of toast, but stopped in midair when he heard his father chuckle after exchanging glances with Vonda.

"So that was your plan all along. Butter me up with a good breakfast and then drop the shopping bomb. Very clever, little girl."

Kyra didn't think her father's joke was funny and quick as a flash turned on her heels and said, "Never mind. I knew you would say no. You never let me do anything."

Before Lee could respond to his daughter's accusation, Vonda looked at Kyra knowingly and shoved a small plate into her hand. And then she gently took her by the shoulders and turned her around, giving her a slight shove toward her father.

Remembering the talk she'd had with Miss Vonda about controlling her temper, Kyra walked over to the table and placed a warm, gooey cinnamon roll in front of her father. Taking a deep breath she said, "Can we at least go to the store in town? I left my toothbrush and my robe at home."

Kyra and Vonda had obviously talked before he came down. He didn't know about what, exactly, but whatever it was Kyra's tantrum seemed to have lost steam. Looking into his daughter's pretty face, Lee could see she was making an effort, and for that he was willing to meet her halfway. "Yes, honey, I'll take you to the store. We can go around noon."

When Kyra left the room to get ready, Lee turned to Vonda, and mouthed, "Thank you."

Katrice wanted the grand opening of Book Wares to be spectacular, unlike anything the town had ever seen. Actually, that wouldn't be too difficult a feat. There was a lot the town of Benton Lake had not seen.

Katrice vowed that her new bookstore was not going to be your typical stuffy, run-of-the-mill literary establishment. Book Wares would be different. It was a venture she'd thought about for a long time but never had the courage to undertake. Well, the time had come for her to take on something new. And so here she was.

As she drove along the increasingly familiar streets of Benton Lake, Katrice shifted from business concerns to thinking about the many reasons she had fallen in love with this town many years ago, even before she had decided to make it her home.

Who wouldn't fall in love with this place? It was the place where she and her sister had spent practically every summer vacation when they were growing up. Katrice had always looked forward to the annual summer visit to their grandmother's. However, her sister Taryn's enthusiasm for spending the summer at their grandma's house had not been the same as hers. Taryn hated being away from the city and saw no fun in swimming and fishing in the lake or chasing fireflies in the evening. She would have preferred spending time at the mall rather than picnicking at the lake. Taryn would spend her summer days perched in a chair on the front porch reading fashion and movie magazines and complaining about being bored. She once told Katrice that when she grew up, her dream was to have a big house as far away from the country as possible, a husband who doted on her, and two kids, preferably a boy and a girl.

At least Taryn's dreams came true.

Just as it had been when she was a child, the town of Benton Lake remained a peaceful and serene place to live. Nestled between the capital city of Columbus and

Cincinnati, the town had practically no crime and boasted a population of just over 21,000 residents. Nearly all of the residential streets were tree-lined and neighbors still looked out for each other. Now this beloved place had become home.

In fact, Katrice felt more at home in Benton Lake than she had felt anywhere for a long time. Never mind that her family and friends thought that she had gone crazy. Who could blame them? A few years earlier, she would have thought the same thing if someone had told her she would quit her job as a college professor, break up with her long-time fiancé, pack up all her worldly possessions and move to a one-horse town, her mother Melinda's favorite description of Benton Lake.

There comes a point in everyone's life when it is time to stop trying to live up to other people's expectations and create some of your own. Katrice was at that point. She had learned the hard way that life is too short to simply muddle through without enjoying one's chosen path.

Katrice's mother had stared blankly at her daughter when she had recited that exact speech to her. As expected, Katrice had to endure the speech that included references to how successful her sister Taryn was, what a good husband and kids Taryn had, and why it was foolish to walk away from a promising career. The bonus speech included reasons from A to Z as to why women today need a good man by their side.

As usual, Katrice's father had been silent and Taryn had sided with their mother, leaving her to defend herself. In the past, Katrice would have given up trying to maintain her independence and wouldn't have even bothered to explain to them that the "good man" they thought she had wasn't the man he appeared to be. This time Katrice had spoken up in her own defense. She had had enough analytical garbage from her family to last a lifetime. She was a grown woman who, until now, had lived her life to conform to the expectations of everyone else without being true to herself.

This time, she stood her ground and announced to her parents that she had given the university and her fiancé notice. At the time she hadn't dared mention that she had also purchased an old building that needed a great deal of repairs and had plans to open a bookstore in Benton Lake. She purposely put off unveiling those two decisions for later.

Why couldn't her family be proud of her for something *she* had chosen to undertake? The only time they had shown approval of something she'd accomplished was when *they* had deemed it the right thing to do. Well, Katrice had grown weary of living her life according to other peoples' expectations and of being afraid to step outside of her comfort zone. For as long as she could remember, everything she had done had been influenced by someone else's approval or because it seemed safe.

She had attended the University of Colorado because her mother insisted they had a better English department than the schools Katrice had chosen. That was also where she'd met Andrew; not only was his father the dean of students, but he was a pre-med student. Her mother had met him during orientation and thought he was the perfect match for her. However, Andrew was looking more for a mannequin than a girlfriend. He already had every detail of his life planned out, down to the two children they would have, where they would live, the two-story brick house with four bedrooms and two and a half baths, and a dog named Bobby. Who named a dog Bobby?

After two months, Katrice concluded that Andrew was boring, anal, and just plain weird. And they had absolutely nothing in common except for their complete dislike of each other.

After completing her master's degree in English, she had accepted a job teaching at a small university in Illinois because her mother convinced her that would be the proper starting point to her career. Katrice had really wanted to accept a position teaching English in the Columbus public school system, which at the time had one of the worst academic records in the state. She had wanted to teach in an area in which she could help make a difference and at the same time be challenged. She also had wanted to teach in Columbus because she would have been close to her grandmother Harriet, who lived in Benton Lake until her death.

It hadn't taken much for Melinda to convince her daughter that teaching in an academically struggling school system ranked as one of the worst ideas she'd ever had, especially when she brought up the gang activity that reportedly plagued some of the schools. To strengthen her argument against Katrice's plans, Melinda reminded her daughter that the amount of time and effort it would take to establish her career wouldn't allow for extra time to run back and forth to Benton Lake to spend time with her grandmother.

Melinda never kept it a secret that she wasn't very fond of Grandma Harry, as her granddaughters affectionately called her. Melinda Ware had always said that her mother-in-law lived life by the seat of her pants and routinely threw caution to the wind. She wanted more stability in her girls' lives. She didn't want them acting on impulse or jumping into decisions without thinking through all possible consequences. Rational people did not live their lives that way she would recite like a mantra. Taking risks and throwing caution to the wind seemed as disagreeable and odd to Melinda as a blizzard in Hawaii.

Forget what my family thinks. Grandma Harry would be proud of me.

She would say, 'It's about time you decided to live your own life. Women today have many more options and opportunities than I had when I was your age. Live life to the fullest. Never settle for less.' Katrice giggled. People would likely brand her crazy if they saw her "channeling" her grandmother.

Browsing the length of the candy aisle, Katrice selected several packages of assorted miniature chocolates, starlight mints, and chewy caramels. The candy would be placed on the counter in the bookstore for her patrons. She was glad that it was all on sale since she needed to watch her spending.

In addition to her house, Grandma Harry had left her and Taryn money. Her wish was that her granddaughters use the money to help make their dreams come true. Taryn had used most of the money their grandmother left them to remodel her kitchen and bathroom and on a family trip to Europe. Katrice was using hers to start her bookstore.

Satisfied that she had something that would satisfy every sweet tooth, she moved on. Shifting the packages from one arm to the other, she tried to ignore the butterflies in her stomach when she thought about everything she had invested to make her bookstore a reality. But mostly she felt excitement and pride whenever she thought about her business venture.

Unfortunately, it looked as if she would be basking in the grand-opening glow and dealing with her nervous butterflies all by herself. The invitation she had sent to her family had yet to be accepted. No one had called, sent a letter, or even e-mailed her to acknowledge her accomplishment. Although they hadn't exactly said they weren't coming, neither had they said they were. In their case, she couldn't assume silence meant acceptance.

Squaring her shoulders and shaking off the disappointment of her family's snub, Katrice headed for the checkout line. With each step, her armload of groceries and packages became more difficult to carry. Wishing she had gotten a cart when she first came into the store, she tried unsuccessfully to balance the packages of balloons, bags of candy, and groceries. The problem with Smithfield's was that she always got carried away when she shopped there. Today was no exception.

She began losing the battle to hold on to her packages when one item slipped from her shaky grasp. Twisting her body to see what had fallen caused another item to fall. A can of soup that had been pressed between her elbow and hip slipped out and rolled down the aisle. A can of tuna, a package of cookies, and a grapefruit followed.

The sheer volume of brands and varieties of coffee available never ceased to amaze Lee. Smithfield's seemed to carry them all—all except his regular brand. He was trying to find an acceptable alternative when a can of tuna landed next to his feet, followed by a can of soup, and then a grapefruit. He followed the trail of groceries to a woman who was struggling to secure her remaining packages.

"Here, let me help," Lee offered, pushing his cart toward her, deftly catching a package of chocolates before it hit the floor.

Katrice leaned against a shelf trying to get a better grip on the few remaining items she had managed to hold on to.

"Thank you," she replied with a half smile, once again regretting that she had not gotten a shopping cart when she first walked into the store.

Katrice studied the helpful stranger cautiously as he transferred her groceries one by one from her arms and off the floor to his shopping cart. She had already met quite a few people in Benton Lake while securing permits and licenses for her business. *Was this someone she'd met before?* He didn't look or sound familiar. Lowering her gaze to secretly get a better look, she concluded he was definitely someone she would have remembered.

"Having a party?"

A deep, strong voice matched an equally strong physical presence—tall but not overpowering. Katrice continued watching the man's movements as he bent to pick up the runaway grapefruit. His legs were long and muscular, shoulders broad, arms chiseled. *Probably spends way too much time in the gym.*

When he straightened up, Katrice had to take a step back to keep from having to tilt her head to look into his eyes. He was actually taller than she had originally thought. His eyes were a deep brown and framed by tightly curled eyelashes. Overall, his features—rich, smooth brown skin, full lips, slightly squared chin—were quite nice.

All of her items were soon in the front of his shopping cart. *Did he just ask me a question?* Willing herself to stop staring she asked, "I'm sorry. Did you just ask me about a party?"

"Yes, you seem to have all the makings for a party. Is it your birthday?" Lee had to hide a smile when he realized that despite her best efforts to appear indifferent the pretty lady had been checking him out.

"My birthday? No, I just didn't mean to get so many things. Actually, I just wanted to get enough for the grand . . . Wait." Suddenly, images of her overbearing ex-fiancé flashed before her. She didn't need to explain herself. Had she unwittingly projected the stereotype of a damsel in distress? Or at least someone too scatterbrained to have gotten a grocery cart when one was obviously needed? She didn't need help. She had no idea who this strange, albeit handsome, man was. For all she knew, he could be Jack the Ripper incarnate.

"You didn't have to do that. I didn't mean for you to stop doing whatever it was you were doing to help me."

Lee detected a slight edge to her voice. "It's not a problem. I'm just here picking up a few groceries. I stopped because you looked as if you could use a hand."

"Well, thanks for offering to help, but I can manage by myself."

"It didn't look that way from where I stood."

In fact, Lee was very appreciative of what he had observed from his vantage point. He had seen someone more alluring than a damsel in distress. Given time, this long-legged beauty would be more likely to put *him* in distress.

Wearing form-fitting jean shorts and a snug top, it didn't take much imagination to see that she had the kind of curves and natural beauty that commanded more than a passing glance.

Katrice began reclaiming her items from the grocery cart. She hadn't asked for his help, and she certainly didn't need it. She knew she must have looked silly with her arms stacked with more packages than she could manage to carry, but she hated appearing helpless, especially to a total stranger.

With her items precariously stacked in her arms, she turned to the stranger, politely thanked him, and marched off.

What was that all about? Lee stood in the grocery aisle watching Katrice walk away. She had gone from pretty to pretty pissed in a matter of minutes. *What had he said to make her so angry?*

"Dad? Is something wrong?" Kyra asked, a puzzled look on her face.

Shrugging, he replied, "To be honest, Ky, I have no idea."

Realizing her father was distracted, Kyra quickly placed a pair of sunglasses and several bottles of nail polish that she'd been hiding behind her back onto the conveyor belt, hoping he wouldn't notice.

Lee was still puzzled by the strange encounter he'd had a few minutes earlier. He tried to comprehend what he could have said to upset the beautiful stranger. Maybe she thought he had been coming on to her. Would that have been so bad? Surely, someone who looked as she did was used to men falling at her feet, although that hadn't been his intention. Judging by the way she'd hurried off he wouldn't have the opportunity now, anyway.

So much for first impressions.

"Why do we need balloons?"Kyra asked after the cashier scanned a brightly colored package and placed it in the grocery bag. "Are we having a party?"

"Huh?"

"I asked if we were having a party."

"Apparently someone is. But I don't think we should count on being invited."

CHAPTER 3

The drive back from Cleveland was a little more tedious than the journey up north had been earlier. Somehow the nearly four-hour drive seemed to be taking a lot longer.

Katrice massaged the kinks in her neck and shoulders with one hand; with the other, she steered the overloaded van down the dark highway, longing for the comfort of her bed.

The dashboard clock read eleven forty-five. Even without seeing the time, her body had already told her it was late and considerably past her normal bedtime. She rolled her window down a few inches, hoping the cool night air would help fend off the drowsiness and fatigue that had dogged her over the past hour.

Katrice wished that she had left Cleveland sooner, but she had lost all track of time, having found so many bargains and deals at the book wholesaler's one-day sale. The old cargo van that she had bought to haul merchandise for her bookstore was packed to the hilt. Everything from books to shelves to signs and framed artwork had been stuffed into the van. She could almost hear the old van graining under the weight.

Yawning, Katrice negotiated the sharp curve that turned into Turner Ridge Road. The nearly deserted farm access road was dark and narrow, but it would get her home a little faster.

Almost home, she thought, catching glimpses of familiar landscape. *Almost home.* She could practically feel the cool, crisp sheets against her skin and the softness of her pillow beneath her weary head.

As Katrice passed the sprawling farm where she had occasionally purchased fresh fruits and vegetables, something on the side of the road caught her eye. She hit the van's high beams to get a better look. Suddenly, the figure came into view. A deer leaped forward and stopped directly in her path. *A deer caught in the headlights.*

Reflectively, Katrice tightened her grip on the steering wheel while simultaneously hitting the brakes. Tires squealed and the van swerved sharply. Just as quickly as the deer had darted into her path, it was gone, narrowly avoiding a collision. Before she had fully recovered, blinding bright lights suddenly bathed the inside of her van. Wide-eyed and still shaking from her near-collision with the deer, she nonetheless quickly realized the approaching vehicle was headed straight for her. Hitting the gas pedal with more force than necessary Katrice turned the steering wheel sharply. The sudden movement sent the van careening onto the shoulder. She heard tires screeching and gravel crunching. Then the aging van sputtered and the motor cut off.

Breathing rapidly, her heart pounding, Katrice still clutched the steering wheel as she uttered a quick prayer of thanks. Not only had she narrowly avoided a collision with the deer and an oncoming car, but the biggest tree she'd ever seen was less than five feet to her left. Realizing that she had barely missed becoming one with the tree, she felt a lump rise in her throat as her heart continued to pound loudly.

Somewhere in the distance she heard a car door slam, followed by the sound of rapidly approaching footsteps on the pavement.

Katrice flung open the van's door, forgetting how close she was to the tree until the sound of metal meeting bark reminded her. Taking a deep breath, she muttered an expletive and squeezed out of the space between the tree and door, prepared to confront the approaching driver.

What kind of maniac was she about to encounter? Probably some kid out for a joy ride, or worse, a drunk driver. Normally, she would never approach a stranger in this manner. However, these weren't normal circumstances. Whoever it was she was about to meet was going to get an earful.

"Are you all right?"

The hem of Katrice's blouse had caught on the door. It ripped when she pulled it free. Her new blouse! Now she was livid!

"You almost hit me!"

"I didn't see you until it was almost too late. You were swerving all over the road and driving left of center. It took everything I had to not hit *you*."

Katrice stepped closer. She couldn't see the speaker but the voice sounded familiar. Stepping even closer and allowing her eyes to adjust to the darkness, she quickly recognized her accuser. *The man from Smithfield's. The handsome stranger who had tried to help her with her groceries a few days ago.*

"It's you," she said, her breathing returning to normal.

The man came closer.

"Are you all right?" he repeated his question, this time more gently as he recognized her.

Seeing the approaching vehicle that had been driving on the wrong side of the road and swerving from lane to lane, Lee thought he was about to be hit by a drunk driver. After seeing the van drive off the side of the road, he felt positive he was going to have an encounter with someone who'd had a little too much to drink or had been driving under the influence of drugs. To his surprise and relief, it was the beautiful woman who had gotten angry with him at the grocery store and marched off after rejecting his help.

She was just as beautiful as he remembered, but a lot more upset.

"I'm fine, considering I almost killed a deer. Then here you come flying around the bend like a bat out of hell, and to avoid hitting *you* head-on I came this close to hitting that tree," Katrice said, pointing at her van and the nearly missed tree.

"You were driving in my lane. And I was not speeding!" Now it was Lee's turn to be angry. How had she turned this whole incident around so that it seemed as if it was his fault? The only thing he remembered seeing were headlights dancing all over the road then coming straight at him. He hadn't seen a deer. How was he supposed to know?

Katrice turned on her heels. Her legs felt wobbly, causing her to stumble slightly. As her anger dissipated, relief and fatigue overwhelmed her.

"Wait," Lee said, starting after her. "Are you okay? Let me help you." No longer angry, he felt compelled to make sure she was all right.

Willing herself to appear more composed than she actually felt, she quickened her steps and began walking back to her van. "No, thank you. Any more help from you and I'd be meeting my Maker." Adding one last dig, she said over her shoulder, "You've done enough."

Standing in the road with his arms folded and his jaw set, Lee watched Katrice pull her van onto the pavement, kicking up dirt and gravel, and speed off. "Keep driving like that and you'll meet your Maker tonight!" he yelled after her.

Lee stood on the side of the road for a few minutes longer before getting back into his car.

"What is it with that woman?" he asked aloud, wondering why he suddenly had the urge to punch a wall, bite nails, and pull the angry and mysterious woman into his arms while kissing her until her long, lean legs grew weak. How could one person manage to be so utterly aggravating and downright mean, but yet be so captivatingly beautiful all at the same time?

Benton Lake was definitely getting smaller and smaller by the day, he thought. Twice he'd run into the same beautiful woman and both times their meeting had ended in complete disaster. Where else would their paths cross? Would he look up and see her sitting next to him in church? Maybe she would be standing in line to buy stamps at the post office. Perhaps he would see her getting her caffeine fix at the new coffee shop his dad mentioned.

One thing was certain—wherever and whenever their next meeting, it was bound to be interesting.

Pulling his car back onto the road, Lee started the trip back to his father's house. What had been an attempt to relax and clear his mind with a late-night drive had turned into an exercise in futility. Not only had he been accused of driving like a *bat out of hell*, he actually questioned whether he had caused the van to run off the road. Oddly, the fact that he knew he wouldn't be able to stop thinking about the mystery woman was the one thing that nagged at him the most.

He wondered if he'd made the same impression on her.

CHAPTER 4

Boredom often brings on complaining, at least when there is a pre-teen in the mix. Kyra and her father had been in Benton Lake for barely a week when she announced that she was bored and needed something to do. Cooking classes with Vonda had come to a temporary halt when Vonda had to go to Cincinnati to help her sister, who'd had emergency gallbladder surgery.

"I need something to do, Dad."

"Hmm?"

Her father was busily jotting down notes on something that looked an awful lot like work to Kyra. She could tell by his irritated look that he was not happy about being disturbed and did not seem to be in the mood for chitchat, either. *Some vacation.* She would have had more fun at summer school.

Kyra frowned and rearranged the sausage links on her plate. She wished that she had gone fishing with her grandfather. On second thought, getting out of bed at five hadn't been on her top five list of fun things to do. At the time, she could see no reason for getting up that early unless there was force involved.

"You said this would be a fun vacation. How is it any kind of vacation when you're still working?"

Lee removed his reading glasses and put down the will he had been working on for most of the morning. He had been preparing the document for one of his father's friends, and he had given very explicit instructions for doling out his possessions after his death. He didn't seem to trust anyone but Lee to put his final wishes on paper.

"Stop playing with your food and eat your breakfast."

"You didn't answer my question," she said, pouting.

"This isn't really work, Ky."

"You don't see me solving algebra problems or writing term papers on my summer break, do you?"

Lee winked. "Keep talking. That can be arranged."

Kyra didn't see anything funny and let out an exaggerated sigh to illustrate her frustration. "I need something to do before I go crazy, Dad."

She had a point, Lee thought. This was supposed to be a vacation, and vacations were supposed to be fun.

"Okay, you're absolutely right. What would you like to do?"

"I'm glad you asked." Kyra pulled a flier from her pocket and placed it on top of the will.

Lee took the flier and read it, placing it back on the table after a few seconds. "You're not old enough to work."

"It's not a job, Dad. Read it. The flier says that readers are needed to participate in a discussion group."

"Where did you get this?"

"It was on the information board at church, and some of the girls said they'd done something like it before at the library and that it's a lot of fun. So can I do it?"

"I don't know, Ky. I'm not even sure where this place is."

"The address is on the front and so is the phone number. Don't you have to drop off that stuff you're working on today?"

"What does that have to do with anything?"

"We could go together and check it out since you have to go out anyway."

Lee wasn't budging and Kyra knew she had to make a desperate, yet heartfelt, plea to get him to consider her request. "Come on, Dad. I don't have anybody to hang out with and there is nothing to do here. I'm going to die if I have to sit in this house one more day. Things are getting so bad that I'm considering going fishing with Grandpa."

Lee read the flier again, more thoroughly this time. Students between the ages of thirteen and sixteen were being invited to join a readers' group, just as Kyra had said. From the basic information listed on the flier the time commitment would be minimal, and, as far as he could tell, all Kyra would be expected to do was read and participate in a discussion. Lee smiled. A forum where his daughter would be able to speak her mind and offer her opinion—how fast could he sign her up? Hopefully this would actually hold her interest longer than a few weeks—unlike ballet, the clarinet, karate, and gymnastics.

"Well?" Kyra knew she was winning when she saw the smile tugging at the corners of her father's mouth.

With his beautiful little girl peering at him with pleading brown eyes, Lee felt cornered and had no other choice but to bend just a bit. "All right, little girl. Finish your breakfast and we'll go by and check this out."

Kyra pushed away from the table and ran over to plant a kiss on her father's cheek. "Thanks, Dad! Oh, yeah, while we're out, do you think we could stop by the mall? I need a new pair of sandals."

Lee rolled his eyes. *When did I become such a pushover?*

CHAPTER 5

The R&B oldies station Katrice had tuned her radio to provided the perfect music to work by. Unpacking and shelving books didn't seem like work at all as she lip-synched and bobbed her head to the soulful rhythms, even though she didn't know most of the lyrics. A new shipment of books had arrived that morning, and she wanted to get everything inventoried and shelved before she went to lunch. Moving along to the beat of the music gave her the energy to do just that.

Katrice marked off entries on a packing slip to make sure she had received everything she'd ordered. The spreadsheet on which she was recording her entries would be entered into the computer in her office as soon as she got the chance. The software that had come with her new computer enabled her to create inventory sheets and payroll logs, as well as design fliers for opening day.

Katrice finished unpacking the shipment and placed the last stack of books on a cart. Wheeling the cart over to the children's section and stopping in front of a partly stocked shelf, she pressed her hand to her stomach to calm the sudden onset of butterflies. Book Wares finally had the look and feel of a bookstore, Katrice thought as she knelt down to transfer the books from the cart to the shelf.

Her bookstore.

The contractor she'd hired after purchasing the store had been a friend of her grandmother's. He had completed all the major renovations ahead of schedule and slightly under budget. New carpet had been installed the week before and all the shelving was in place, as were the tables and chairs for the coffee nook. The children's section needed a few added touches, and a shipment of how-to books had yet to arrive. Other than that, everything was on target for the grand opening on Friday, she thought with rising excitement.

She had just shelved the last book and stood to stretch when a song on the radio caught her attention. She turned up the volume. Closing her eyes, she leaned against a stack of boxes, letting the music set the mood for her daydream. She envisioned customers browsing up and down the aisles looking for books by their favorite authors. Other patrons would be enjoying coffee and literary conversations in the bookstore's coffee nook. She imagined children listening attentively while being read to in the children's corner and teachers looking for books to add to their students' must-read lists. She could almost hear the lively conversations of students and friends meeting for an afternoon cup of coffee or tea in the coffee nook after their classes.

Being this close to getting her business off the ground was beyond exciting; it was intoxicating. But it wasn't just the opening that was making her feel this way. For the first time in years Katrice felt free, free to make her own decisions without regard for what her parents, sister, or her ex-fiancé Greg, thought was right. Book Wares belonged to her, and she alone would decide how to run it. It felt good to take responsibility for herself and her life, every bit of it. She even loved that Grandma Harry's house now belonged to her and that Benton Lake was now the place she called home. She had turned her dream into reality, and everything felt right. No feelings of fear or trepidation; no second thoughts.

Tucking her daydream away; she decided it was time to get back to work. But first, she turned up the volume even louder and grabbed a permanent marker. Holding it to her mouth, she began belting out a tune sung by Patti LaBelle. Although her vocal talents were nowhere near Miss Patti's, Katrice sang with just as much conviction and joy.

No, she didn't have a new dress or a new hat as the song lyrics described, but Katrice Ware definitely wore a new attitude. And it fit her to a T.

As she swayed her hips and belted out the parts of the song that she could remember, Katrice allowed herself to get carried away. Easily drowning out Patti, Katrice became so caught up in her new attitude that she didn't notice she had a captive audience.

As the song neared its end, the sound of someone loudly clearing his throat stopped Katrice mid-twirl. Standing with her mouth open and 'microphone' marker tilted in midair she stared wide-eyed at a man and young girl standing in her bookstore.

The man who ran her van off the road.

"We knocked, but I guess you didn't hear us." Kyra tried to be polite, sensing the awkwardness of the situation and wondering if anything ever embarrassed adults.

Katrice's face burned as surprise quickly turned into embarrassment. How could she have forgotten to lock the door? Forget the door, she thought, looking into the faces of her audience. *What sane person dances around singing into a marker?* She wanted more than anything to find the nearest crack in the floor or hole in the wall and crawl into it.

Could she have looked like a bigger fool in front of him?

Scrambling for something to busy herself with, she turned the volume down on the radio and stepped behind the counter, quickly unwrapping a package of bookmarks. "I was just tidying up." *Could she sound more lame?* "As you can see, we're not open for business yet. Is there something I can help you with?"

Lee didn't utter a word, but the smile tugging at his lips spoke volumes.

Katrice stacked the bookmarks a few more times before she deciding to shove her restless hands in the pockets of her jeans. She didn't know what to say, but the silence was anything but golden. Then she had a thought that caused her to stand straighter and assume an air of defiance. *This is my bookstore. I can sing into markers, dance, or jump off the roof if I want to.* Except that at the moment she really wanted the floor to open up and swallow her.

"If this is a bad time, we can come back later."

Katrice lifted her chin and turned to face Lee, who wore a mischievous grin that she couldn't help noticing; nonetheless, she tried her best to ignore it—and him. "No, not at all. I'm Katrice Ware, the owner. I'm in the process of getting everything ready for the opening. Is there something I can do for you?"

Still appearing amused, Lee introduced himself and his daughter. "I'm Lee Oliver and this is my daughter, Kyra. I believe we've met before. At Smithfield's. Sort of. I tried to help you with your groceries and you mistook my kindness for something other than its true intent."

Katrice's face grew warm.

Maybe she didn't remember, he thought. He certainly hadn't forgotten her. "We met again on Turner Ridge Road the other night. Remember? I tried to explain to you that I was not trying to run you off the road. Somehow I don't think I was very convincing."

Of course, she remembered. How could she have forgotten? Even if she hadn't remembered the occasions *when* they'd met, she certainly hadn't forgotten *whom* she'd met. How could she forget him? He had been on her mind ever since he had bent over to pick up her fallen groceries.

He had a daughter. Did that mean he was married? Divorced? Widowed? Or a *baby daddy*?

Did she really care? After all, he probably had already pegged her as a lunatic. She had thought about her reactions to both of their previous encounters again and again since they'd happened. Her reactions had been a bit out of character. Lee had only been trying to help her in the grocery store. And the night she'd almost hit the deer, he seemed to be trying to be helpful then, too. She could only imagine how she must have appeared to him with her torn blouse, exaggerated gesturing, and wild accusations. She couldn't quite pinpoint why she had reacted the way she had. She blamed it all on fatigue and stress. *Definitely not her normal behavior.*

Heck, who was she kidding? There was no normal reaction when she was around this man.

Lee nudged Kyra to encourage her to speak up after a moment of awkward silence.

Kyra pulled a piece of paper from her back pocket and said, "I'm here to find out about the discussion group."

"The discussion group," Katrice repeated inattentively. "Oh, right. The flier. Okay, sure." Katrice came from behind the counter and approached Kyra, making a point not to look at her father. She had almost forgotten about the fliers she had placed around town hoping to attract young readers to the bookstore. "I'm looking for people who like to read. Are you an avid reader?"

Kyra nodded enthusiastically.

"Good. Being in the discussion group is pretty easy, and hopefully will be a lot of fun. You and a group of other kids around your age will be responsible for reading books and sharing your opinions of them."

"What if I don't like the book?"

"That happens. If you read a book that you don't like, then you can explain what it was that you didn't like about it. Members of the discussion group will meet once a week, or more if you need to, and discuss the books you've read to get the entire group's opinion. There might be a few times when the local newspaper would like to feature a review in the literary section. Other times my staff and I will share the opinions of the group with customers when they ask for recommendations. Sound like something you'd be interested in?"

Kyra was ready to accept, but she still needed her father's approval. "Can I, Dad?"

Lee hadn't said a word up to this point. He had only been half listening to the exchange between Katrice and his daughter. He'd actually been paying more attention to Katrice than to the details about the discussion group, taking note of her pretty smile, flawless mocha skin, and large, expressive brown eyes. Her curly black hair sported auburn highlights and had been pulled into a disheveled ponytail. She had been wearing her hair the exact same way when he had seen her at Smithfield's, except now several tendrils had escaped, adding a touch of softness to her appearance. Even prettier than he remembered, she now seemed slightly more at ease—at least when speaking to Kyra.

"There are no strings attached," Katrice offered when she noticed an odd look on Lee's face. "I just thought this might be a fun way to get kids more involved in reading. Besides, it's something to do while school is out."

Kyra practically held her breath waiting for her father's answer. When he finally nodded, she breathed a sigh of relief.

Katrice smiled at Kyra and led her over to the counter. "Okay, let's get down to business." She pulled out a small stack of books from under the counter and handed them to her. "These are the books I've set aside I'd like you to review. You don't have to read them all at once, but if you could finish this one before next week, I can set up the first meeting with you and the other book club members shortly after that."

After flipping through a few pages of one of the books, Kyra read the back cover. "I don't think I've ever read anything by Sharon Flake. This sounds like it might be pretty good."

Kyra and Katrice talked about the review process and authors they both enjoyed reading. Lee was a little surprised that Katrice had read many of the same books as Kyra, but that probably wasn't unusual for a bookseller, he reasoned.

While they talked, Lee looked around the bookstore. Katrice was a distraction, and he definitely didn't need his daughter to witness him ogling her. Part of helping his daughter to grow into a well-adjusted adult was to show her first hand a level of respect that all women deserve and should expect. Getting caught eyeing Katrice's round backside wouldn't do it.

Lee was impressed with the terrific job Katrice had done in transforming the former bakery into a bookstore. A small area to the right of the entrance looked as if it might be a café. There was space for about two or three small tables. Just past the café was the counter. Bookshelves lined the walls to the right and opposite the counter, stopping at what Lee thought might be a doorway to a storeroom or office. The center aisle was clear, but more bookshelves were on either side of the aisle. Peering through some of the empty shelves, Lee could see an area in the back of the store that was vacant.

He liked what he saw. Even though it wasn't quite ready for business, the place had a nice, cozy feel to it. Lee had never really been a dedicated reader, but he thought he might enjoy spending time at Book Wares, albeit not necessarily for its literary offerings.

"Dad, I just saw Amber and her mother go into the ice cream shop across the street. Can I go over and talk to her for a few minutes?"

Kyra had met Amber Reynolds at church on Sunday. She was the daughter of the pastor, and she and Kyra had hit it off instantly. She seemed like a good kid, but Lee had asked Vonda about her just to be sure. As far as he could tell, Amber didn't exhibit the characteristics that some preachers' kids were infamous for—angels around their parents but absolute devils around their friends.

"Okay. Just for a little while, though. Remember, don't go anywhere else without checking with me first."

"Thanks, Daddy! Thanks, Miss Katrice."

Kyra ran out the front door, leaving him alone with Katrice. A chance for redemption, Lee thought. Their first few meetings had gone badly, and he wanted the chance to make up for it. Now he had the opportunity to show her that he was a good guy.

"I almost forgot to pay for the books. How much do I owe you?"

Katrice grabbed a stack of magazines off the counter and began placing them on a nearby rack. "There's no charge. Kyra doesn't realize that she's doing me a big favor. I had the idea for the book discussion group, but I don't really know that many kids around town. I think she'll be a wonderful addition to the group. She's tailor-made—smart, articulate, and enthusiastic, and she seems to enjoy reading."

Lee shoved his hands in his back pocket and smiled. "Yes, she's all of those things and more. It's the more that I have trouble with sometimes."

Katrice thought about her sister's children and what a handful they could be. "She seems like a good kid. Be grateful."

Katrice continued working but could feel Lee watching her. She made a point of appearing really busy. Unfortunately, he didn't take her subtle cues to leave.

Reaching down to lift a large box up to the counter, Katrice nearly dropped it when she realized, too late, that it was much heavier than it appeared. Lee quickly stepped forward and reached out to grab the box.

Agitated, she turned and said, "I can handle this myself, thank you."

Lee put his hands up in a defensive gesture. "So I've been warned." He'd done it again. What was it about him that agitated her so much?

"Look, Mr. Oliver—"

"Lee. Please, call me Lee."

"I'm really busy. I have a lot to do before I open my shop."

Redemption chance number two. Lee spoke up before he realized that he shouldn't have. "I'm free after lunch.

I'd be happy to help. It's my way of saying I'm sorry about what happened the other night."

"That's kind of you, but I am more than capable of doing this on my own, and you don't owe me an apology." Katrice didn't add that after she had calmed down, she had felt silly about the way she'd treated Lee. Again, she blamed the whole episode on fatigue and stress.

Lee groaned. *Another strike.* "I wasn't implying that you weren't capable. I just wanted to—" Just then Kyra came running back into the shop.

"Dad, the church is having a game day today and Amber invited me to go with her. Can I? Her mother said she could give me a ride."

"Today? What time?"

"It starts at one."

Lee looked at his watch. It was ten minutes shy of one o'clock. "What about our lunch date?"

Instantly, Kyra's expression changed from delight to dismay. "Oh, yeah, lunch. I forgot." Just that morning she had made such a fuss about being bored and wanting to go somewhere or do something. When her father had mentioned that they might go to lunch after stopping by the bookstore and maybe to Smithfield's after that to look for sandals, she had been excited. But that was before she had been offered something more exciting.

Kyra's excitement waned long enough for Lee to recognize that she was trying to think of a way to get out of going to lunch with him. He knew he would give in without much of a fight, but he refused to be a complete

43

pushover. Truth be told, he was glad his daughter had made a friend.

"I'm really hungry and I thought once we finished lunch we could go to Smithfield's to look for a new swimsuit or whatever you said you needed. Then after that, I thought we might go to a movie or even fishing."

Kyra's face dropped. "Sandals."

Lee could barely contain his amusement. He was laying it on pretty thick.

"Can't we do that tomorrow? Not the fishing part, but maybe go to the movies and then to get sandals?"

A smile tugged at Lee's mouth. He had to admit the tension between them had subsided a bit, and it had been a whole twenty-four hours since Kyra had gotten upset with him over something insignificant. "All right, go ahead. Tell Mrs. Reynolds that I said hello, and remember to thank her for the ride."

Kyra was practically out the door when her father reminded her to call when the activities were over.

Still pretending to be busy, Katrice quietly observed the brief exchange between Lee and his daughter. She wondered just how long Kyra had had her father wrapped so snugly around her little finger.

Lee let out an exaggerated sigh. "Imagine being stood up by a twelve-year-old. Now I'm really in a tough spot."

"Hmm, that's too bad," Katrice replied nonchalantly.

"Looks like I'm in need of a lunch date."

Katrice stopped stacking magazines long enough to throw a curious glance in Lee's direction. "And you're telling me that for a reason?"

"Come on, even really busy independent business owners have to take time out for lunch. You do eat, don't you?"

Katrice shook her head. Going out to lunch with this man was reason for pause. He was a distraction, and distractions had no place on her agenda right now. More important, this was a whole new life for her, and she couldn't afford to let old habits creep back in and cloud her way of thinking. While Lee didn't appear to be like Greg—selfish, domineering, and condescending—she didn't want to take any chances. She'd had enough of that behavior to last a lifetime. Besides, her vow to occasionally step out of her comfort zone didn't mean that she had to act foolishly. What did she know about this man? *Practically nothing.* Yes, he had shown that he could be charming and polite. And, she had to admit to herself, he was easy on the eyes.

Okay, if she had to be honest, the man had the kind of looks that would turn more than a few heads. He had certainly turned hers the first time she saw him. And the body—well, any month on a beefcake calendar would sizzle just because his image graced the page. She quickly dismissed that thought, as she knew all too well that possessing good looks, charm, and manners didn't necessarily rule out a host of bad habits or troubling traits.

Good sense prevailed. "No, thank you," Katrice replied curtly. "I'm not hungry, and I have way too much work to do."

Katrice turned her back to Lee and continued working. Maybe if she kept busy and didn't talk to him, he'd become discouraged and would finally leave her alone. She hoped that would be soon as she closed her eyes and inhaled the scent of his cologne. The heady scent and his presence had an odd effect on her. She scolded herself for becoming so easily distracted.

It bothered her that she found herself attracted to this man. She needed to stay focused, and not on Lee.

Please go. You're an unwanted, good-smelling distraction.

But instead of hearing the front door open signaling Lee's departure, she heard footsteps coming up behind her. Not knowing what to expect, she tensed up.

Enough is enough. She had work to do and she would never get everything finished in time for the grand opening with Lee hanging around.

Katrice turned around to confront him when the footsteps stopped and she found herself standing a little too close for comfort. All personal space had ceased to exist. Another whiff of his cologne, coupled with the fact that she could practically feel the heat from his body, sent her head reeling. She reached over and caught the corner of a bookshelf and held on for support. Thrusting her chin upward, she refused to let him see that he had rattled her.

Placing an errant strand of Katrice's hair back into place, Lee tried to imagine how she would look with cascading curls framing her face. Her hair was soft and thick and he wanted more than anything to run his fingers through the dark tresses, but he knew better. She looked annoyed. He couldn't quite pinpoint why. He thought how strange it was that what he saw on the outside seemed so different from what she chose to reveal. He knew from experience that sometimes it was easier to bury your feelings than to acknowledge them and let them reach the surface. It would be interesting to know Katrice's true feelings. If he used her past actions as an indicator to judge how she felt about him, he'd have to say that she just flat out didn't like him. However, at this moment he looked deeper and thought differently. There was no denying the fact that he felt an attraction, and he knew she felt it, too.

"Pretty lady, you truly are a mystery to me. I keep asking myself what it is about me that irritates you so much. I have gone out of my way to be nice to you. I use my best manners, remember to smile and say 'please' and 'thank you' and you still treat me like the smelly kid in kindergarten who ate paste."

She wanted to respond, but she couldn't, especially with him standing all up in her personal space! It was hard enough for her to keep her reaction to him in check, let alone think of something intelligent to say. All she could do was stare and pretend that she didn't notice how sexy he looked or how good he smelled. Standing close enough that she could see his long, curly eyelashes, the taut muscles beneath his T-shirt and the exact width of his chest, it was all Katrice could do to keep from licking her dry lips and running her hands along the outline of his chest.

This man occupied areas of her personal space she hadn't shared in a long time, and it made her both nervous and tingly inside. The fact that she caught yet another whiff of his cologne mixed with a scent that she knew was uniquely Lee Oliver didn't help matters in the least.

Somebody needed to step back. Unfortunately, at the moment she didn't think her mind could will her legs to carry her far enough away to make a difference.

This man was fine. She was not the kind of woman who typically cared whether a man looked good or not, but Lee Oliver couldn't be ignored. He had the kind of good looks that made a sistah brag to her girlfriends and at the same time cut her eyes at any woman who let her eyes rest on him too long. Aside from his appearance, he had other characteristics that appealed to Katrice, although she wouldn't admit it to anyone. During the brief times she had been in his presence, she'd found he could be funny, polite, and quite the gentleman. He also appeared to have a good relationship with his daughter, an added bonus. While he didn't wear a wedding ring— she had covertly checked the ring finger at Smithfield's— neither he nor his daughter had mentioned a mother. However, the absence of a wedding ring only partly ruled out that he could really be a cheating scumbag.

Okay, she established that Lee Oliver possessed good looks and charm. *Big deal.* Was she expected to swoon? Maybe the old Katrice would have remained silent and slightly mesmerized, but the new Katrice reached down deep inside and forced herself to speak her mind. She lifted her chin slightly higher and replied in a voice that didn't sound as solid as she would have liked. "Listen, I'm not sure what you have in mind, but I'm not some country bumpkin who gets weak in the knees at the sight of a handsome face. Nor am I a shrinking violet incapable of taking care of business all by herself. What I am is a busy woman who has a lot to accomplish in a very short period of time. So if you don't mind—"

Lee smiled and Katrice noticed a faint dimple appeared in one cheek. Katrice sighed ever so slightly and swallowed the rising lump in her throat.

Handsome had just clicked up a notch to *absolutely gorgeous.*

Hold up. Wait a minute! She could not and would not allow herself to get sidetracked by a handsome face—or broad shoulders and a dimple, she told herself.

Lee recognized a front when he saw one, and Katrice was indeed putting on a front. She pretended to be annoyed with him, but he sensed something else. It wasn't especially warm in the shop, but beads of perspiration had formed on her nose.

She felt it, too.

Lee wasn't the kind of man who lost his head over a pretty face, but Katrice intrigued him. Part of her irritated the hell out of him with her misreading of his intentions and the way she so easily threw his offers to be nice back in his face, but another part excited him. However, at this moment he only had one thing on his mind—leaning forward to taste her luscious lips. Standing this close to her he couldn't help noticing again how pretty she was. The rubber band thing that struggled to restrain her curly hair had allowed several more tendrils to escape, which gave her a rather appealing disheveled look.

Her pretty brown face was devoid of makeup except for the faint remnants of a shade of lipstick that he couldn't quite make out. In his book, Katrice was a natural beauty. From head to toe, everything proved to be to his liking. Even her ears, adorned with tiny gold hoops, looked irresistibly kissable.

Lee felt surprised by the urge to pull Katrice into his arms and kiss her until she was breathless. Thankfully, he remembered his manners. She seemed the type who studied self-defense and wouldn't hesitate to break out a move on a brotha. Fighting was not how he wanted her to expend her energy.

Instead of taking the approach that most appealed to him, Lee closed a little more space between them.

Katrice inhaled.

Just how close does he need to be?

Could this woman possibly know how sexy she looks right now?

What is he up to?

I don't ever remember wanting to kiss anyone this badly. She has the sexiest lips I've ever seen.

Is he going to try to kiss me? He wouldn't dare. Would he?

Stealing a kiss would be worth whatever wrath she would wish on me later.

He's going to kiss me.

Waiting for what she felt would be a bold but not necessarily an unwelcome move by Lee, Katrice willed herself to remain still. She practically dared him to kiss her.

As Lee lifted his hand to her shoulder, she felt her body tingle in anticipation. Would he take her by her shoulders and pull her into his body? She exhaled and closed her eyes as she waited for his lips to find hers. Time seemed to stand still. However, surprise quickly replaced anticipation when instead of feeling strong lips against hers, she felt something brush softly against her shoulder.

"That ought to help," Lee said softly. "You should be able to move around a little more freely and get your work done."

Lee turned to leave and Katrice looked at her shoulder and shot him a questioning look.

"That chip on your shoulder," he said, "must have weighed a ton."

CHAPTER 6

Arrogant! No other word could accurately describe Lee Oliver. Well, maybe there were a few others, but Katrice didn't want to entertain such thoughts·just now.

She could not believe his nerve. He'd actually accused her of having a chip on her shoulder. How in the world had he formed that opinion? He didn't know anything about her. She didn't have a chip on her shoulder. And she had never had one.

Maybe he felt intimidated by her. Some men were like that. Seeing a woman in control of her own destiny could be threatening to some men.

Who am I kidding? Who in the world would be threatened by me?

His accusation still stung but not as much as her unexpectedly anticipating a kiss she instinctively knew would have rocked her to her very core. Those feelings that reinforced her feeling that she needed to steer clear of Lee. Above all, she had to keep a clear head and stay focused on creating a life free of stress and drama, and stay focused on living an independent life. Even if he hadn't exhibited the same behavior that she had endured with Greg, Lee was still a distraction, something she did not need in her life right now, no matter how enticing.

Stubborn! Irritating! Mean! And sexy as hell!

Those had been Lee's recurring thoughts since leaving the bookstore. His latest encounter with Katrice left him shaking his head, more perplexed than ever. Once again he had been on his best behavior, and Katrice had accused him of treating her as if she were a country bumpkin incapable of taking care of business. How could she have taken his invitation to help out around the bookstore as anything but a gesture of goodwill? There were no ulterior motives. He was simply being a nice guy. Any gentleman would have done the same thing. His intentions had not been influenced by anything other than a common sense of decency. Well, for the most part. She did look awfully cute throwing her hips from side to side and singing along to the radio. He had wanted to kiss her so badly that his body had reacted in a way that both surprised and confused him.

Shaking his head to clear his thoughts, he told himself he couldn't afford to get all worked up over someone who thought him contemptible.

So what had triggered the attitude? Pulling into the parking lot of the church, he was once again pondering that question.

How could someone be so pretty and prickly all at the same time? As he began to calm down, something hit him: Maybe it wasn't he at all. Katrice's reaction to him might well be learned behavior. *Could he be paying for the misdeeds of another man or could she really be that—*

"So can I go?"

Lee took his eyes off the road and his mind off Katrice long enough to glance at Kyra sideways. How long had she been talking to him? He barely remembered her getting into the car.

Man up and get yourself together.

"Can you go where, honey?"

Kyra pouted when she realized her eloquent plea to accompany Amber and her mother to Cincinnati on Friday had not been heard. This wasn't the first time her father had been staring off into space while she was talking to him.

"I just told you where. You weren't listening."

Lee shifted restlessly. No, he hadn't been listening. He had been thinking about Miss Katrice Ware and what he could do to change her mind about him.

"I'm sorry. I had something on my mind. Where is it you want to go?"

Kyra took a deep breath. She knew this was going to be a tough sell, so she had to make an earnest plea or else she would miss out on what she hoped would be a fun trip.

"Amber and her mother are going to Cincinnati, and they wanted to know if I could go with them. It would just be for the day and we would be back around nine o'clock. Mrs. Reynolds said she would give you a call tonight to explain the details."

"When?"

"Friday, Dad. I already said that."

"Friday? That's the grand opening of Book Wares."

Kyra gave her father a confused look. "I know, but I don't have to have my books read by then, do I? I thought I had until next week."

Lee shook his head in an attempt to rein in his scattered thoughts. "I'm sorry. You're right. You don't have to have them read this soon. I was just saying that Book Wares opens on Friday, that's all."

Kyra wondered why her father was acting so strangely. It wasn't so much that he had practically ignored everything she'd said over the past five minutes. Something seemed to be bothering him. She had noticed it when he picked her up from the church. It seemed to Kyra that he was agitated. Since she knew she hadn't done anything to upset him, she didn't worry about it too much. She decided it would be best if she left him alone with his thoughts so she could spring her other requests on him at the right time—the trip with Amber and her mother was actually a shopping trip and she would need some money to take with her.

While her father stared blankly at the road ahead, Kyra made a point of keeping her head turned to the side so he wouldn't notice the pink lip gloss she had on. After he glanced in her direction to tell her to fasten her seat belt, she felt pretty confident she had pulled off her little makeup coup, much to her delight. In her father's book, lip gloss was makeup and he had warned her on more than one occasion that he didn't want to see anything that remotely looked like makeup on her face until she had reached the ripe old age of sixteen. To Kyra, sixteen seemed light years away and she had to be the only girl on the planet who couldn't at least wear lip gloss. Amber did.

Something else strange had happened when her father had picked her up, Kyra thought, as she craned to admire her "new look" in the car's side mirror. Not only had he not noticed the lip gloss, he hadn't made a fuss when she changed the radio station from jazz to hip-hop, a form of music he really detested. On top of that, he had mentioned the grand opening of the bookstore as if she hadn't been standing there when Katrice mentioned it.

Maybe his weird behavior could be blamed on old age. Some of her friends had parents that were older than her dad, and Kyra had heard stories about their strange behavior. Forgetting things and repeating the same stories over and over probably wasn't too far behind for her dad. He didn't actually do any of that now, but maybe it was just a matter of time.

Well, whatever had caused her father to act so strangely, Kyra hoped it lasted all summer, especially if it meant he would be a little less strict.

CHAPTER 7

The evening sun had long since set when Katrice arrived home. She and two of her new employees had stayed late at the bookstore to make final preparations for the next day's grand opening.

Just thinking about it had Katrice worrying that something would go wrong. While everything didn't have to be perfect, close to perfection with no major mishaps would work just as well.

Going over her list of things to do for about the hundredth time, Katrice wanted to be sure that she hadn't forgotten a thing. Special gifts with purchase items had been set aside for the first customers of the day. Specialty coffees ordered from Seattle had arrived a few days earlier and were lined up for sale on the shelves in the coffee nook. Bookmarks, fliers announcing upcoming events, and other promotional materials were scattered throughout the store. Complimentary bowls of foil-wrapped chocolates had been placed at the checkout counter.

There was nothing left to do except to show up tomorrow, open the doors for business, and pray for paying customers.

Katrice sat on the couch and checked her phone messages. There were the usual messages from telemarketers urging her to try satellite TV, support a charitable cause, or calling to congratulate her on the fabulous vacation she'd won to some sunny and exotic location. She laughed. Between spending time getting Book Wares up and running and fixing up her house she could barely remember the last time she had watched TV, let alone take a vacation. Taking any time off would be a pipe dream for about the next five years or at least until Book Wares started to show a steady profit.

The last message instantly turned Katrice's mood from light to somber.

"Hi, Katrice. This is your mother. I was just checking to make sure you were

all right. Your father and I haven't heard from you in a while. I told him I thought you were busy taking time to sort things out with your life. I spoke with your sister yesterday and she and the kids are doing fine. Robert is working hard, as usual, and we haven't seen him in a while. Would you believe he just bought her a new car? She took me for a ride in it yesterday. It was like riding on a cloud. I swear, that man spoils her so. Good news! Taryn has been chosen to head the annual fundraiser for the Women's Clinic. That's sure to keep her busy over the next year, not to mention all the people she'll be meeting and the valuable connections she'll make. One more thing. I spoke with Greg the other day. You really need to give him a call, Katrice. He's not taking the breakup well and frankly, I still don't understand what is going on between you two.

Well, honey, I've got to run. Call when you get a moment."

No mention of Book Wares. No questions about her move to Benton Lake. Nothing indicating her mother cared about how things were going in her life or even what was important to her. She had been here since January. Even now, six months later, her family still treated her move as something she would "get over" and move on afterward. *Typical.*

Katrice didn't bother to save the message. Why should she? Did she really need another reminder of her family's complete lack of support? She rose wearily from the couch and went to the kitchen to make something to eat.

Her mother still refused to acknowledge that she chose to do something different with her life. Why couldn't she come to terms with the fact that she and Taryn had different lives and goals? Marriage, children, and the whole society thing simply did not fit as comfortably into Katrice's life as it did Taryn's. Those things were Taryn's desires. At least that is what her sister pretended she wanted. Katrice had to wonder if deep down inside Taryn really knew what she wanted.

Katrice remembered the last time she had visited her sister's family. She had gone to visit them for a week before moving to Benton Lake. Taryn had spent the first two days chiding her little sister for giving up a promising career, leaving a good man, and trading what seemed like a comfortable life to settle down in a place that held no promise for anything deemed worthy of Katrice's time and talent. The rest of the week she had waged a full-fledged campaign to prove how perfect her life was with her husband, Robert, who worked sixty to seventy hours a week providing the things Taryn felt they needed to prove how successful they were. In Katrice's opinion, Taryn and the kids had more clothes, trinkets, and gadgets than was necessary. It made Katrice sad to see how much Taryn spoiled the kids and how rotten they were becoming. Although she hadn't mentioned her concern to her sister, she wondered how much longer Robert would allow Taryn to put everything and everyone else before their relationship.

Katrice knew Robert loved her sister and the kids, but she had wanted to tell him to stop giving Taryn and the kids material things and spend more time at home with them. She felt sure that was the reason her nephew was such a handful; he needed time with his father. Unfortunately, Taryn spent so much time trying to be mother of the year it seemed as if she had forgotten that raising children meant more than cramming their lives with activities. Taryn and Robert's two children were so busy being shuttled back and forth to piano, soccer, voice, and swim lessons that Katrice had barely spent any time with them. The few moments she did spend with her niece and nephew required exceptional patience.

Although she loved them dearly, she had to admit that her six-year-old niece and eight-year-old nephew were turning into absolute brats. They whined and complained about the least little thing. They were disrespectful to their mother and would only mind her when she threatened to tell their father. However, most nights when Robert came home he was too exhausted to do anything with the children, let alone discipline them.

Katrice could see the strain on her sister's marriage, but Taryn seemed oblivious to it all. Apparently, Taryn felt that appearances were more important than the life she actually led. At the end of the visit, Katrice had left feeling grateful that she wasn't being forced to live her sister's "perfect" life.

Sitting back on the couch, Katrice balanced her dinner plate on her lap and got comfortable. Between bites of her sandwich and munching on chips, she leafed through her mail and mentally went over the details of the grand opening one more time. She had intended to decorate the shop with colorful balloons, but couldn't find the packages she thought she'd purchased from Smithfield's. Oh, well, being more organized and staying mindful of unfinished tasks were things she continually worked to improve. Hopefully, her employees would be better at it than she.

Geneva, the woman she'd hired to work mornings and afternoons, had been scheduled to meet her early to open up the shop. Katrice had been lucky to find her. A retired teacher, Geneva was warm, friendly, and the type of person who would make customers feel at home at Book Wares. She had been one of the first to apply for three of the part-time positions Katrice had posted.

The next person hired was Patrick. A shy and somewhat serious young man, he had explained to Katrice that he was taking time off from college to find his purpose in life. That was the reason he had given for wanting to work at Book Wares, and the fact that he needed a steady income. Katrice knew Patrick's purpose in life probably had very little to do with selling books or working in a coffee shop, but he had impressed her with his candor, friendly attitude, and odd sense of humor. From the varied employment history listed on his résumé, Patrick did not seem to be the type of person to stay on a job long, but Katrice had a good feeling about him and decided he would be worth taking a chance on. He, too, would be a welcome addition to Book Wares.

Millicent Vanderpool was the last person Katrice hired. It had taken careful consideration when it came down to making a hiring decision about Millicent.

A twenty-two-year-old college dropout who had attended three different colleges in three different parts of the country in the past four years did not seem to be someone who would be of much use to Katrice. To add further validity to her doubts, Millicent's fields of studies had been as diverse as her colleges. From what Katrice could gather from her résumé and their initial interview, Millicent had studied everything from philosophy to Latin to ceramic engineering. In addition to her incomplete and unusual college career, her appearance also caused Katrice a bit of concern.

Sporting black spiked hair, a ring through her eyebrow, a stud directly below her bottom lip, and a tattoo of an elf on her ankle, it had taken a little effort for Katrice to focus on Millicent's qualifications rather than on her appearance. But once Katrice really talked with her, it took only a moment for Millicent's love of books, her outgoing personality, and fresh outlook on life to shine through.

Millicent had shared with Katrice that her family didn't approve of her lifestyle. Both her parents were professionals and had planned for their daughter to one day have a career that would be financially and personally fulfilling. Millicent had other plans; she just couldn't articulate them. At least she had a simple philosophy by which she lived her life: try everything at least once, be true to yourself, and not end up like her parents.

Katrice washed her dinner dishes and placed them on the rack to dry. Completing her nighttime ritual of watering plants and checking the locks on the front and back doors, she headed upstairs to bed, hoping for a good night's sleep, a spectacular grand opening, and that one day she, too, would create such a philosophy.

CHAPTER 8

Katrice stood in front of Book Wares clutching an armload of books. Smiling brightly and dressed casually in dark pants and a light-colored sweater, she appeared relaxed, carefree, and genuinely happy.

Oddly, even in the grainy black and white newspaper photo she had the ability to quicken Lee's heartbeat. He'd read the accompanying story five, maybe six times that evening already and was reading it once again.

"You like her, don't you?"

Startled, Lee looked up from the newspaper to see Kyra peering over his shoulder with a knowing smile on her face. He quickly folded the newspaper and stuck it under a pile of contracts he had been reviewing.

"What are you talking about?"

"Come on, Dad. Give me some credit. I'm not a little kid anymore. I noticed how you were staring at Miss Katrice when we went by the bookstore. You were being extra polite and saying things that you normally don't say." Kyra rolled her eyes playfully and stood in front of her father. "I was kind of embarrassed but I kept it to myself. My dad has a crush. I thought only seventh-grade boys looked that goofy when they were around girls they liked. Guess it happens to old people, too."

"Oh, now I look goofy? And I'm old, too?"

Kyra grabbed an apple from the fruit bowl on the counter and walked over to her dad, placing her hand reassuringly on his shoulder. "No offense, Dad, but you've had that goofy look for a while now. I thought it was just old age, but now I know you've been hit by a monster crush."

Lee removed his daughter's hand from his shoulder. "Can you stop with the old stuff, please? Besides, *mature* people don't have crushes."

Kyra took a bite of her apple and shrugged. "If you say so. I just call it like I see it."

"You don't see anything, little girl. And don't talk with food in your mouth," Lee admonished, hoping to steer clear of the current conversation and on to a less awkward topic.

"Ask her out. She probably likes you, too."

Lee stared at Kyra's back as she walked out of the room happily munching on her apple and contentedly sticking her nose in his business. Wasn't it just yesterday she was playing with dolls and needed her father to scare the bogeyman away? All of a sudden she's giving relationship advice. His little girl was indeed growing up.

Sighing, Lee pulled the newspaper out from under the contracts. He wondered if he really should take his daughter's advice. Did Katrice like him, too? She certainly didn't act like it. Judging by their previous encounters, it was more likely she would sooner drive a stake through his heart than to share a steak dinner with him.

She certainly was pretty, he thought, looking at the newspaper photo again. Good thing he hadn't said that aloud. He smiled, thinking he actually did sound as if he was in the seventh grade.

He became thoughtful as he returned to studying the image in front of him. If he thought for one minute about following Kyra's advice, he would have to approach the situation with care. Katrice still remained a mystery to him. She appeared warm and friendly when she dealt with Kyra, but she treated him as if he were Jack the Ripper. Well, little did she know, mysteries fascinated him. Unraveling the mystery of Katrice Ware would be no exception.

Leaning back in his chair, Lee absentmindedly flipped through the pages of the contract he had been preparing for one of his father's friends. He needed to drop the document off tomorrow to obtain a signature. Perhaps he'd stop on his way back home and pick up something interesting to read.

Taryn had to place her hand over the mouthpiece of the phone to remind her children she was talking and to please keep the noise down. As usual, they ignored her.

"No, Mom, I haven't spoken with Katrice in a few weeks. It seems as if she's been so busy with this reshaping of her life, or whatever it is she's supposed to be doing, she doesn't have time to keep in touch with her family anymore. I won't even mention that foolishness about the bookstore. I can't imagine why anyone in her right mind would want to live in Benton Lake, let alone try to establish some kind of business there."

"What is going on in that girl's head?"

Melinda Ware was truly baffled by the differences between her two daughters. Taryn, her eldest by three years, had a nice, hard-working husband, two beautiful children, and a lovely home in the suburbs of Chicago. She actively participated in her children's lives, remained supportive of her husband's career, and kept involved in her community. Katrice had never seemed to be interested in any of that. In fact, she seemed to abhor it.

Even as children, Katrice and Taryn had been very different. Taryn had been outgoing, charismatic, and ambitious, while Katrice was quiet, studious, and kept to herself so much that Melinda often wondered if her youngest daughter would ever make it in the real world.

Melinda sighed. "Greg called a few days ago. Poor dear. He's so confused by Katrice breaking off their engagement and leaving town that he doesn't know what to do. I tried to find out what happened between the two of them, but he was as tight-lipped as Katrice. All he would say was that he loved her and wanted a chance to prove his love for her. He asked me if I knew what was going on in her life. Frankly, I really couldn't say. She's apparently too busy to return our phone calls."

Taryn's attention was drawn away from the conversation when she heard a loud ruckus. Identifying the source of the commotion, she inwardly groaned. Her son had his sister pinned to the floor as the two of them fought over a toy.

"Uh, Mom, I have to go. I think someone's at the door," Taryn lied when her daughter let out a wail as her brother pulled her hair.

"Okay, dear, kiss the babies for me and tell Robert that your father and I said hello."

Melinda placed the phone on its cradle and studiously ignored her husband as he sat across from her, scowling over the top of the evening newspaper.

"Melinda, I wish you would stop treating Katrice as if she is some lost soul that needs to be rescued. Did it ever occur to you that she doesn't return your phone calls because she doesn't want to be criticized?"

"Oh, Vincent, you don't understand," she said, waving her hand absently at her husband. "You've never understood."

"What is it you think I don't understand? That our daughter is ambitious? Or that she has decided to try something different with her life? Maybe it's that Katrice is trying to live her own life without your stamp of approval?"

Melinda shot her husband a scathing look.

"Melinda, Katrice is not doing anything wrong. Making the type of changes to her life that she did may not have been anything that you or I would have done, but so what? She's not us. I'm proud of her for making a decision to shake up her life a little bit, especially if she wasn't happy. How many people are brave enough to do that? Instead of supporting her you make it sound as if she's sold all of her worldly possessions, shaved her head, and joined a cult. The girl quit a job that no longer challenged her, moved to a different city, and is starting her own business. Seems like just cause to be proud of her, if you ask me."

"I just want her to be happy."

"Who said she's not happy?"

"How can she be happy rambling around in a drafty old house? And what about the fact that our daughter is living in a one-horse town among strangers with no one to look after her?"

Vincent could only shake his head as he gave his wife a look that left no doubt that he thought she had characteristically blown things out of proportion. If he had learned nothing throughout his years of marriage to Melinda, he knew one thing for sure: As far as Melinda was concerned, when it came to her daughters there were no boundaries.

"What is that look supposed to mean?"

"You need to mind your own business."

"But I just—"

"Leave it alone, Mel. Our baby girl is all grown up. She may not be living the kind of life you or I would have chosen for her, but she is living the life that *she* has chosen to live. I think we need to support her, and be there for her when and if she needs us."

With that said Vincent took his newspaper and left the room. Staying would have meant having to endure his wife's defense of her behavior.

After her husband left the room, Melinda sat on the couch with her arms folded and thought about what he'd just said. It was no wonder Vincent didn't share in her belief that Katrice had lost her mind. Katrice was just like his mother.

Harriet Ware had been the type of woman who threw caution to the wind without regard for the consequences.

Well, Melinda wanted her girls to be more levelheaded than that. The absolute last thing she wanted was for daughter to end up the lonely old woman Harriet had become.

As a mother, Melinda felt it her obligation to make sure her daughters had the best. She also knew that she had to keep them from making costly mistakes, especially ones that she felt she could easily prevent.

Melinda got her purse and fished out her address book. Knowing her husband would be furious with her for what she was about to do, she closed the door to the den and placed a call that she hoped would put an end to the mess Katrice had gotten herself into.

CHAPTER 9

Geneva sidestepped a group of teenagers flipping through gossip magazines and went behind the counter just as Katrice finished waiting on a customer. As the assistant manager of Book Wares, she and Katrice shared many of the same tasks as well as the same expectations for the budding business.

"Finally, a moment to breathe," Geneva exclaimed as she leaned against the counter.

While Katrice couldn't have been more delighted with the steady stream of customers they'd had since the doors opened earlier that morning, she, too, was delighted to have a few minutes to catch her breath.

"I'm glad I caught up with Millicent this morning. She agreed to come in a little earlier to help out. I don't know if we could have handled everything without her."

Geneva nodded in agreement. "It's a good thing, too. I don't know what's in that coffee, but folks couldn't get enough of it today. Patrick could barely keep up with the orders. Although I do have to say I'm really impressed with his ability to keep a cool head under pressure."

Thinking about the earlier rush in the coffee shop, Katrice agreed. There was more of a demand than she had expected for the fresh-baked goods and gourmet coffee. She and Geneva were too busy to lend Patrick a hand, but Millicent had readily stepped in when she saw the line getting long. While Patrick waited on customers, Millicent filled orders. The two of them worked well as a team, which pleased Katrice and further reassured her that she had made smart hiring choices. "I've already put an ad in the paper for another part-time person to help out in both the coffee shop and the bookstore. Until then, we'll all have to give a little bit of extra time and effort if needed."

Geneva nodded in agreement.

After taking a quick break, Katrice went back to work and began restocking a popular series of picture books that were selling almost as fast as she could place them on the shelf. As she moved from that task and on to another, time seemed to fly by. As she finished ringing up a customer's purchase, she asked Geneva to send Millicent on break while they experienced a bit of a lull.

"I think we've sold almost all of those home-improvement books," Geneva remarked, nodding in the direction of the nearly empty bookstand located by the cash register. "I might have to buy one for my husband. Since he's been retired, he has a lot more time on his hands that he doesn't know what to do with. Hopefully, he'll begin to make good use of his time and start some of the projects he's been putting off over the years."

"What does he do during the day when you're working?"

"He works out at the gym on Mondays, Wednesdays, and Fridays. He bowls on Tuesdays with some other retirees from his old job and he reads in his spare time."

Katrice nodded thoughtfully, wishing she had more time to read some of the books she spent the better part of her day logging into inventory, shelving, and bagging for her customers. "Tell him he's welcome to come here any time. He can even use your employee discount."

"I can't promise that he'd be a big customer, but every little bit helps. Speaking of which, I have to admit your idea of featuring a group of local authors for a book signing on the same day as the grand opening had me a little worried at first," said the animated Geneva. "But I'll be the first to admit that you struck on a good idea. Did you see the line of people waiting for the cookbook author? I had never heard of him before today, but my curiosity got the best of me and I bought one of his books for myself."

Smiling, Katrice admitted that she, too, had wondered if her idea had been a little overzealous. Fortunately, everything had gone off without a hitch.

"I'm just happy the authors had a chance to promote their work."

"I looked over the calendar of events you gave me last week, and I'm predicting more busy days like today."

"I certainly hope so," Katrice replied, more to herself than to Geneva. She felt the all too familiar flip-flop in her stomach when she thought about how much of her meager savings and inheritance she had invested in the bookstore and how important the success of Book Wares was not only to her ego but also to her livelihood.

Turning out the cover of a popular book on stock-market investing, Katrice looked around the store to see what else needed to be done. Nervous energy fueled her desire to keep busy.

Taking in the activity inside the bookstore, she noticed that the earlier crowds had thinned a little, but business seemed to remain steady. A few patrons in the coffee shop enjoyed iced coffee and freshly baked scones. Over in another corner of the store that would soon feature morning and afternoon storytime for preschoolers, a young mother sat reading to her two small children. The overstuffed chairs Katrice had found at an Amish furniture store in one of the neighboring towns proved to be the final touch that had been needed to give the area a cozy and welcoming feel. She had even purchased one of the chairs for her own home.

Katrice couldn't help smiling as pride and a sense of accomplishment enveloped her simultaneously. Despite her family's reservations and hurtful lack of support, she had done the right thing. And in her heart, Book Wares had already proved to be a success.

Just then her stomach growled and she remembered the box of granola bars in her desk drawer. They were calling her name. Before taking a break, Katrice put out a new supply of promotional bookmarks and tidied a bookshelf.

"Excuse me."

She inwardly sighed. *Break time and the granola bars were going to have to wait.* Turning to greet a customer she asked, "Hi, may I help—"

Lee Oliver looked amused when Katrice's offer to help trailed off at the sight of him.

"Help me?" he finished for her.

Katrice turned her back to Lee and busied herself straightening a book on a shelf. *What was he doing here?*

Lee heard her sigh and wondered if it stemmed from exasperation or something else.

"I don't imagine that you'll be in business very long if this is the way you treat your customers. By the way, you just turned that book upside down."

Glancing sideways at the book she had just put on the shelf, she realized with a noticeable degree of annoyance that he was right. Grabbing the book with a little more force than she intended, she accidentally knocked several other books off the shelf and on to the floor.

Lee made no attempt to help pick them up.

Katrice knelt down and picked the books up, carefully placing them right side up on the shelf. When she finished she turned to face Lee and placed her hands on her hips. Annoyed that he was still there, she asked, "So are you a customer or are you here for another reason?" *Wrong choice of words.* There should be no other reason for Lee to be standing in her bookstore looking and smelling so divine other than to buy coffee or a book.

"Now that depends."

She felt a little silly for overreacting to him, but she just could not relax around this man. Looking around for help, she saw Geneva was busy ringing up a customer and she remembered Millicent was on a break. Well, regardless of what she felt, he was a customer and would be treated as such. She couldn't afford to treat him, or anyone else, rudely. Dropping her hands and her defensive attitude, she asked, "What can I do for you?"

Lee folded his arms across his impressive chest. "I'm going to be very careful when I answer your question. I seem to have a knack for saying the wrong thing around you, and I don't want that to happen today."

Her hands went back on her hips. "Then I guess you'll need to choose your words carefully. Just a hint, keep your inquiry to something simple like 'Where can I find a book on . . .' or 'What's your most expensive coffee and can I buy a pound of it' and we'll be fine."

Lee didn't bother to hide his amusement. As hard as she tried to remain annoyed with him, he could tell it was proving to be a bit of an effort. He wasn't quite sure why she felt the need, but he decided to leave that alone for now.

As she stood before him with her hands on her slender but adequately curvy hips, he paid particular attention to her smoldering dark eyes and berry-hued lips. Clearly, she had no idea how beautiful she was. Today she wore her hair in a loose twist that combined two looks—practical and pretty. Lee shifted his attention to the gold contraption that held her hair together, longing to reach out and free the thick, curly strands and to feel her soft mane sliding through his fingers. He wondered why she never wore her hair loose. *Could her hair possibly be as soft as it looked?* He imagined it smelled of springtime or rain . . .

Control, he warned himself.

Clearing his throat and willing his voice to sound normal, Lee said, "Actually, I am looking for a book."

To Lee's ears his voice sounded odd, but Katrice didn't seem to notice. He watched with amusement as one hand slid down her side and then back up to her hip. He was learning that this is what she did when she was annoyed.

Katrice didn't know what to think. Lee pretended to be shopping for a book but he suddenly seemed distracted and his voice sounded odd, almost . . . sexy. Could he be teasing her or worse, flirting?

She turned her attention away from him for a moment and looked around the shop. She needed to collect her thoughts and focus on something besides Lee. This man seemed hell-bent on driving her crazy. Or maybe she was making herself crazy. His intentions might actually be legitimate; maybe he really had come to the bookstore to purchase a book. Either way, she reminded herself, she had to earn a living. His money was as good as anyone else's. If she treated him like a customer, maybe he would buy something and go away, she reasoned.

Turning her attention back to Lee she asked, "Is there a particular book you're looking for?"

"How about a mystery? I was hoping you could suggest something stimulating."

Stimulating? Was this a play on words? She tried to read his expression. If he wasn't being serious, then she had to be. She did not have time for games. Her main focus was on running a successful business, not flirting with this broad-shouldered, mocha-hued, good-smelling brother with the sexy voice and flirty dimple that made her heart flutter every time it highlighted his handsome face.

Be serious. No time for games. Too much to do.

This time it was Katrice who cleared her throat before speaking. "Well, uh, we have a new release by one of my favorite authors I think you might find stim—enjoyable. It's a politically based mystery set in New York during the sixties."

Lee followed Katrice to the shelves housing mysteries, listening to her describe the book's plot along the way.

At first, nervous rambling marked her description, but as Katrice allowed herself to become absorbed in the plot of one of her favorite books, the critic, lover of literature, and genuine fan took over.

"The author is very good at staging several characters to look as if they are the perpetrator so you never really know who committed the crime until you're almost at the end of the book or at least I didn't. He also likes to sprinkle cleverly placed clues and several twists and turns throughout the book to keep you guessing. One thing I really liked was the way in which he described New York City during one of the most interesting times in history. In my opinion he included just the right amount of detail, without bogging down the story. When I read I want to be pulled into the story; this author does that from page one. This is definitely a page-turner. I don't think you'll be disappointed," she said, handing the book to Lee.

"Wow, you're good." He meant that. For a few minutes she had drawn him into her world. He found that he actually looked forward to reading the book. "Are you a history buff, too?" he asked wanting to keep her engaged in conversation.

"What do you mean?"

"You mentioned something about the sixties being an interesting time in history."

Katrice shrugged. "I wouldn't say I'm a history buff, but there are certain times in history that are more exciting than others."

"Fascinating."

Lee smiled. Dimple.

Katrice flushed.

"Is there anything else I can help you with?" she asked when he made no move toward the counter to check out.

Much to his disappointment, the climate had suddenly gone from helpful and friendly back to distant and guarded. "Well, yes, there is."

What now? How much longer could she be expected to stand within inches of this man and not lean in and get one good whiff of the cologne that had teased her nostrils the moment she had turned to face him? To further turn the tension up a notch his hand had brushed hers when he had taken the book from her. She could have sworn that he had done it on purpose, but the brief contact had sent a shower of tingles straight up her arm. Apparently, he hadn't felt a thing as he stood in front of her looking calm, collected, and absolutely scrumptious.

"I'd like to invite you to dinner." *Whoa! Where did that come from?* He'd meant to be a bit more subtle and a lot more suave but his mouth and brain weren't working in unison. Consequently, the dinner invitation just tumbled out.

Dumbfounded, Katrice stuttered when she asked, "Y-you want to do what?"

"I'd like for you to have dinner with me."

"Why would I want to do that?" *I can hardly stand here talking to you without imagining things that I shouldn't be imagining. Trying to eat might prove to be a complete disaster.*

In searching for the right words, Kyra's advice was the first thing that had come to mind. *Ask her out.* He couldn't tell Katrice that his twelve-year-old daughter had suggested the date. He needed to think of something fast, and Kyra's advice wasn't exactly what he wanted to repeat.

Lee gazed away from Katrice for a moment. When he looked back at her, he realized that he had caught her off guard. "There are a few reasons that come to mind. One, we can celebrate the grand opening of Book Wares. Two, I want to thank you for helping me out with Kyra. She is halfway through the first book you gave her and is pretty excited about participating in the discussion group. I think the experience is going to be good for her and will give her chance to make some new friends and keep busy this summer. Last, but certainly not least, I want another chance to make a good impression since my other attempts have failed miserably."

This time, Katrice looked away from Lee's intense gaze and tried to shift her attention to the top button of his shirt, hoping to be less distracted by the inanimate object. It didn't work. "You don't have to do that," she said quietly.

"Why not?"

"Because I don't think this is just about your daughter or my opening the bookstore."

Lee smiled slightly. "So what do you think this is about?"

Sigh. That smile. That blasted dimple! Katrice could feel her face growing warm. "I can't really say for sure."

"Then why don't you have dinner with me and find out for yourself?"

"You know, there are lots of other women in this town that would be much better company."

"That's a matter of opinion. And I can't think of anyone I'd rather share a meal with than you."

"I find that a little hard to believe."

"Well, believe me when I say there's something about you that I find interesting. It's not just that you're beautiful, smart, and ambitious. There's more. I can't quite put my finger on it, but if you give me a chance, I'd like to find out."

He thinks I'm beautiful? Instantly, her hand went up to smooth her hair. She could tell he was trying to gauge her reaction to what he just said. Clasping her hands together, she pretended to appear unaffected. "Did it ever occur to you that I could be happily married with ten children?"

Lee nodded thoughtfully. "Fair enough. That would be true, except for the article in the paper."

Katrice looked puzzled.

"Yesterday's paper featured a rather intriguing article about young, *single* entrepreneurs. Who knew we'd have any of those in Benton Lake? Anyway, a certain young woman who fit that description—young *and* single—was featured in the article. There was even a picture. Does any of this ring a bell?"

Busted. She wanted to wipe the smug look right off Lee's face. *Arrogant!*

"Katrice, phone," Geneva called from behind the front counter.

While she was gone, Lee pretended to scan an assortment of magazines on a nearby rack. However, it wasn't the glossy covers that held his attention. It was a sexy lady with long legs, pretty brown eyes, and a spicy attitude.

Idly flipping through a fitness magazine, he couldn't stop wondering what it was about her that had piqued his interest. As far as he could tell, the feeling still wasn't mutual. Katrice had made her feelings for him crystal clear on more than one occasion. With everyone else she appeared cordial, helpful, and pleasant. With him, she maintained an air of barely concealed contempt. Not since high school had he had to work this hard to impress a woman. It was humbling.

There had been a few glimpses of Katrice that belied her attitude toward him. When she had allowed herself to relax around him earlier, he had seen a softer, less prickly side to Katrice that had drawn him in a little deeper. Then there was the touch. He wasn't sure if she'd felt it, too, or if the whole thing had been his imagination working overtime. Their hands had touched briefly when she handed him the book. In that moment, a spark had passed through him, going straight to his heart, and causing an unexpected flutter and sending a surge of electric pulses through every nerve ending in his body.

Well, regardless of what he thought he felt or witnessed, it would have to remain tucked away for now.

Waiting for Katrice to finish her phone call, Lee continued to feign interest in the magazine. Then a change in her tone caught his interest. Trying to keep from eavesdropping on her conversation proved difficult, especially when he picked up on what seemed like distress in her voice.

When the call ended, Katrice slumped against the counter and sighed.

Concerned, Lee covered the distance from the magazine rack to the counter in just a few strides.

"Is everything all right?" he asked, trying to temper the concern in his voice.

"Hmm?" Katrice had retrieved a notebook from under the counter and was frantically flipping through the pages.

"Is something wrong?" Lee asked again.

Katrice looked up and stared blankly at Lee for a moment, and then her expression suddenly changed. The worry lines on her forehead disappeared and Lee could have sworn he saw a mischievous glint in her eye.

She closed the notebook and returned it to its place under the counter. "Maybe not," she replied. "Were you serious about dinner?"

"Yes," he replied hesitantly.

"Well, there's a chance that I might reconsider your offer if you'd be willing to help me out."

Although pleased at the prospect of having dinner with Katrice, Lee knew he had better choose his next words carefully. "You're asking for my help and if I say yes, you'd reconsider my offer to take you out to dinner? This should be interesting, if not frightening. First, will this favor require me to stand in the middle of traffic wearing a blindfold or something similar but equally dangerous?" Lee asked, placing the mystery novel Katrice had recommended on the counter.

"No, nothing dangerous or crazy. I promise."

Did she just bat her eyes at him?

"Then what?"

"Can you be here tomorrow around one? On second thought, make it one-thirty. Oh, yes, and before I forget, I have another book for Kyra. It's not for the discussion group, but I think she'll enjoy it. It's an advance copy from the publisher, so it's no charge."

After bagging his purchase and Kyra's book, Katrice came from behind the counter. "I really appreciate your willingness to help." Patting him on the shoulder, she said, "By the way, your book is on me."

With a wink and a smile, Katrice left to help another customer, leaving Lee to wonder what he had gotten himself into.

CHAPTER 10

Marshall Oliver was four years older than Lee, and two years older than his other brother, Sean. When they were kids, Marshall had taken his role as the big brother seriously. Even though they were now adults, he still did.

Marshall arrived in Benton Lake early Saturday morning for a surprise visit, and the first thing he did after walking into his father's house was to place his younger brother in a headlock. Much to their father's chagrin, this had been the brothers' customary greeting since childhood.

At the sight of the two men, both well over six feet tall and with a combined weight of nearly four hundred pounds, tussling, Sam issued a stern but jovial warning about playing in the house. The warning hadn't changed much over the years, although now was much less stern.

"Been working out? It's not as easy to take you down as it used to be."

Lee picked up the pillows that had fallen to the floor and returned them to the sofa. "That's 'cause you're getting old, bro," he replied, taking a seat.

Marshall plopped down beside his brother and playfully punched him in the arm. "I'll show you old."

Sam shot his sons a warning look on his way to the kitchen. "You break it, you buy it."

"Hey, where's my niece?"

"Sleeping. She went to Cincinnati yesterday and got back pretty late last night. Nothing short of an earthquake is going to get her out of bed until around noon."

Sam soon returned to the living room to summon them to breakfast.

Over a hearty meal of sausage, eggs, home fries, grits, and biscuits, the three men caught up on the happenings in each other's lives. Marshall, who owned a construction business, was on his way to Indianapolis for a trade show. Lee and Sam thought it odd that he'd made a detour to Benton Lake from the Cincinnati suburb where he lived, but neither of them said anything. Something else Lee found odd: The trade show was a week away, and Marshall had announced that he would be taking a few days off until then to do absolutely nothing. Eighty-hour workweeks and infrequent vacations defined Marshall's life, not days leisurely spent doing nothing.

"So how's Marisa?" Sam asked Marshall, refilling his coffee cup.

"History."

"What? How'd that happen? I thought the two of you were headed to the altar," Lee joked.

Marshall quipped, "You know me better than that. It's going to take more than a pretty face and a nice as—"

Sam cleared his throat loudly.

"Uh, I mean, a nice set of legs to get me to make that kind of commitment."

"Commitment. Hmm. What is it about that word that sends a grown man running for the hills?"

ALICIA WIGGINS

Both Marshall and Lee looked at their father as if he were speaking a foreign language.

In his defense Marshall spoke up. "I'm not afraid of commitment. I'm just happy with the way my life is right now. Besides, everyone is not cut out for marriage. I think I definitely fall into that category. Trust me, life is a whole lot easier to deal with once you recognize that little character flaw."

"I see," Sam said, leaning back in his chair. "Can't say that I agree with you, though. As I see it, everyone has a soul mate, son. I don't think you should give up on love because of a few bad relationships. Just a word of advice; keep hope alive."

Unmoved, Marshall said, "Dad, hope is on life support, and I think someone just tripped over the cord."

"So what's on tap for today?" Lee asked, feeling a need to change the subject before he and his brother had to endure a speech from their father on the trials and tribulations of finding and maintaining a lasting and meaningful relationship.

Sam was well qualified to school his sons on the dos and don'ts of such a relationship. He had married the boys' mother right out of high school, and they had lived happily, with a good portion of ups and downs, as husband and wife for nearly forty years until her death just several years earlier. Sam had loved his wife dearly but felt he had been doubly blessed to have found Vonda.

"Aren't you going to take Mrs. Parkins' will over to her this afternoon?" Sam asked, flipping through the morning paper.

87

Lee nodded. He had prepared a will for Mrs. Parkins and performed other legal services while on vacation. His father had secured enough work for him writing wills, reviewing contracts, and answering legal questions to last for most of the summer. But Lee didn't mind. Most of the people he was helping didn't have access to legal advice from someone they felt they could trust. He happily provided a much-needed service.

"Do you want to ride over with me?" Lee asked his brother. "I have to make another stop when I'm finished with Mrs. Parkins, but I can drop you off at the gym. If you like, we can even play golf or basketball later."

"Sounds good. I have my clubs but I didn't bring my basketball shoes. I wouldn't mind working out, though. Loan me a pair of your sneakers, and you can drop me off at the gym before you run your other errand." Marshall helped himself to more home fries. "Do you think Kyra might want to hang out with her uncle today?"

Lee grabbed the last biscuit before his brother could and smirked. "She's been invited to a pool party and is going to the movies with her friend after that. I hate to be the one to break it down like this, but as much as she loves you, I'm afraid you come in a distant second compared to her friends."

CHAPTER 11

Lillian Parkins didn't receive many visitors, but when she did, she made the most of it. Lee patiently discussed the details of the will he had prepared for her, making sure all of her wishes were documented and would be carried out to her exact specifications. After she was satisfied that her worldly possessions would be properly distributed between her loved ones and her church and had signed where required, Mrs. Parkins insisted on serving lemonade and homemade ginger cookies to her guests.

It took very little coaxing to get the brothers to sit down in Mrs. Parkins's living room for cookies and ice-cold lemonade made with real lemons. With as much interest as they could muster they listened to stories of Mrs. Parkins's grandchildren's achievements, neighborhood gossip, and church news.

As one o'clock neared Lee did his best to wrap up the visit. He could tell she was lonely, and made a point of scheduling another visit with her very soon. Standing on her front porch with a take-home bag of ginger cookies, Lee and Marshall each placed a kiss on Mrs. Parkins's rose-scented cheek and thanked her for her warm hospitality.

She practically gushed. "You two boys have grown up to be such handsome and delightful young men. If only I were forty years younger," she said with a wink.

Marshall and Lee felt like young boys again, thanking Mrs. Parkins once more for the cookies and promising to visit again.

As they drove away, Lee asked his brother, "Do you remember when we were kids and at Halloween how Mrs. Parkins used to give out the best candy?"

"I can't say that I remember that, but I do have some pretty fond memories of Mrs. Parkins's niece from Florida." Marshall clutched his chest dramatically and let out a low whistle. "Remember her?"

Lee nodded and smiled fondly.

"Summer vacation didn't mean much until she showed up. Wonder how she turned out?"

"According to Mrs. Parkins, she is now a doctor and practicing medicine in the impoverished areas of Central and South America. I think she's been in Honduras for about the past year or so."

Marshall turned to his brother. "You're kidding. A doctor, huh?"

Nodding, Lee laughed. "Trust me, it's the truth. I'm told she went to college, later joined the Peace Corps, and apparently found her calling during a stint in Uganda caring for war orphans."

Marshall looked surprised.

"What were you expecting? A model or actress, right?"

"Yeah, something like that."

"Maybe if you hadn't been so busy drooling over her legs and other physical attributes that I'm too much of a gentleman to mention, you would have recognized that she had beauty, brains, *and* ambition."

Marshall shrugged and bit into a cookie. "Who knew?"

Driving along for a few minutes in silence, Lee grabbed a cookie.

"So are you going to tell me what's going on?"

"What do you mean?"

"For starters, you show up here in Benton Lake for a few days of R and R, and you expect us to believe you're a reformed workaholic."

"Is the pot calling the kettle black?"

"This isn't about me, Marshall."

"It's not that serious. Business is slow right now, and this seemed to be the best time to take a few days off."

"Dad might buy that, but I don't."

Marshall looked out the passenger-side window, hoping his brother would drop his line of questioning.

"Okay. So explain to me why you're attending the trade show. When is the last time you attended one of those things? Don't you usually send your partner, Harlan, to trade shows and conventions?"

"I told you, business is slow and I thought I would take a few days off. Besides, there's no law that says I can't go to trade shows."

"That sounds good, but you're going to have to try again."

Shifting his weight, Marshall wondered when his little brother had become so intuitive. "Sometimes you just need to come home for a while. This is one of those times."

"Does your need to be home have anything to do with a certain ex-wife's wedding?"

Surprised, Marshall turned to his brother. "How did you hear about that?"

"Someone that Sean knows also knows Tiffany and he mentioned it to him. Why didn't you tell me that your ex was getting married again?"

"Because I keep telling myself that I don't care."

"Do you?"

"In a strange sort of way, yes, though I can't really explain why. It took a year after our divorce before I stopped pretending that I wasn't hurt our marriage had ended. I made a point of dating as many women as I could during that time to prove that just because Tiffany didn't want me anymore, someone else still did."

"Tiffany was a gold-digging, selfish, spoiled brat who proved to be incapable of loving anyone other than herself. You were simply a means to an end for her, and nothing more."

Lee had been waiting a long time to say that to his brother and now seemed like the perfect time. He had disliked Tiffany almost from the moment he'd first met her. From her flashy clothes and expensive jewelry to her overbearing personality, Lee still wondered what it had been about her that had hooked his brother.

It hadn't taken long after Tiffany and Marshall were married for her to put into place a plan to distance him from his family. It was typically Tiffany who declined family get-togethers. She made it known in no uncertain terms that she hated coming to Benton Lake, referring to the town as a dusty, boring farm town stuck in the middle of nowhere. When she did come for a visit, she spent the entire time complaining and whining about being bored. To add insult to injury, Lee, Sean, and Sam were rarely invited to visit their home.

It had taken a while for Marshall to finally come to the realization that Tiffany simply did not love him. Her feelings were strictly wrapped around Marshall making possible a lifestyle that she couldn't afford on her own. Marshall's construction business was moderately profitable so he could—and did—give his wife anything she wanted and then some. However, he soon realized the more he gave her, the more she wanted. Squarely facing that realization had been a hard pill to swallow, and the hurt he felt from the discovery still stung. Marshall had not trusted his heart to another woman since.

"It didn't occur to you to give me your opinion of Tiffany *before* we were married? That bit of information would have saved me a lot of heartache and money."

"Would you have listened?"

Marshall thought for a moment and then replied, "Probably not."

"That's why I didn't say a thing. So home is where the heart heals?"

"Something like that."

"Hope it works for you, man. I really do."

Lee dropped his brother off at the gym and drove straight to Book Wares. He knew his brother would be okay; Tiffany was now someone else's problem. Time spent away from his daily routine should be good for him and should help him forget the lingering bad memories from his marriage. Coming home certainly seemed to be working for him. He felt more relaxed and at ease than he had in a long time. He hoped it worked for Marshall as well.

Lee's thoughts easily transitioned from Marshall to Katrice as he pulled into the small parking lot behind Book Wares. He tried not to be too concerned about what she had planned for him that afternoon, but was confident that whatever it was he could handle it. Another chance to be around her was an added bonus. He had to admit he enjoyed being in her company despite her tendency to show him only her abrasive side.

The bookstore buzzed with activity. Patrons in the coffee shop chatted, read, and enjoyed gourmet coffee and fresh baked goodies. The aroma of something freshly baked met Lee at the door, making him forget all about the half dozen or so cookies he had just eaten at Mrs. Parkins's.

He was a few minutes early. He looked around the shop but didn't see Katrice. As he made his way to the counter to ask the clerk for her, a young woman with spiked hair and what looked like blue lipstick asked if he needed help. Had she not been wearing a blue smock emblazoned with the shop's logo and her name stenciled across the pocket, he would have never guessed she was an employee.

It took some effort not to gawk at the young woman, who looked as if she had just stepped out of a heavy-metal video. She appeared to be in her late teens or early twenties, just at that age when shock value and expressing yourself were more important than fitting in. *Was this what he had to look forward to with Kyra?* He prayed not.

"Hi, I'm looking for Katrice. Is she around?" Lee tried to keep from counting the young woman's piercings but he couldn't help himself. *Eleven.*

The clerk nodded enthusiastically. "Yes, I think she's expecting you. By the way, I'm Millicent," she said cheerfully and extended her hand.

Lee shook her outstretched hand, being careful not to squeeze too tightly and risk disturbing the gold ring that went through the skin between her thumb and index finger.

"If you don't mind my saying so, you're not quite what I expected," she said with a slight giggle. "This should be really cute. Please follow me."

Exactly what was she expecting, and for what?

In the back corner of the shop, Katrice sat in the middle of a small group of children sitting on a brightly colored rug. The children were listening intently to her remarks.

"You all are in for a very special treat today," she said. "This is Mr. Oliver, and he has been kind enough to be our volunteer reader today." Katrice looked at Lee with an encouraging smile and held up three books. She hoped he wouldn't bolt for the door and would be true to his word and help her out.

"Who likes dinosaurs?"

A chorus of "me" rang out.

"And who wants to learn about all the different kinds of fish in the ocean?"

Another chorus of "me."

Katrice stood and gestured toward a chair that Lee thought had been made for a kindergartener.

"This is what you chose for me to help you with?" he whispered to Katrice as the children waited anxiously for storytime to begin.

Katrice smiled sweetly and replied, "Be careful what you ask for."

With fifteen pairs of eyes on him, Lee carefully lowered himself into the chair Katrice had placed in front of the children; he prayed that it wouldn't give way.

"Which one are you going to read first?" one of the few boys in the group asked.

Lee slightly shifted his weight in the chair while balancing the books on his lap. He decided there was no getting comfortable; he would have to make the best of it. He looked over at the boy, who he guessed to be about four years old, who had asked the question.

"Well, let's see what we have here: dinosaurs, using good manners, and the ocean. Should we start with dinosaurs?"

All heads nodded in agreement.

Lee started reading the story of a young dinosaur who wanted to hurry and grow up. He wanted to be tall enough to reach the juiciest leaves on the highest trees just like his dad, but he couldn't because he just wasn't tall enough yet. The children laughed when Lee animated his voice to reflect that of a gruff male voice and when he made it higher to sound like the mother's voice. By the time he finished the third story about manners, the children wanted more.

Lee had forgotten how active the imaginations of young children could be. One little girl had asked if dinosaurs ate anything else besides leaves. More specifically, she wanted to know if they liked cookies.

Although he had only read three books, the entire storytime experience had taken close to thirty minutes, especially with the children asking questions and with Lee's added theatrical embellishments.

Katrice feigned indifference when she heard giggles mixed with *oohs* and *ahs* coming from the children's area. When Millicent commented on the wonderful job Lee was doing with the children, Katrice simply smiled and nodded nonchalantly. She'd actually thought the same but didn't want to be the one to mention it. If she absolutely had to admit it, she would say she was impressed that he had done such an excellent job.

He was good with the children. Greg hated being around them.

The university where she had taught ran a tutoring program for elementary aged children. She volunteered with the program and had tried to persuade Greg to do the same. After practically begging him to commit at least one day a week to the program, he reluctantly agreed. The experience for the children was a disaster. He was impatient and cold to the children and none of them wanted to work with him. He barely lasted three days.

"Where have you been hiding him?" Millicent asked.

Katrice looked up and noted with a bit of annoyance Millicent's dreamy expression. She groaned inwardly. Millicent apparently thought the two of them were an item.

Making a show of appearing uninterested, she replied, "I haven't been hiding anyone. He's just someone who expressed an interest in helping out. So I put him to work."

Geneva joined Katrice and Millicent at the counter. "Good choice for storytime reader. I thought one of us would have to fill the spot today."

"So did I." Katrice hadn't wanted to think about it, but she had halfway thought Lee wouldn't show up. If he hadn't, her other alternative would have been to draft Millicent or Geneva to read stories to the children. But that would have been a problem if they had gotten busy, and they had.

So everything had turned out nicely. Now she would have to be a woman of her word and keep her end of the agreement.

The sound of applause signaled that the reading session was ending, and Katrice returned to the children's area. Parents were collecting their children and buying copies of the books Lee had read to them. One enthused mother told Katrice her son had enjoyed the stories and assured her they intended to be regulars. She bought copies of all three books.

Once the reading area was cleared of the children and their parents, Katrice began tidying up. She sensed Lee observing her from his little chair, but she refused to acknowledge him just yet. He had done an outstanding job and he knew it. It wasn't that she didn't want to acknowledge that he had helped her out in a jam; she just didn't want him to be so cocky about it, glimpsing his smug expression from the corner of her eye.

"What time do I pick you up for dinner?"

Katrice finally turned to face Lee. She bit her bottom lip and wondered how someone could look so smug and devilishly handsome at the same time. She wished she had the ability to be oblivious to him, but he made it so darned difficult.

"About that—"

Rising to his feet, Lee braced himself for an excuse. "Don't tell me you're trying to back out of our deal."

Is that an option? She looked around the shop, desperately hoping to find an excuse to get out of going to dinner with Lee.

There was nothing. "No, it's just that the shop doesn't close until six tonight."

Relaxing, Lee smiled.

Katrice's resolve began to crumble.

"Is that all?" he asked, relieved. "Well, I know Benton Lake is small, but I'm sure we'll be able to find a restaurant that's still open after six."

Katrice crossed her arms and thought for a moment. *Maybe spending a few hours with Lee over dinner wouldn't be so bad after all. This was dinner, not a lifetime commitment. Besides, a deal was a deal.* "You're right," she conceded. "What was I thinking?"

I could probably guess.

"You can pick me up . . . here . . . around six-fifteen, no, six-thirty."

"See you at six-thirty."

Lee practically walked on air as he left the shop, whereas, Katrice sat down wearily on the little chair in the reading corner and asked herself, "What have I gotten myself into?"

Staring at a list of minor tasks that needed her attention, Katrice gave up trying to make heads or tails of the variety of paper and type of ink cartridges she needed to purchase for the shop. No matter how she tried to focus on other things, she could not stop thinking about Lee. Her thoughts didn't just center on their upcoming dinner, but the man in general.

He puzzled and intrigued her. She was having a hard time trying to figure out how he had gotten under her skin, and why she had allowed it to happen. With his charm, good looks, and that blasted dimple, he seemed to be the kind of man that could make her mind stray off of the carefully defined path she had set for herself. Here she was distracted by him when her concentration should be strictly on the success of her bookstore. Instead, she was wondering about things that really should be of no concern to her at all.

One thing she wondered about was Lee's marital status. Did he have a wife? He didn't wear a ring, but that didn't mean much at all. Was he divorced or separated? He didn't seem the type to cheat, but who could tell these days? And what had brought him to Benton Lake for the whole summer? What did he do for a living that would allow him to take that much time off from work?

Her curiosity extended to Lee's daughter, secretly admiring their relationship. Lee struck her as the type of father who would move heaven and earth to make sure his child was in a safe, happy, and secure environment. While Katrice knew her own father loved her, she sensed there were limits to how far he would go to demonstrate that love.

Katrice leaned back in her chair and closed her eyes, letting her imagination roam. Did they share the same taste in literature, music, food? Did they have similar world views? Had his childhood been a happy one? Did he have pets or a favorite color?

What was the name of that sexy cologne he wore?

Sighing, Katrice leaned forward, resting her elbows on the desk. Since she allowing her mind to wander, Katrice figured she might as well go all the way. *What would it feel like to lean her head against Lee's broad chest and feel his arms wrapped around her? Were his lips as soft as they looked? What made him laugh? Upset? What turned him on?*

This is crazy. Forcing herself to return to a realm where reality ruled, Katrice returned to to-do list.

Her track record in previous relationships had reinforced her need to be careful and selective. Even before Greg, Katrice had never been in a relationship where she hadn't been the one making major compromises; each time losing a little more of her true self. As far as she was concerned, fifty-fifty relationships where the give and take was equitable did not exist and she had grown weary of looking for that pot of gold at the end of the relationship rainbow.

"I didn't give up everything to move here and then turn around and repeat bad habits," she reminded herself before putting Lee out of her mind and, hopefully, as far away from her heart as possible.

CHAPTER 12

The evening sun was just beginning to set over Benton Lake. The hustle and bustle of the earlier part of the day had transitioned into the lazy calm of a summer evening.

Katrice had just finished vacuuming the children's story area when she heard a knock on the shop's door. She didn't need to look to know it was Lee.

Six-thirty on the dot. Lee may be a bit on the arrogant side, and he seemed to delight in trying her patience, but the man was prompt.

Katrice unlocked the front door to let Lee in. "Give me a second to put away the vacuum cleaner and straighten up the counter," she said.

"Is there something I can do to help?"

"No, I can manage on my own."

"How did I know you were going to say that?"

"Because you're a know-it-all," she said under her breath.

After putting the counter in order, Katrice got her purse, set the alarm, and turned off the lights. Standing on the sidewalk pretending to look for something in her purse, she asked, "Where are we going for dinner? I could follow you in my car to save you the trouble of having to bring me back here later."

Amused, Lee ignored the implied rejection of riding with him in his car. He had already decided where they would have dinner, and it was only a short walk from the bookstore.

"What do you think about Hanover's?"

"Hanover's? I don't think I've ever eaten there. I've been meaning to, but just haven't taken the time to stop in."

"I've been there for lunch a few times. They have pretty good barbecued chicken, and homemade bread that practically melts in your mouth."

Barbecued chicken did sound good. Actually, anything edible sounded good. This had been one of those days when Katrice had been too busy to have a proper lunch. The granola bar and apple that had been her lunchtime meal had failed to ease her hunger pangs. And a few cookies from the coffee nook hadn't done much, either. She needed a real meal, and Hanover's seemed to be the place to get it. And so she quickly agreed to Lee's suggestion.

Hanover's was a locally owned restaurant whose menu featured steak, barbecued chicken and ribs, and some of the best chicken and dumplings Lee had ever eaten. Not too fancy or too casual, he had chosen it as much for its charm and ambiance as he had for its delectable food.

Lee and Katrice were seated in a small booth near the back.

"Relax," Lee said when he saw Katrice biting her lip and playing with her napkin. "I don't bite."

"It's just been a long day, that's all. I'm a little tired."

Katrice folded her hands in her lap and tried to relax. She didn't want to enjoy Lee's company and wished the evening would go by quickly. If she wasn't careful, she might actually find him even more likable. Under normal circumstances that wouldn't be a bad thing, but she didn't feel as if she could truly trust her emotions just yet. With Greg, she had allowed her heart to lead her. In return, he had taken her through the kinds of trials and tribulations that had left deep scars. She had vowed to never let that happen again.

"I started the book today."

"What book?" she asked, having temporarily zoned out.

Lee wondered where Katrice had drifted off to. At first he thought she was being rude, trying too hard to show indifference to his company. But detecting a slight change in her expression, he thought he caught a glimmer of sadness shadowing her pretty face. He sensed something or someone had caused her pain. Knowing that tugged at his heart, even though there was very little he could about it.

"The mystery. Remember the book you recommended?"

"Oh, yes. I'm sorry." *Come back to the present and leave the past behind.* "Do you like it?" Katrice asked, willing herself to at least be polite and attentive.

As Lee talked about the book's plot she lowered her guard enough to relax and enjoy the atmosphere of the restaurant and Lee's company. Several times she attempted to maintain eye contact with Lee, but each time the intensity of his gaze forced her to look away.

"Is it warm in here to you?" she asked, draining her glass of water.

"Not really," Lee replied with a slight smile.

Feeling nervous and awkward, not to mention transparent, Katrice looked down at her lap. She didn't want to focus on how handsome Lee was, but how could she not? Fortunately, experience and her grandmother had taught her to look beyond the surface. However, that created another problem: Lee had revealed enough to make her curious about what lay beneath that cool, calm exterior.

"You were right about the author setting up several potential suspects."

Katrice nodded and smiled with genuine interest. As he continued talking about the story, she was finding it easier to maintain eye contact, even though his gaze was still intense. Looking straight into her eyes, he seemed to command her undivided attention and was willing to give his in return.

When she spoke to him, he actually paid attention and appeared interested in what she had to say. Katrice remembered her one-on-one time with Greg, most of which had been spent repeating herself or wondering if he was even paying attention. Other times, she simply gave up, deciding that trying to have a conversation with him just wasn't worth the effort. Even when they were supposedly spending quality time together, Greg always seemed preoccupied, anxious even. But what distressed her most about Greg could be summed up quite easily; he didn't value her opinion, only occasionally humoring her when he realized he had no other option. That lack of respect had gotten progressively worse over time, and Katrice had grown weary of trying to prove herself to him. And for what? In the end, she realized it just wasn't worth the effort, especially once she discovered the reason behind his behavior.

"For a while I had the waiter at the Italian restaurant as the triggerman, but after reading chapter three, I could see that he's not the one."

Lee was definitely different. Katrice couldn't pinpoint all the differences between him and Greg, or anyone else she'd dated, but she didn't feel the need to. For now, she was satisfied knowing that Lee was different.

She had learned a few things about him, but he still made her wonder about so much more. With his good looks and charm, why pursue her? To her knowledge there had been no signals given off that would have led him to believe that she found him attractive or was even interested in him, at least none that she could recall. Maybe he enjoyed a challenge. After all, Katrice hadn't exactly fallen at his feet at first sight. In fact, she remembered, with a bit of embarrassment, she had been anything but pleasant.

"I'm leaning toward the antique shop owner. He's the only one so far without an alibi."

Something else puzzled her about Lee. Why did it seem like the man always showed up when things were going astray or when she appeared to be in the midst of some kind of near disaster? She hated appearing helpless. After all, she neither needed nor wanted his help. She thought he somehow knew his timely appearances annoyed her. She could swear he got a kick out of it.

"I can hardly wait to get to the end."

Katrice smiled. She had barely heard anything he'd said, but he went right on chatting about the book.

Lee was hardly unaware that Katrice was lost in thought. He wondered if she still regretted having made the deal with him. If so, he needed to change that.

"Listen, we got off on the wrong foot when we first met . . . and a few times after that. I'm not quite sure why, but I would really like it if we could start over."

"Oh, really? At what point?" Katrice picked up her water glass to take a drink, but it was empty. Annoyed, she asked, "Are we starting before or after you knocked the chip off my shoulder?"

Lee smiled sheepishly. He couldn't have missed the sarcasm in her voice if he tried. Well, if he needed to take the first step toward a fresh start, then he would. Clearly, he would have to make a heartfelt and sincere apology if he ever hoped to gain Katrice's friendship. "I'm sorry about that. That's not like me at all. But you were being so . . . mean and defensive."

Katrice looked squarely at Lee. "Mean? Am I mean because I want to do things for myself or because I refused your help?" She tried to keep the edge out of her voice, but it found its way back in anyway.

Lee threw his hands up in despair. "There you go again. Everything I say to you comes back as an accusation."

"As an attorney, I would think you would have relatively thick skin and would be able to handle accusations with ease. Offering a suitable defense should be second nature and as effortless as greeting a neighbor on the street," Katrice retorted.

Lee didn't even bother to hide his amusement. "How'd you know I'm an attorney?"

Busted! She had said too much, but the words had come tumbling out so fast. How could she now explain that she knows he's a thirty-eight year old attorney who works for legal aid in Columbus, is a widower, is partial to homemade cookies, and has two brothers, one younger and one older? Of course, all of that had been way more information than she'd pretended she cared to know about the man, but thanks to her neighbor, Lillian Parkins, his blood type and shoe size were about the only things she didn't know about Lee Oliver.

Mrs. Parkins had stopped by the bookstore that afternoon and Lee had been all she had talked about. The older woman thought the world of Lee and his brothers, but seemed particularly fond of Lee. According to Mrs. Parkins, Lee was nothing short of amazing.

Katrice had wanted to ask Mrs. Parkins about Lee's wife, but she didn't know a good way to bring up the subject without seeming nosy. Mrs. Parkins had offered just a few details about her. She did mention that his wife had been ill for several months before she died.

What she had been like? Was she pretty? Smart? A loving wife?

Katrice thought of some of Grandma Harry's stories about her husband, Katrice's grandfather, who had died shortly after Taryn was born. Grandma Harry always said he was a good man who worked hard, loved his family, and treated her like a queen. When she was a little girl, Katrice never really understood the look that came into her grandmother's eyes when she talked about her late husband or the reason she never remarried. It wasn't until she had grown up and had experienced a few relationships that she finally understood; her grandfather had been the love of Grandma Harry's life.

Had Lee's wife been the love of his life?

Trying to buy time, Katrice was giving unusual attention to adding sugar and lemon to her iced tea. Lee expected an answer, and she planned to give him one, but this time she would have to choose her words more carefully. Finally, she responded offhandedly with, "I think someone mentioned it."

"Really?"

"Yes."

"Who?"

"Can't remember. You know how people in small towns talk about everyone else's business."

Lee was amused. From what he had learned in the short time he knew her, Katrice Ware could pull off many things, but indifference wasn't one of them. Although he didn't buy her explanation, his gut instinct warned him that it would be best not to let her know that, at least not now. He was secretly flattered. She didn't dislike him as much as she pretended.

"What?"

"I'm sorry. I didn't mean to stare," Lee said. "I think I just figured something out about you."

"Go ahead, enlighten me. I'm pretty sure I won't be able to stop you from saying whatever is on your mind, anyway."

"I realized that you're not as mean as you pretend to be."

Katrice feigned indifference. "I'm not pretending to be anything. I am what you see. There's no pretense here."

Lee, leaning forward, caught and held Katrice's gaze. "Part of that is true, but I sense there is more to you than meets the eye."

Just what did he think he saw?

The waiter appeared and placed a basket of warm bread on the table. The intensity of the moment vanished as quickly as it had appeared. Thankful for the interruption Katrice saw it as a reprieve of sorts, an opportunity to take control—of what she wasn't really sure.

Lee removed the cloth covering the rolls and offered the basket to Katrice.

Katrice inhaled the rich aroma of freshly baked bread and was tempted to not even wait for the waiter to finish taking their orders before pouncing.

After the waiter left, Katrice spoke before Lee had a chance to, hoping to steer the conversation in a different direction.

"So tell me, how do you like small-town living?"

Her desire to change the subject was obvious, but Lee decided to be nice and play along. "Actually I grew up in

Benton Lake. I lived here until I graduated high school and went to college."

"Where was that?" she asked, biting into a buttery piece of bread.

"Central State in Wilberforce. After I graduated from Central, I went to law school at Case Western. After passing the bar, I ended up practicing law in Columbus."

"Is that where you live now?" She felt silly asking the question, since she already knew the answer. Thankfully, he didn't know that she knew and this seemed to be a safe topic.

Lee nodded. "Kyra and I are here for the summer for some R and R. What about you?"

Caught off guard Katrice asked, "What *about* me?"

"It's your turn. What brought you to Benton Lake?" he asked.

"How do you know I haven't always lived here?" she asked, buttering another piece of bread.

"I grew up here, remember? Don't think that for one minute I wouldn't have remembered someone as pretty as you."

Heat rushed to her face as she tried to hide the effect of his compliment. She took a sip of tea to wash the bread down, which had suddenly become hard to swallow.

"Is that a line?"

Lee smiled. "A line? No, not at all. One thing you'll learn about me is that I say what I mean and I mean what I say."

Katrice took another sip of iced tea. *What was he getting at?* "Is that a warning or something? Or maybe I should be taking notes."

"Maybe, if that will help you get to know me better."

"Am I missing something here?"

"I certainly don't think tonight is going to be the last time we see each other. Do you? The more we learn about each other, the better. I'm thinking the next time we go out, you can pick the activity or the restaurant or both. It's up to you."

Katrice laughed in spite of herself. "Next time? How very thoughtful of you to have everything already planned out to save me the trouble. We haven't even made it through tonight's dinner. Who said there's going to be a next time? And if you haven't noticed, the bookstore keeps me pretty busy, which doesn't leave much time for other things."

"You still have to eat. And the bookstore is closed on Sundays."

Unable to think of a snappy comeback, Katrice did the only thing she could do; she grabbed and buttered another piece of bread.

Under the restaurant's soft lights, Lee listened to Katrice once again changing the subject. This time the topic was the weather.

He openly studied her as she talked about an article she'd read on global warming. Keeping his hands still to resist the urge to reach out and release the clasp that restrained her curly hair, Lee wished he could see those curls softly framing her face.

113

Listening without real interest, he wondered if Katrice thought she was pretty. He certainly did. He couldn't imagine her fussing with her hair or makeup or obsessing over color palettes. To him, she was a natural beauty with smooth skin, sparkling eyes, and the most kissable lips he'd ever seen. She clearly didn't see his adoration for her or how much he enjoyed listening to her talk, even if the topic was as mundane as the weather. He even loved the way she wrinkled her nose when she tried not to laugh.

Lee didn't know who or what had damaged her confidence, causing her to be defensive and forever on guard. But he wanted her to know that she could relax around him and be herself without fear of being judged or ridiculed.

"I don't think I'm the only one enjoying myself this evening. Judging by the way you inhaled the bread, I would say you enjoyed the meal as well."

Katrice looked at the empty breadbasket and was mortified. *Did I eat all of that bread by myself?* "I was hungry," she blurted out, feeling the need to offer an explanation. "We were so busy at the shop today, and I didn't get a chance to eat a proper lunch."

Lee laughed. "Don't apologize. I was just teasing you. I'm glad you enjoyed your meal. It's nice to have a meal with a woman who doesn't spend the evening pushing food around on her plate and worrying about how many carbs and fat she has consumed."

Katrice smiled shyly. "Under normal circumstances, my appetite is pretty fierce and includes lots of carbs, fat, and other things I probably shouldn't be eating. But today, my lunch consisted of an apple and a granola bar, eaten in under ten minutes. Not very filling."

Concerned, Lee asked, "Don't you have enough help at the bookstore? It's not a good idea to get so wrapped up that you don't have time to sit down and eat lunch."

"Oh, no, most of the time it's not like that at all," she assured him. "I have a really good group of people working for me. I think I've been pretty fortunate to have found people who enjoy sharing their love of books as much as I do and who don't really have to be supervised. They're all very hard-working and seem to be as committed as I am to making Book Wares a success. As for myself, I just have to learn how to manage my time more effectively or at least bring a sandwich from home."

Aside from the weather, the topic of her bookstore seemed to be safe territory. Katrice really opened up when she talked about it and her staff, Lee noticed. It was then that she seemed relaxed and happy. He listened with interest as she continued.

"It's funny, but Geneva, who is my assistant manager, Millicent, and Patrick, who works in the coffee shop, don't realize that they are a big part of making my dreams come true. Every time I walk into Book Wares, I have to remind myself that it's my bookstore. I know this may sound silly, but I've wanted to open Book Wares or something very similar to it for a long time."

"Dreams aren't silly. Without them life wouldn't hold much purpose or pleasure. What took you so long to make this one happen?"

Katrice hesitated. What could she say? That she had been a spineless jellyfish for years and had let others make decisions for her? Or she had been so busy pleasing her family and fiancé that she almost lost sight of what mattered most to her? Maybe he'd like to hear how at thirty-two years old she had decided to take charge of her life and live on her own terms while at the same time managing to alienate her family.

Hmm, any of those would go over well.

Instead of revealing the real reason, she opted for a nonspecific answer. "I guess everything happens in time. At least that's what my grandmother used to say."

The waiter reappeared and topped off Lee's coffee. At Lee's suggestion, he came back a few minutes later to see if they wanted to order dessert.

Lee took the dessert menu from the waiter and scanned the selections. "Did you save room for dessert? Apple pie and vanilla ice cream sound good. Or how about a slice of chocolate cake?" he asked, hoping to prolong his time with Katrice.

"Are you kidding? After almost polishing off that whole basket of bread I couldn't finish my chicken, which, by the way, had to be the biggest piece of chicken I have ever attempted to eat. Please, don't let me stop you from ordering dessert."

Frankly, Katrice didn't believe Lee could eat another bite of food. Her entrée had included what looked like a half a chicken, a healthy portion of rice pilaf, and a mound of steamed vegetables. More than half of her dinner would be going home with her in a doggy bag.

Lee had prime rib, which was so big it had been brought out on its own plate, a baked sweet potato, a huge salad, and a bowl of soup. He'd eaten every bit of it.

Disappointed his evening with Katrice was coming to an end, he motioned to the waiter to bring the check.

Katrice reached for her purse.

"Don't even think about it," he warned.

"Will you at least allow me to leave the tip?"

The look he gave her was answer enough.

It was dark when they left the restaurant, and the street-lights cast triangular beams of light every few yards along the way back to the bookstore. The streets were quiet, even though other people were out walking. For a while Lee and Katrice walked in comfortable silence, enjoying the night sounds that one only hears in the country.

"Thanks for what you did today."

Smiling to himself, Lee accepted her thanks. Actually he had had fun reading to the children. "I wondered when you were going to mention that."

"Well, now seemed like a good time."

"Can I ask you a question?"

"Can I stop you?"

"No."

"Ask away."

"Did you really need my help today or was that all part of a setup?"

Katrice stopped walking and turned to Lee. "No, I really did need help, as much as I hate to admit it. The person scheduled to read to the children called yesterday and said she couldn't make it."

"There you go again. What's so wrong with asking for help when you need it?"

"It's not asking that's the problem. Appearing helpless and always needing help, that's the problem. I don't want to live my life that way."

"Katrice, that's not how I see you. In fact, helpless isn't anywhere near how I would describe you."

If you only knew.

Changing the subject, Katrice started walking again and asked, "Where's your daughter this evening?"

"You do that a lot, and it's really not a good habit."

"What?"

"You change the subject when we talk about something that makes you uncomfortable."

"That's because I'd rather not talk about me. So where's your daughter this evening?"

Lee sighed. Katrice could be stubborn, but so could he. "She went to the movies with one of her friends. After I see you to your car and make sure that you're safe, I'm going to pick her up."

When they reached the driveway of Book Wares, Katrice began rummaging in her purse for her car keys. "I'll be okay from here. I'm just in the parking lot behind the building. I always park under the streetlight, so I should be fine if you need to leave to pick up your daughter." She didn't know if she should offer Lee a handshake or give him a peck on the cheek. Both seemed awkward, so she did neither. "Uh, thanks for dinner. I had a good time."

She started walking, but after just a few steps, she was stopped by a firm hand on her shoulder. The pressure of Lee's hand wasn't meant to cause pain, but it did get Katrice's attention. He turned her around to face him and under the bright security light on the side of the building, she could see his eyes blazing. He seemed angry.

"For one minute would you please stop this 'I am woman, hear me roar' battle cry? There are all kinds of strange people in this world who don't care if you're parked under a light or in a dark alley as long as you're alone. This is Benton Lake, not Heaven. It's going to take all of two minutes to walk around this building with you and make sure that you're safe. Is that understood?"

Lee spoke firmly, but Katrice refused to let him bully her. She lifted her chin defiantly. *Who did he think he was to speak to her that way?* She was more than capable of walking to her car alone. Any idiot could do that. She had been doing it before she met Lee Oliver, and she would still be doing it long after he was gone. "What if I don't want you to walk with me? This isn't the first time I've done this, you know."

Why did she have to be so stubborn? Lee shoved his hands in his pockets and took a deep breath. One minute this pretty lady could be charming and pleasant; the next, she bared her claws and practically spit nails. And for no apparent reason! Why did she feel as if she had to act so tough? And why did he allow her to test his patience? Once again he had the urge to punch a wall and at the same time take her into his arms and kiss her until she was breathless.

Regardless of how he currently felt or the reason Katrice seemed to derive pleasure in irritating the hell out of him, his gaze had not wavered and he refused to back down.

Shrugging, he replied, "Well, the way I see it you have two choices. We can both walk to your car and I can make sure that you leave here safely or I can throw you over my shoulder, carry you to your car, and make sure that you leave here safely. Either way is fine with me, even though I think I would enjoy the second option a lot more."

He couldn't be serious. Or could he? He appeared irritated, but he'd also just made a joke. At least Katrice thought he was joking.

She didn't know him well enough to judge accurately, and she really didn't want to take the chance of being slung over his shoulder like a sack of flour. Her mind raced. Standing her ground had seemed important a few minutes ago, but calling his bluff might prove dangerous.

"Fine," she snapped.

Lee and Katrice made the short walk to her car in silence.

"Keys please."

She practically threw them at him. He unlocked her car door and held it open for her, gesturing to the driver's seat with a grand motion.

Katrice swept past Lee and got into the car. She reached over to close the door, but Lee put his hand out, preventing it from closing.

Now what? He probably felt compelled to give her a lecture about maintaining the speed limit and obeying the local traffic laws. Prepared to give a snappy comeback for whatever he was about to say, her breath caught in her throat at the change she saw on his face. She continued to hold her breath as he leaned in, his eyes never leaving her face.

His jaw was taut and he wore a look of sheer determination.

Had she pushed too hard?

"Allowing me to be a gentleman doesn't make you any less independent nor does it take anything away from you. When you're with me, always expect that I'll treat you with respect, but just as important, I'll treat you like a lady. The sooner you accept that the better."

Katrice parted her lips to respond but never had a chance to say a word as Lee lowered his head and pressed his lips to hers. Before she could react, she found herself caught up in a kiss that took her breath away. She suddenly felt lightheaded, and a longing she hadn't felt in a long time emerged with a force that seemed to match the intensity of Lee's kiss.

Staring out the driver-side window, she couldn't say who had closed her car door and exactly when it had happened. The kiss that just seconds before had stirred her soul had ended as quickly as it had started.

"Good night, pretty lady. Pleasant dreams," Lee whispered and turned to leave.

Katrice started the car and began her drive home. Passing one street after another, she practically drove on autopilot, making the correct turns but not paying attention to anything else. She couldn't shake the feeling that with his kiss, Lee had unleashed something that she thought she had under control. Whether or not that was a good thing remained to be seen.

CHAPTER 13

"How could you say that?" fourteen-year-old Bettina asked.

"Easy. Why else would Trey skip school and start stealing?" a quiet boy asked, joining the discussion for the first time. "You didn't get it?"

"Trey was going through a lot of drama with his mother and brother. That's why he did all that stuff so his mother would get mad at him and send him away to live with his dad," Kyra chimed in.

Shelving books near the area that doubled as the story-time and discussion group space, Katrice listened to the exchange, pleased with what she saw and heard. She was decidedly satisfied with her decision to start the teen book discussion group. Not only had they all read the book, but from what she could gather from their comments, most of them seemed to enjoy participating in the discussion.

She had chosen Millicent to be the moderator and was pleased to see her young employee enjoying the experience. When the discussion ended and everyone had a copy of the next selection, Millicent joined Katrice at the front counter.

"Wow! Those kids are sharp. I don't remember being anywhere near that intuitive at their age. At first they all seemed a little reluctant to speak up, and I was afraid they hadn't read the book. So to get things moving I asked questions and then gave them my opinion of certain parts. They slowly began to open up and voice their own opinions. We could probably have gone for another hour, easy."

"For what it's worth, I think you did a great job, and the kids seemed really comfortable with you. I walked by a few times and heard some of the remarks. I thought for a minute there was going to be a *boys-versus-girls* kind of battle."

"I know! That Bettina is pretty opinionated, but I like her spunk. At least she isn't easily intimidated. Next time, I think we'll have to set up some ground rules at the beginning. Once we establish that all opinions count, things will go a little more smoothly. I hope."

Geneva, passing by the counter on her way to the back office, announced, "Fine brother on the premises."

Katrice and Millicent had been so caught up in their conversation they hadn't noticed anyone entering the store. It wasn't until Millicent giggled and nodded her head toward the café that Katrice noticed Lee talking to Kyra but looking in her direction. She looked away.

It had been three days since Katrice and Lee had dinner together. She had thought about that night on several occasions. The meal they'd shared. The conversation. The confrontation. The kiss.

She could feel him staring, even if she couldn't see for herself. Making eye contact with Lee wasn't exactly a disagreeable prospect, but she just didn't want to give him the satisfaction of intimidating her with a stare-down.

"I think someone is trying to get your attention," Millicent offered, trying without success to stifle a giggle.

Katrice frowned at Millicent. *Okay. Just turn around, smile, wave, and look away.*

"He's coming this way," Millicent whispered.

Katrice wasn't ready to face Lee. No one had ever kissed her with as much tenderness as Lee had. *What other skills did he possess?* She still remembered the feel of his lips on hers, his taste, the way he smelled up close and how he—

Stop it! Yes, she wanted to be a little more impulsive and take chances, but she also had to be sensible.

She grabbed a stack of books from behind the counter and was retreating to her office when she collided with Geneva, who was returning from the same direction.

"I'm sorry!" both exclaimed.

"Let me help," Lee offered, kneeling and picking up the books Katrice had dropped in her hasty retreat. He placed the books on the counter and pointedly greeted Geneva and Millicent.

The two women exchanged knowing glances and left for other parts of the bookstore, leaving Katrice alone with Lee.

Looking around desperately for something to do and failing, she retreated behind the counter and grabbed a notepad, pretending to compile a list.

Lee noticed she was nervous, and he was both amused and flattered at the thought. To his mind that meant that she had felt something the other night when they kissed. He knew he had.

Leaning against the counter, Lee cleared his throat. "Do I make you nervous, or are you this wound up all the time?"

A-R-R-O-G-A-N-T! she scribbled on the notepad. Then she stopped writing and looked up. "I'm not nervous or wound up, thank you very much."

"Good, I thought the kiss we shared the other night might have something to do with your behavior, but I stand corrected."

No, he did not just put their business all out in the street!

Katrice looked around to see if anyone had overheard him. "*We* didn't share a kiss. *You* were being a bully and took advantage of a situation."

"Funny, that's not how I remember it."

"Really? Well, a new book on herbal supplements just arrived today. I'm sure there's a section in it on remedies that help with memory loss."

Lee threw his head back and laughed.

Hearing him laughing Katrice couldn't help laughing, too, in spite of herself.

Katrice's smile lit up her face and her laughter touched a part of his heart that had been empty for a long time. It was a good feeling, and one he had truly missed.

"Now that you're in a good mood again, is this a good time to invite you to lunch?"

Lee's smile was mischievous and Katrice wondered what he had up his sleeve. She hadn't heard from him in three days. Now he shows up and wants to take her to lunch. Why, for a repeat performance of the other night? She didn't know if she could handle another one of Lee's kisses.

"What part of that arrogant mind of yours houses the notion that I would want to join you for lunch?"

"Arrogant? Is that what you think of me?" Lee clutched his chest, pretending to be hurt.

Katrice nodded. *Among other things.*

"We're going to have to discuss that later. For now, would you see me in a better light if I told you Kyra asked me to invite you to lunch with us?"

"She did, huh?" she asked sarcastically, looking at Lee with open suspicion. "How do I know you're telling the truth?"

Lee leaned in close so that only Katrice could hear. Looking dead serious, he said, "You can always count on me to tell you the truth. I will never lie to you, Katrice."

At lunch the chitchat flowed smoothly. From the time they left the bookstore, Kyra and Katrice had not stopped talking. Lee simply listened, interjecting an occasional thought when asked a question. He didn't mind; he was actually enjoying the interaction between his daughter and Katrice. Kyra was fascinated with the places Katrice had traveled. Katrice had everyone laughing when she told a story about traveling to Peru and dining on guinea pig, which she thought was pork.

"You know, we're going fishing on Saturday. Do you think you might want to come with us?" Kyra unexpectedly asked.

Where had that come from? Lee wondered

"It'll be fun," she continued before either adult had a chance to respond. "There's going to be a picnic and everything. I'm sure my grandfather won't mind."

Lee had considered inviting Katrice to the outing, but wasn't sure if Kyra would be uncomfortable with her there. Now he had his answer.

Lee and Kyra looked at Katrice expectantly.

"I don't know," she said. "I don't want to intrude."

"Oh, it won't be an intrusion, will it, Dad?" Kyra wondered why she had to do all the work and why her father kept missing her obvious clues to take the lead in encouraging Katrice to join them.

"I haven't been fishing since I was a kid," Katrice said, thinking about the summer outings at the lake spent with Grandma Harry and Taryn.

"It's like riding a bike, only more disgusting. Once you know how, you never forget, even if you try really hard to forget."

Lee looked at his daughter and smiled. She returned his smile and understanding finally dawned. His daughter was fixing him up on a date. And she was good.

"Well, Katrice, how about it?" Lee asked.

"Yeah, how about it?" Kyra repeated.

Katrice thought about the invitation. She could use a break from the bookstore for a little while, and a picnic did sound nice. The weather over the past week had been gorgeous and she hadn't been able to enjoy one bit of it. She didn't want the summer to pass by without doing something fun.

"Pleeeease," Lee and Kyra chanted.

"All right," she said laughing. "I'll just need to rearrange schedules at the bookstore. If I can do that without interrupting everyone else's plans, then I'll go."

Lee felt an odd sense of loneliness when Katrice announced she had to get back to work. Where had the time gone? He didn't want Katrice to leave and tried to think of a reason to get her to stay.

"How about another cup of tea?" he asked.

"I can't," she said. "I really need to get back."

Lee consoled himself with thoughts of seeing her again on Saturday.

"I had fun today," Kyra announced on the ride home. "The discussion group was fun, too. I didn't want to say anything at first because I didn't know anyone there, but then everybody started talking and it ended up being nice. I have another book to read for next time."

"Do I need to send money so you can pay for the books they're giving you?"

"No, Millicent—that's the lady with the tattoos and stuff—said the publisher sent them and they won't cost us anything."

"I see."

Riding along the streets of downtown Benton Lake, Lee began humming along to a song on the radio. Her father's humming almost always turned into full-blown singing. Kyra would rather not be subjected to that. Annoyed, she slipped on her headphones and turned her music up. When they were almost home, they had to stop when the gate on the railroad crossing just ahead of them began to flash and descend. Kyra removed her headphones.

"I like Katrice. She's nice."

"*Miss* Katrice," Lee corrected.

"Dad, she said I could call her Katrice. Apparently, she's not as old school as you are about those kinds of things. Anyway, I think you made a good choice."

"Excuse me?"

"You know, for a girlfriend, or whatever old people call someone they like."

Lee looked over at his daughter, who was doing her best not to laugh.

"Very funny, little girl. Do I need to remind you to mind your own business? *Miss* Katrice and I are just friends."

"Whatever. You're in denial. That's why I had to make a move to invite her to go with us tomorrow."

"Yeah, we need to talk about that. What made you invite her?"

"I thought it would be fun. Besides, she doesn't have any family here. That has to be kind of lonely, don't you think?"

"Although a good motive, is that the only reason?"

Kyra shrugged. "Yes and no. I happen to think that you really like her and she likes you, too."

Curiosity made him dig a little deeper. "What makes you say that? We barely know each other."

Kyra turned and looked directly at her father. "Do you really want to know?"

"I asked you, didn't I?"

"Well, it's kind of hard to explain. Let me just talk about you because I don't really know Katrice all that well yet. I think you like Katrice because you seem to spend a lot of time hanging around the bookstore. I know you like to read and all, but even I can see something else is going on. Nobody makes as many trips to the bookstore as you do, Dad."

Am I that obvious? Lee wondered, feeling slightly embarrassed.

Kyra continued. "When you're around Katrice, you're like a different person. Kind of the way you used to be with Mom. It's hard to explain, but you seem happy."

Lee stole a quick look at Kyra, who was watching the last few railcars roll by.

"That's not a bad thing, because I want you to be happy and it seems as if you haven't been for a long time. At first, I thought it was because of me."

Lee turned into Planter Street and was soon pulling into his father's driveway. He turned off the engine and turned to face his daughter. "Why would you think you caused me to be unhappy, Ky?"

"I don't know. You changed after Mom died. For a long time you seemed so sad. No matter what I did to try to change that, good or bad, you just still seemed unhappy."

Lee reached over and cupped his daughter's chin. Looking into her expressive brown eyes, he said, "Honey, you're the one person in my life who brings me joy and happiness all wrapped up in one lovable bundle. Through the good, the bad, and the not so good, I will always love you and be happy simply because I have you in my life. If you don't remember anything else, remember that."

"I guess I know that now. Maybe I've known it all along."

"How did I get so lucky as to have a daughter as wonderful as you?"

Kyra got out of the car and started walking toward the house. Stopping, she turned slightly and said over her shoulder, "I've wondered that same thing myself. You know, since I'm so wonderful, do you think we could go shopping this weekend?"

Laughing, Lee rolled his eyes and replied, "Did I say wonderful? Hmm. Give me a chance to rethink that."

CHAPTER 14

Despite her earlier reservations, Katrice was having a good time. She had spent a few hours at the bookstore that morning before Lee picked her up and had rearranged Geneva's and Millicent's schedules to ensure adequate coverage while she was away. When they learned the reason for the schedule changes they were happy that Katrice was finally taking a much-needed break, but they couldn't resist engaging in some good-natured teasing.

Katrice had been a good sport about it, but eventually had to put a stop to their eye-winking and giggling. It only ended after Geneva and Millicent made Katrice promise to give them all the details of the day when she returned.

Not knowing what to expect, Katrice had been a little nervous about meeting Lee's father. Would he be friendly like his son and granddaughter or would he be distant like her family? Just in case, she had concocted a good excuse that would allow her to leave early should the situation call for it.

Thankfully, she hadn't needed it. After introductions and unexpected yet welcome hugs from Sam Oliver and his lady friend, all her fears were set aside.

Turns out, Sam had known her grandmother through working together on the town's council and spoke highly of her.

"Harriet was a nice lady and truly cared about this town and the people who live here," Sam told Katrice. "You know, I wondered what was going to happen to her house after she passed away. I'm glad there's someone living in it who cares about the house and who will look after it."

"Lee tells us that you own the new bookstore in town and business has been pretty good."

"Well, so far so good," Katrice responded. "At first I was a little nervous about opening the bookstore. It seemed as if most people in town thought Book Wares would be too fancy, with the coffee shop and all. But once people actually stopped in to see the place for themselves, they were eager to return."

"Hmm. Too fancy for Benton Lake? I wonder who would've thought such a thing," Lee remarked, looking meaningfully at his father.

Sam cleared his throat and avoided eye contact with his son.

Vonda handed Katrice a cold drink and said, "That's just folks talking who are afraid of change. Frankly, I think your bookstore brought a breath of fresh air to this town. I recommended it to one of my clients, who had nothing but good things to say after her girls attended storytime. Another of my clients was really impressed with the wide selection of romance novels that you carry.

Those aren't really my cup of tea, but she said you have something for every taste."

"Believe it or not, those have been some of my hottest sellers. You wouldn't believe the following some of those romance authors have. A few of the really popular authors are actually from the tri-state area. Maybe at some point I can get them in for a book signing."

"Seems like a good idea. I hear you have a pretty nice coffee shop, too. My client mentioned something about some cookies with chopped almonds on top. She couldn't stop talking about them."

Katrice nodded and laughed. "I know exactly which ones you're talking about. Those are a big hit with adults and kids. We can hardly make enough of them. The recipe was actually my grandmother's."

"Hey, you're holding out on me," Lee said to Katrice. "I don't remember any almond cookies."

Vonda winked at Lee. "Apparently something else sweet at the bookstore caught your fancy."

Katrice blushed and Lee smiled bashfully.

Sam and Vonda were nice people. Katrice thought it was cute the way they held hands while fishing. They seemed comfortable together and very much in love. What they shared wasn't the giggly, giddy kind of love, but one that exuded trust, respect, compassion, and a sense of stability. At least that was the impression she had after spending time with them.

The only person Katrice hadn't met was Lee's brother Marshall. According to Lee, Marshall had consumed way too much alcohol and had partied just a little too hard the night before and was nursing quite a hangover. Katrice wondered if he shared the likeability of Lee and his father.

After a delicious meal of fried chicken, ham sandwiches, potato salad, and fresh fruit, Katrice was more than content to sit at the edge of the lake enjoying the view and munching on Vonda's homemade butterscotch oatmeal cookies. She made a mental note to get a copy of Vonda's recipe. She didn't have a great deal of time to practice her baking skills, but she hoped that once her hectic schedule eased up a bit she would have time for some of her hobbies.

Kyra and her friend Amber had gone off exploring. Vonda and Sam were taking a walk. They hadn't had much luck catching fish and had decided to try again later. Lee and Katrice were alone for the first time since they'd arrived at the lake.

"Are you having fun?"

Katrice nodded. She hadn't felt so carefree and relaxed in ages. "As a matter of fact, I am. Thanks for inviting me."

"Thanks for accepting my invitation."

"Your family is nice," she said pensively.

"Yeah, they're all right. I think I'll keep 'em."

Katrice leaned back on the blanket and rested on her elbows, letting the sun's rays warm her face, for a minute ignoring the potential damage of UV rays and the risk of sun-damaged skin. "No, trust me; they're more than all right. I don't think you realize how special it is to have the kind of relationship you have with your father and daughter. Not every family can do this," she said, gesturing toward other picnickers and people fishing. "I know some families that would have been at each other's throats before the grill got hot."

Katrice laughed, but it sounded empty to Lee's ears.

"What's your family like, Katrice?" he asked, trailing a blade of grass down her arm. He wanted to kiss her but thought better of it.

Katrice lay all the way back on the blanket, tucking her hands behind her head. She looked up at the clouds and thought about how she should answer Lee's question. *Her family?* She'd rather talk about the mating habits of locusts. "You know, if you squint your eyes and turn your head slightly to the left, that big cloud over there looks like an elephant."

Lying alongside Katrice, Lee rested on one elbow and studied her closely as she stared into the afternoon sky. She seemed lost in thought, and he wondered why her eyes reflected such sadness.

"What's wrong?" he asked, stroking her cheek and resisting the impulse to pull her into his arms.

Katrice turned and looked up into Lee's handsome, caring face. The tenderness she saw touched her heart. As she suppressed a wave of self-pity that threatened to surface, she thought without envy that Lee truly did not realize his great fortune in having such a wonderful family. He was surrounded by people he loved and who willingly returned that love. After spending time with them today, Katrice felt a longing that she fought to suppress, but the love Lee and his family shared was contagious. She wanted the same thing, not just for a moment but for a lifetime.

Pushing up on one elbow, she smiled as cheerfully as she could manage. It simply was too nice of a day to be weighed down by such heavy thoughts. "I don't have any cares or worries today. And if I did, I'm pretty sure that one of Vonda's cookies would make me forget all about them."

Katrice was very good at avoiding his questions, but Lee would be put off for only so long. One day he hoped she would trust him enough to open up and share with him whatever was causing her such sadness. Until then, he knew he would have to be patient.

Lee sat up and pulled Katrice into his arms in one swift move. Before she had a chance to protest or question his actions, he leaned in and placed a gentle kiss on her lips, followed by a more passionate one. "I've wanted to do that all day."

"You have?" she asked, surprised but not displeased.

Lee nodded and kissed her again, not allowing the effects of the previous kiss to fully fade. This time his kiss was more lingering as he took what Katrice so willingly offered—an intoxicating sweetness that was uniquely hers.

"I'm sorry," he said to a dazed Katrice.

"Why?" she asked quietly.

"Because I'm about to lose all credibility as a gentleman if I don't stop." Lee released her, stood, and walked over to the cooler for a cold drink.

While his back was turned, Katrice touched her fingers to her lips, still feeling the way Lee's tongue had traced the outline of her lips and how good he tasted. Her body had reacted to his kisses and touch in a way that left her questioning certain decisions. Had she been neglecting her heart and the need to feel wanted in a misguided attempt to be tough? In her mind, being tough meant keeping her focus and not leaving herself open to possible heartbreak. Sadly, that same toughness could cause her to miss out on a pretty wonderful experience with someone special.

Lee rejoined Katrice on the blanket and positioned her so that she could lean against his chest and look out at the lake. She closed her eyes and decided to simply enjoy the moment and delay scrutinizing her life and mixed-up emotions until later.

For a while she simply reveled in her surroundings, allowing herself to fully relax. As a child she'd had a lot of fun swimming in this very lake and playing on its shores. Those were carefree and fun times. The memories that were created with her grandmother and sister would forever hold a special place in her heart. Today, she was adding a new memory.

Lee and Katrice sat in comfortable silence and watched the activity around them. Katrice observed a couple sitting at the end of a pier and began to focus on them. She couldn't hear their conversation, but she could tell they were enjoying each other's company in that intimate way people in love tend to do. A gentle touch, a caress, an affectionate smile were all universal signs that spelled love.

"May I ask you a personal question?" Katrice asked after a few minutes of watching the couple.

"Boxers," Lee replied with a chuckle.

She flushed. Thank goodness her back was to him.

"Sorry," Lee said, trying to be serious. "Ask away. My life is an open book."

"What was your wife like?"

Katrice felt Lee's body tense.

He hadn't been expecting that particular question, although he didn't think it odd that Katrice would ask about Paulette; he just didn't think it would happen today. But if he were in her position he would want to know, too. Typically when he dated and the subject of his marital status came up, he would simply say that his wife had passed away after being ill for some time. Most women didn't press him for more details beyond that.

Katrice hoped she hadn't crossed a line. "If you'd rather not—"

Lee looked out over the shimmering lake. There had been a time when he couldn't talk about Paulette and the void left by her death. Although lately, he'd felt differently about the loss of his wife, more at peace. He couldn't quite understand why or even begin to explain it, but maybe this was what his father had meant about being ready to move on to another phase in his life.

Katrice felt him relax.

"No, it's okay. I'll tell you about Paulette." Lee gently turned her back around to lean against his chest. "Several years ago, I attended a fundraising dinner for some charity that I can't remember. It was one of those stuffy affairs with a dull speaker and boring people, and it seemed to take forever to end. Well, one pleasant surprise turned out to be the food. It was excellent. It just so happened that I had been put in charge of finding a caterer for a co-worker's retirement luncheon. I don't know who picked me for that job or even why I accepted the responsibility, but I did. Being the newbie, I was probably trying to prove I could be a team player. Anyway, when the event ended, I hung around to get the name of the caterer. No one seemed to know. So I thought I would ask someone from the kitchen staff. On my way to the kitchen, I spotted this young woman carrying a tray piled high with dishes. I thought she was a member of the staff and could give me some info about the caterer. Well, me being the gentleman that I am, I saw that she was struggling with the tray of dishes so I tried to help by running ahead and opening the kitchen door for her."

"Let me guess, you tripped and fell, causing her to drop the dishes?"

"Not exactly, but you're not too far off. Let's just say that I ended up wearing cheesecake and lasagna on my suit."

Katrice tried not to laugh, but the image of Lee sitting under a pile of dishes covered in food was too comical to resist the urge. "Sounds like the beginning of a beautiful relationship."

Lee nodded and smiled. "Yes, it was. It turned out that Paulette owned a small restaurant and had catered the event that night. Once she forgave me for being a clumsy oaf and making a big mess, we began dating. We were married the following year. We had a good life together, thirteen years, lots of good times and a few that weren't so good.

"When Paulette was diagnosed with cancer, I thought my whole world would come to an end. When she died it pretty much did. The woman I had planned to spend the rest of my life with had suddenly and cruelly been taken away from us. I was in a bad way for a long time. Paulette had been a good wife and mother and I didn't know how to make life go on without her."

"But you did," Katrice said softly, admiring Lee for his apparent fortitude.

He nodded. "I had to think of Kyra. She had lost her mother. She didn't need to lose her father, too."

"I'm sorry," Katrice said, turning to face Lee. But where she expected to see sadness, she instead saw peace.

"Thank you, Katrice."

Then the two of them sat quietly for a while longer, lost in their own thoughts. Finally, Lee reached into the picnic basket, taking out two cookies. He offered one to Katrice and asked, "Are you ready?"

She accepted the offering and took a bite of cookie. "For what?" she asked. "A nap? That had to have been the most sinfully delicious meal I've ever eaten, but I'm afraid I ate more than I normally do. Now I'm feeling pretty lazy."

Lee got up and walked over to an old beat-up cooler that Sam had set apart from the picnic supplies. He rummaged through the cooler and retrieved a dirty-looking container. He walked back, holding the container in one hand and two fishing poles and his tackle box in the other. "Let's see what kind of angling skills you have."

"To be honest with you, I'm not that good at fishing."

"That's okay. On a scale of one to ten, with ten being a bass master, where do you think you fall?"

"About a negative three."

"Looks like I've got my work cut out for me. Do you want me to bait your hook or do you want to do it yourself?"

She placed her cookie on a napkin and wrinkled her nose. "Ugh, I forgot about that part. Can you do it, please?"

Lee pulled a fat night crawler from the container and attached it to the end of one of the fishing hooks. "I thought you said you used to fish when you were a kid."

"I did, but it was with a stick, some string, a hook, and bologna for bait."

Lee shook his head and laughed. "You're kidding. I find it hard to believe you ever caught anything."

"I said I went fishing as a kid. I never said I caught any fish."

Lee stopped what he was doing and looked down at Katrice. "Never? Not even one fish?"

"Nope. My grandmother and sister were the only ones who ever caught anything. The problem may have been with my bait. I could never bring myself to sacrifice a worm, even though I hate them, so I always used bologna as bait. Guess fish aren't big fans of lunch meat."

Lee laughed harder.

"What?"

"Come here." He took Katrice's hand and pulled her up. He then placed a gentle kiss on her lips.

"What was that for?" she asked, touching her lips with her fingers.

"Because I just can't seem to get enough of you. Besides, that kiss was meant to provide encouragement. In case you didn't know, today is your lucky day. I can feel it in my bones."

"Why is that?" she asked, seeing the playful glint in his eye.

"'Cause I'm going to show you that with the right bait, you can catch just about anything."

CHAPTER 15

The small deck off the kitchen was one of the things Katrice loved most about her house. Her grandmother had it built about fifteen years ago because she wanted a place to commune with nature—or so she'd said. Katrice thought the real reason was so she could spy on her neighbors unseen.

For Katrice, the deck not only provided the perfect place to sit, unwind, and enjoy a cup of tea in complete solitude, but it also offered a serene spot to occasionally enjoy a sunrise or sunset while reflecting on life. She and her grandmother had shared many such evenings and early mornings. Katrice missed those times when life seemed simpler and her worries were few. She especially missed her grandmother, who could always put things into perspective and who never allowed life's little annoyances to derail her.

With her grandmother, Katrice never felt the all-consuming need to please or seek acceptance. She could make mistakes without being ridiculed or concerned that her missteps would be seen as major transgressions. She could simply be herself.

Resting her head against the cushion of the lounger, Katrice recalled her grandmother talking about life "back in the day." Grandma Harry never missed an opportunity

to stress the importance of hard work to her granddaughters. She also stressed the need to immerse themselves in
literature of all kinds as well as the importance of paying
attention to world events. She believed doors that were
closed to the women of her generation would eventually
open, and she wanted her granddaughters to be prepared.

*Yes, I miss my grandmother, but I feel closer to her living
in this old house we both loved so dearly.*

Emerging from her reverie, Katrice resumed reading
the Sunday edition of the Benton Lake *Citizen Journal*.
Leisurely enjoying a cup of tea while reading every section of the newspaper was a rare pleasure. If she could she
would spend every Sunday morning this way if she could.
But some bookstore-related task usually made that
impossible—checking stock, drafting work schedules,
ordering supplies, reconciling the books. It was never
ending. In fact, the work schedule for the following week
still needed to be finalized. And then there were resumes
to look over. Today, however, she had decided she would
indulge in a work-free day.

Basking in the beauty of her surroundings, Katrice
was thankful her grandmother had had the foresight to
landscape her property with large shade trees and thick
hedges along the property line. The heavy foliage provided a barrier to the outside world, as well as enhancing
the property's beauty. With the exception of a partial
view of Mrs. Parkins's house, Katrice could enjoy the
wonders of nature in blissful solitude.

It was still too early for most people to be awake.
Absent were the sounds of lawn mowers, traffic, and chil-

dren playing. The only sounds Katrice heard were birds singing, the chattering of cicadas, and a dog barking off in the distance. She folded her newspaper and allowed her mind to drift off to a peaceful place. A gentle breeze caressed her skin, and the early-morning sun warmed her face.

It would be wonderful to spend a lazy morning in the arms of someone who loved her, and to feel needed, appreciated, and cherished. She could also picture herself with a family for whom she cooked their favorite meals, read bedtime stories, and chased fireflies in the backyard. Most of all she could envision giving and receiving unconditional love and having the man of her dreams loving her in a way that left no doubt that she was his and he belonged to her.

Katrice had never experienced that kind of love but she imagined it to be wonderful, and maybe just a little frightening. To be able to give of yourself—mind, body, and soul—was something she didn't know if she would ever be capable of. It all sounded wonderful, but was she being naïve?

If she were to be completely honest, she would have to wonder if she would allow room in her life for dreams to become reality. The bookstore took up almost all her time, and prospective husbands weren't exactly lining up at her front door. In fact, since she'd been in town, she hadn't noticed very many prospects at all. However, truth be told, she'd been too occupied with other matters to notice much of anything.

Well, not exactly true, she thought, smiling. Lee Oliver had been rather noticeable. More so than she would have ever imagined a mere mortal could be. Even without sight, hearing, or sense of smell, she probably would still have noticed Lee. The man had a way about him that commanded attention and evoked thoughts that she only read about in romance novels. Sometimes she could sense his presence even before she actually saw him.

She remembered their dinner at Hanover's. She had been nervous that evening, not the kind of nervousness she had experienced on her first date with her high school crush. This had been different. Lee had been a perfect gentleman. He'd made small but interesting talk and had been an attentive listener. He had made her feel special.

A great deal of her nervousness had stemmed from her awareness of Lee's masculinity, which was not in the overtly sexual way the media portrays men He was what she had always thought of as a real man. The way he carried himself, articulated his thoughts, and treated her said he was all male, in every sense.

Then there was the kiss in the parking lot at Book Wares. Just thinking about it caused liquid heat to pool in the bottom of her stomach. The kiss had been simple, but unexpected, particularly with the earlier threat of being slung over his shoulder still looming.

Hmm, the kiss. Nice could not adequately describe it. Scorching and tantalizing were better adjectives. Touching her bottom lip with the tip of her finger, Katrice could feel Lee's lips on hers, could almost smell his enticing aftershave, and feel his body heat. Even now, days later, she could still feel the effects.

Why had she allowed him to kiss her in the first place? Not just in the parking lot, but at the lake, too. Kissing someone she barely knew could be considered impulsive and impractical, totally out of character for her, definitely not something she would have done in the past. However, the present was a new chapter.

Whatever the reason behind her behavior, she knew she needed to be careful. Lee was no ordinary man.

"Enough!" she chastised herself.

Taking a sip from her cup and finding that her tea had become cold, she tried to think about something other than how Lee Oliver made her feel. Katrice picked up the newspaper and tried to focus on the lead story. But after rereading the first paragraph three times in a row without knowing what she had read, she finally gave up.

This wasn't the first time thoughts of Lee had caused deeply buried feelings to surface. Watching him read to the children at Book Wares and seeing the interaction he had with his daughter had made her wonder if she had misjudged him. Could he be the kind of man who made dreams come true? Particularly *her* dreams? Could she trust him and be true to herself, without pretense or major compromises?

"Enough," she chided herself again. *She* was making her dreams come true. No man could make her happy. She, and she alone, would be responsible for her own happiness.

This mantra sounded good in theory but lonely in practice. Katrice grabbed her newspaper and teacup. She had a business to run and a life to get in order. As far as she could see, there wasn't room in her life or her heart for anything else, especially not a fleeting summer fling.

Hanging shelves on a Sunday morning wasn't something Lee would have scheduled, but Mrs. Parkins had called Sam, who in turn volunteered his son for the job. Since Lee had promised to take Kyra and her friend to the church picnic later that afternoon and also had an appointment to prepare a will for one of his father's friends the next day, Sunday morning became the ideal time to hang the shelves.

Lillian Parkins had a wonderful old house. Large, airy rooms with lots of windows allowed the morning sun to fill the kitchen and dining room with bright, cheerful light, while the afternoon and evening sun illuminated the living room and brightened the front porch. Another feature of Mrs. Parkins's home that Lee just recently discovered he especially liked was of the view of her next door neighbor's house.

Katrice was the "nice young lady next door" Mrs. Parkins had mentioned. Funny, his father never mentioned that Katrice's grandmother had lived next door to Mrs. Parkins.

From the vantage point of the kitchen window, Lee had caught her this particular morning enjoying her morning coffee and reading the newspaper out on her deck.

When Mrs. Parkins left the room Lee moved closer to the window to get a better look. By no means was he nosy or anywhere near a Peeping Tom, but these were circumstances that called for a little creative action. In his mind, taking a few minutes to enjoy the natural beauty in his line of vision, which included Katrice, certainly didn't make him a voyeur; it only meant that he knew what he liked.

Lee quickly moved away from the window when he heard Mrs. Parkins approaching.

"I'll be in the living room with the newspaper if you need anything," she called in passing.

As he unpacked his tools, he reflected on his growing attraction to Katrice. He had enjoyed their time together at the lake, and she had, too. She had even caught a fish with his help. He had baited her hook and had shown her how to cast her line. And then, not more than five minutes after her line hit the water, she hooked a fish. Lee had stood behind Katrice with his hand over hers to help her reel in her catch. He could still feel her supple body pressed against his. Lee's heart raced just thinking about their brief contact.

"*Ouch!*" Distracted, he had closed the lid of the tool box on his finger.

"Are you okay in there?" Mrs. Parkins called out.

"Yes, I'm fine." *Pay attention to what's going on inside, not outside.*

Katrice was unlike any woman he had ever known, but he couldn't quite put his finger on exactly how or why he felt this way. She had the ability to wear his patience down to a nub, but other times she could be warm, funny, and caring, but only when she let her defenses down. He had seen her softer side at the lake.

He thoroughly enjoyed her company, even if she'd felt compelled to constantly remind him that she could be Super Woman, or a close facsimile, if he crossed some invisible barrier. In spite of it all, she was constantly on his mind.

Working quickly, Lee had the shelves put up in less than an hour. He then asked Mrs. Parkins to make sure the job had been completed to her satisfaction.

"This is wonderful," Mrs. Parkins exclaimed. "You do such beautiful work, Lee, and it hardly took you any time at all. How can I ever thank you?"

"No thanks needed. It was my pleasure. Is there anything else you need before I go?"

Mrs. Parkins looked around her kitchen and soft wrinkles formed around her eyes. "Well, do you think you have time to look at my kitchen sink? It's been draining rather slowly, and I don't want to have to call a plumber. You know how expensive plumbers can be, and I never know if they're telling me the whole truth about the problem or not."

Before answering, Lee looked outside. He breathed a small sigh of relief. *She was still there.*

"Uh, sure, I'll take a look." He turned on the faucet and sure enough, the water drained slowly. He checked for obstructions and finally found the cause of the problem. But fixing the clogged drain took a little longer than he had anticipated. When he finally finished, Lee packed up his tools and prepared to leave. This time when he looked out the window facing Katrice's backyard, she was gone.

Mrs. Parkins thanked Lee and made him promise to stop by for dinner one night so she could at least fix him a home cooked meal to show her appreciation.

After placing his toolbox in the trunk of his car, Lee came around to the driver-side door, but hesitated before getting inside. He checked his watch, calculating how much time he would need to get cleaned up and make it to church on time. He had to make a quick decision. "Sometimes you just have to step out on faith, brotha," he told himself.

CHAPTER 16

Toweling off after a leisurely bubble bath, Katrice felt refreshed and relaxed. She had taken some special "me" time that morning and, so far, had not regretted one moment of it. She especially enjoyed watching the sun rise. Yes, there were schedules to check and orders to place, but she was determined to do absolutely nothing today.

Katrice sat on the side of her bed and smoothed her favorite moisturizer over every inch of her body. She thoroughly enjoyed the feeling of being pampered, even if she was the one doing the pampering.

Looking down at her toes, she frowned. They could use some polish. *Maybe bright red to match my mood,* she thought with a giggle. But as soon as she uncapped the bottle, the doorbell rang.

Mrs. Parkins occasionally brought over homemade apple cinnamon muffins or some other mouthwatering baked goods that Katrice had no willpower to resist. Her mouth practically watered at the prospect of enjoying one or two of those delicious muffins with a cup of English breakfast tea. She raced down the steps to answer the door, prepared to see Mrs. Parkins holding a basket of muffins. She was surprised to see Lee instead.

Not a completely unwelcome intrusion, thoughts of warm muffins vanished at the sight of the luscious brown hunk standing in front of her. How did he know where she lived? He had picked her up at the bookstore when they'd gone to the lake and had taken her back there afterward to pick up her car. *Welcome to life in a small town.*

Feeling her mouth go dry, she thought that it surely had to be a crime for someone to look that good in a pair of jeans and a simple T-shirt this early on a Sunday morning. Or any morning, for that matter.

Lee's breath caught at the sight of Katrice, a vision of loveliness in a short silk bathrobe. His heart raced as his reaction to her threatened to overwhelm him. He tried to swallow but his throat felt dry. *Damn, she looked good.*

Her hair was pulled atop her head in a messy pony-tail and her skin looked soft and radiant against the subtle peach color of her robe. His first impulse was to reach for her and kiss her partially opened lips while he loosened her hair and indulged himself in the softness and warmth of her skin. But he realized that if he didn't practice restraint, he could possibly risk a slap across his face, or worse.

"Hi," he managed to croak. He cleared his throat.

It was clear that he had caught her by surprise, and she him.

"I hope I'm not disturbing you. But I was next door doing some work for Mrs. Parkins and I saw you out on the deck."

She hadn't noticed anyone watching her. The hedges that straddled her and Mrs. Parkins' border were kept a bit shorter than the hedges that lined the back end of her yard, something Katrice had never thought much about until now.

"You were spying on me?"

"No, no!" Lee said quickly. "I wasn't spying. I was doing some work in Mrs. Parkins's kitchen, and I happened to look outside and saw you . . . on your deck . . . when I was in the kitchen . . . doing the work." He felt silly repeating himself, but he couldn't seem to will his mouth to say the right things.

Katrice crossed her arms. She tried to hide her amusement. Lee was clearly flustered. Men didn't usually get flustered around her. Greg had never been. He'd always kept his emotions in check, which Katrice never thought much about until now. It felt good knowing that she had the ability to throw him off his game, even if it was just a little, especially since she was usually the one who was ill at ease.

"So you thought you'd drop by to tell me you were watching me from my neighbor's window?"

Lee sighed. This wasn't going well at all. He wished Katrice would uncross her arms. That simple act had exposed enough cleavage to send his pulse racing. She probably had no idea that she was killing him slowly. He almost groaned out loud.

Look away. Lee lowered his head, and ran his hand over the back of his neck. Big mistake. Long, curvaceous legs were now in his direct line of vision. Even the woman's feet were sexy! He was coming undone.

He resorted to clearing his throat again.

Katrice noticed a fine layer of perspiration on Lee's forehead. He seemed extremely ill at ease. *Would asking him inside and kissing him until both of their bodies begged for more also make him uncomfortable?* Where had that come from?

"Are you all right? Do you need some water?"

This time it was her voice that sounded strange.

He needed water all right, but in the form of an ice-cold shower. If he didn't say what he came over to say soon, any restraint he'd shown so far would quickly disappear.

"No, thank you. Actually, I came over to invite you to church and to the annual picnic following the late-morning service."

"Church?" She instantly felt ashamed. Here she was having lustful thoughts and the man had only come over to invite her to church.

Looking past Katrice and focusing on a nick in the wood of the doorjamb, Lee nodded. "That is, if you don't have other plans. Church starts at eleven-thirty. The picnic starts around two. It's the church on Maple Avenue."

Lee had started backing down the porch steps as he spoke.

He seemed a little unsteady. She held her breath, hoping he didn't trip.

He did, but quickly regained his balance.

"Hope you can make it," he said over his shoulder as he turned around and walked quickly back to his car.

Katrice watched Lee pull away. He had barely missed hitting the large rock at the end of the driveway as he sped off. He seemed to be in a great hurry.

What came over him?

Before closing her front door Katrice, examined the doorjamb, running her fingers along the weathered wood. Shaking her head, she started back upstairs to get ready for church. *What in the world was so interesting about the doorjamb?*

After warning Kyra to stop talking to Amber with his *I-mean-business* look during the service, Lee looked to the back door of the church. He had done this several times and it had not gone unnoticed by Marshall.

"Are you expecting someone?" Marshall whispered to his brother.

"No. Why?" Lee asked nonchalantly.

"Because you've looked back at the door at least ten times. I know today's sermon is about the Second Coming, but . . ." Marshall nudged his brother and laughed.

Lee now looked straight ahead to escape further scrutiny from his brother, doing his best to ignore Marshall. He wondered if Katrice had decided against accepting his invitation to join him at church. If she did come, he hoped her choice of wardrobe would be a lot less revealing than the peach robe. A layer of perspiration covered his brow as he remembered the short robe and everything it had failed to hide. Retrieving a fan from the back pocket of the pew in front of him, Lee forced himself to pay attention as the church announcements were being read.

After the announcements, the head usher asked visitors to please stand so they could be welcomed. Lee couldn't resist turning around to see if Katrice was one of the fifteen or so people standing. When he didn't see her, he stole another glance at the back of the church and scanned the pews to his left and right once more in case she had decided not to stand for the visitors' call.

After the guests had been greeted, the minister stood to deliver his sermon, referencing several scriptures that he asked the congregation to record and study later. Most people complied. Lee sat motionless, not because of indifference but something much simpler.

Lee caught only snatches of the sermon. The minister's words normally served as a source of inspiration and guidance to him, but not today. The only thing Lee felt today was an unyielding sense of disappointment.

Standing in front of the mirror, Katrice was trying to decide whether the brown flats or the white sandals looked better with her outfit. She had changed outfits three times but had yet to find the right thing to wear—or at least the one outfit that wouldn't give the impression she was trying too hard.

Unbuttoning her shirt, Katrice tossed aside the tan shirt that had looked cute hanging in the closet but plain and boring once she had put it on. On her bed was a growing pile of unacceptable ensembles. Sighing, she went back to her closet in search of something else to wear.

By the time she finally settled on an appropriate ensemble—one that would work for a church service and the picnic but also flattered her less than curvaceous figure—it had gotten too late to attend church service. After calculating the distance to the church, she figured if she hurried she could still make it to the picnic.

Taking one last look at her appearance, she was satisfied that she had made a good choice with the pale blue linen pants and beige top. She found a pair of comfortable and cute sandals that worked well with the ensemble. A pair of small white gold hoops finished off the look. Spritzing on the companion fragrance to the body lotion she'd applied earlier, she also applied a coat of toffee-colored lipstick before heading downstairs.

On her way down, Katrice stopped short when she remembered her cell phone on the charger in her bedroom. She retrieved the phone and hurried back down the stairs. Hearing a knock the front door, she thought Lee might have gotten tired of waiting for her and decided to come and pick her up. She did a quick check of her lipstick and hair in the hall mirror before answering the door. Taking deep breaths, she tried to keep from smiling too broadly. She felt a lightness and giddiness that she hadn't experienced in years. It felt good. Without analyzing it too much, she knew it had to do solely with Lee.

Katrice then turned the knob and opened the door. A warm breeze rushed in and her smile faded as a cold chill snaked down her spine. The lightness she'd felt just seconds before floated away with the breeze when she heard the words, "Hello, sweetheart."

CHAPTER 17

Marshall tossed his brother a beer and took a seat across from him on the patio. The two brothers chitchatted for a while about the trade show Marshall would be attending the next day.

"It's been good being home."

"Yeah, it was nice having someone to hang out with, especially since I barely see Kyra anymore, what with all of her pool parties and sleep-overs."

"So what do you plan on doing with the rest of your summer? Dad doesn't seem interested in anything that doesn't include fishing or Miss Vonda."

"I don't know. It's been nice taking one day at a time and doing absolutely nothing except preparing the occasional will or reading over contracts. At least I'm keeping my legal skills sharp with all the business Dad has lined up for me."

"Not to mention your new vocation—carpentry. I heard about the work Dad volunteered you for at Mrs. Parkins's. Maybe you need to remind him that you're on vacation."

Lee shrugged. "Naw, it's cool. If I didn't have that to do, I would probably go crazy. Just between the two of us, I don't think I'm cut out to sit around listening to birds chirp and watching grass grow."

Listening to the anxious chirping of crickets and the familiar night sounds that reminded them of their childhood and summers gone by, Lee and Marshall sat in comfortable silence for a while. Lee had been quiet all through dinner and most of the evening. Marshall knew something was bothering him, but he also knew from experience that he would probably have to pry it out of him. Although he had some idea of the root cause of Lee's drooping shoulders and puppy-dog appearance, he felt it was time for a heart-to-heart with his little brother.

"Your beer is getting warm."

Lee looked down at the unopened beer he had placed on the ground and said, "That's okay; I didn't really want it, anyway."

"So, who do you think is going to have the better season this year, the Reds or the Indians?"

"Don't know."

"Yeah, it's hard to speculate at this point. Maybe later on this summer we can catch a Reds game. How's that sound?"

"Sure," Lee said listlessly.

Just as Marshall suspected, Lee preferred to suffer in silence. "Are you going to tell me what's going on or am I going to have to beat it out of you?"

Lee half smiled at his brother's attempt to cheer him up. Back in the day, he would have readily accepted the challenge, and they likely would have had to be pulled apart by their father as they wrestled in the dirt. Now Lee simply stretched out his long legs on the lounger and issued his own warning. "You know better than to try that. You might outweigh me, but I'm much quicker, a little younger, and probably stronger than you."

Marshall chuckled. "Care to put your theory to the test?"

"I'll take a rain check."

"So why have you been moping around all evening?" Marshall asked when his attempts to bring his brother out of his apparent bad mood seemed to be failing. "You barely said two words at dinner."

Lee just sighed and answered, "It's nothing."

"Really? Does this 'nothing' have anything to do with the pretty lady at the bookstore?"

Surprised, Lee shot his brother a quick look, taking care not to give too much away with his response. "What are you talking about?"

"Kyra told me you have a big-time crush on the owner of the new bookstore." Marshall finished his beer and gave his brother the famous Oliver smile, followed by a wink. "Can't say that I blame you, bro. She doesn't look like any bookworm I've ever seen. Nice set of legs, too."

Marshall was baiting him and Lee knew it. It was an old game, one that Lee had lost many times during childhood, but not now. A lot older and with much thicker skin, he could resist for as long as he needed to.

"I'm not going to have this conversation with you, Marshall. I think now would be a good time to change the subject." Lee opened his beer and took a long drink. It had grown warm, but he didn't seem to care. "What were you doing looking at her legs?" Katrice hadn't mentioned that she had met Marshall.

"Whose legs? I thought we were talking about something else."

The muscles in Lee's jaw tightened.

"You were expecting her to come to church this morning, weren't you? That's why you kept looking back at the door." Marshall finally understood.

Lee sat wordlessly sipping his beer and staring out into the darkness.

Realizing he'd struck a nerve, Marshall decided to be serious. "Hey, you know I'm just messing with you, don't you?"

Lee continued staring straight ahead, refusing to respond.

"Seriously, Lee, what's going on? All kidding aside."

Lee finished his beer and tried to decide just how much he should confide to his brother. In the past, Marshall had been a good sounding board for most things. Lee could count on his advice regarding stock picks, cars, vacation spots, and other seemingly less important matters. But affairs of the heart were another matter. Men didn't typically discuss such things with each other, or with anyone else for that matter. Lee and Marshall were no different. Lee was thus a little reluctant to have that kind of discussion with his brother now.

Marshall sensed his brother's reluctance to talk and decided to do his best to be sympathetic and attentive. "Listen, Kyra already told me that the two of you have been out a few times. Ky even said that she likes her, if that means anything to you. And Dad has mentioned the frequent trips you've made into town, presumably to see Miss Bookstore."

"Her name is Katrice, Marshall. And didn't I say I wanted to talk about something else?"

"Okay, okay, don't get your shorts in a bunch I was just trying to jumpstart the conversation, that's all. I think you need to talk about this. Get your feelings out in the open. You'll feel better. I promise."

Lee eyed his brother suspiciously. "Have you been in therapy or something?"

"Come on, Lee. I'm trying to be sensitive here. Help a brotha out."

"You're scaring me, Marshall."

"Look, just tell me about Katrice."

Maybe what Marshall said made sense. He might feel better saying some things out loud instead of keeping them bottled up.

He decided to give it a try. *Why not?* "What do you want to know?"

"Whatever you want to tell me."

"Katrice owns a bookstore. She lives next door to Mrs. Parkins. She enjoys reading, her fishing skills are a little sad, and she's a nice lady."

"Sounds good so far, but not being able to fish can't be really high on your list. Okay, what else? Keep going."

Lee sighed and looked sidelong at his brother to gauge his sincerity. Was Marshall's concern genuine? Did his brother really want to listen to his troubles? He hoped so.

Lee continued, this time releasing a little more information about the woman who had captivated him.

"Okay, Marshall. Here goes. I met this lady when Kyra and I first got into town. We were in the grocery store one afternoon, and I spotted her struggling to carry an armload of groceries. You should have seen her. Cans were rolling down the aisle and stuff was falling all over the place. The whole thing was a big mess."

"Did you help her out?"

"I tried, but when I offered she refused and actually became offended."

"Why? What did you do?"

"That's just it. I didn't do anything except to help her pick up her groceries and try to spark a conversation. I thought I was being a perfect gentleman. I didn't make a pass at her or try to seduce her or anything like that. Believe me, I'm still trying to figure out what I did wrong."

Marshall crossed his feet at the ankles and looked thoughtful. "Okay, bad first impression. It's over and done with. Don't sweat it 'cause there's nothing you can do about it now. What happened next?"

"The next time our paths crossed was late one night when I was coming home. For some reason I couldn't sleep that night and thought a drive would help me relax. I remember coming around Turner Ridge Road traveling east, and she was heading west."

"And?"

"And she nearly wrapped the rickety old van she was driving around a tree. I ran off the road when I tried to avoid slamming my car into hers." Lee put his hand up to stop an impending question. "Don't ask. No one was hurt. That's all you need to know."

"Okay, even worse second impression."

Rubbing the back of his neck, Lee rolled his eyes and remarked, "Tell me about it."

"Let's see, so far you've accosted this lady in the grocery store. Then you almost mowed her down with your car. I'm almost afraid to ask how the two of you ended up going out to dinner or to the lake."

"Well, about the dinner, to make a long story less excruciating, she was in a jam at the bookstore. I did her a favor and she agreed to join me for dinner as a way of saying thank you."

"I'm not even going to ask for details."

"Thanks. I appreciate that," Lee said sarcastically.

"And the picnic?"

"Kyra's idea. A set-up by my daughter. Can you believe it?"

"She's a smart kid. Takes after her favorite uncle. So you like Katrice, I take it, and I'm guessing she probably has feelings for you, too."

Lee nodded. "That's the vibe I get from her—sometimes, anyway. I definitely have feelings for her, and it's not a crush or lust or anything fleeting like that. It's a little hard to explain, but the woman drives me crazy most of the time, and the crazier she makes me, the more I want to be around her."

Marshall looked puzzled.

"I know. That probably sounded really crazy but it's not as complicated as it sounds. Let me explain it this way. I like being around Katrice. It's not just because she's interesting, pretty, and has the longest, sexiest legs I've ever seen. There are other things. I enjoy our conversations and the excitement and passion in her voice when she talks about her business and the plans she has to make it a success. We can talk about anything under the sun and never get bored. She even asked about Paulette."

"Really?"

Lee nodded. "I was able to talk to her about our marriage and the feelings I had for her without things getting weird. Even with all that, I feel there's so much more to this woman and I want to learn everything about her. What makes her laugh. What makes her sad. Her favorite color. What her family is like. The kind of food she enjoys, her favorite movie, and how she could be this wonderful person and still be single. I'm telling you, man, five minutes around her and you'd feel the same. She's funny, sweet, smart, and sexy, all in one great package."

"But?"

"What makes you think there's a but?"

"'Cause you're sitting here with me drinking warm beer instead of being with her."

"Yeah, talk about crazy. I'd love to be spending time with her right now. But for some odd reason, she thinks she has to be tough and in control all the time. You know, if she gives in a little it might mean she's weak, or something like that. It drives me nuts. I can't open a door for her or walk her to her car without ticking her off. I think I may have said or done something today when I stopped by and invited her to church. But once again, I don't know what I did wrong."

Marshall nodded and tried to come up with a piece of brotherly advice that he could impart on his little brother. He had nothing.

"You know, even though she puts up this tough front, I think it's just some kind of protective shield that she's created because she's been hurt or disappointed or both. I don't know the specifics, but I'd be willing to bet that I'm paying for another man's sins."

Marshall rubbed his chin. "Hmm. This might be kind of tough, little brother. That whole scorned-woman-been-done-wrong thing ain't no joke. Without knowing what this lady's past was like, you might be facing a lot more than you bargained for. Are you up to the challenge? And if so, what are your intentions? Summer fling? Long-distance love? Buddies? Buddies with benefits?"

"I haven't thought through all of that just yet. Hell, I'm still working on not looking like a drooling idiot when I'm around her."

Marshall finished his beer and rested his hands behind his head. "Sounds like you got it bad, little brother."

"You think?" Lee asked sarcastically.

"Want some advice?"

Lee braced himself for the 'love 'em and leave 'em' philosophy his brother was becoming famous for.

"I suggest you let Katrice know how you feel about her. Be up front and honest. Understand that you might have to wade through some layers of mistrust and pain carried over from her past. If she's worth it, be patient and go for it."

Surprised by his brother's candid and sage advice, Lee sat up and looked at him questioningly. "Okay, imposter, what did you do with my real brother?"

Marshall pulled up to his feet. Tossing his beer can to the trash, he turned to his brother before going into the house. "Life is too short to spend it being alone and regretful. If you can find someone to share it with, that makes it all worthwhile."

CHAPTER 18

"Aren't you going to invite me in?"

Katrice choked back the bile that had risen in her throat and was threatening to make her gag. "What are you doing here?"

"I'm here to see you, sweetheart. Talk about explaining the obvious."

"Things aren't always the way they seem," Katrice remarked sarcastically.

Greg ignored the remark and asked again, "Are you going to invite me in or would you prefer I take you into my arms right here on the front porch and kiss those beautiful lips of yours in front of the whole world? I'll bet your neighbor would get a big kick out of that." Greg bent his head toward Mrs. Parkins's yard and winked.

Katrice made no attempt to hide her disgust as she looked past Greg and saw her neighbor peering over the hedges with clippers in her hand. She stepped back, mumbling, "Come in."

Greg sauntered into the foyer and surveyed the surroundings. "Nice place. Not quite what I expected but very *homey*."

Katrice couldn't believe the overwhelming sense of hurt and anger that she felt upon seeing Greg. The lies, the deceit, the complete obliteration of trust—everything he had dragged into her life over their last year together—still gnawed at her down to her very soul.

"What are you doing here, Greg?"

"I told you. I'm here to see you, *darling.*"

Katrice cringed. Greg made a point of using his most condescending tone and referring to her as "baby" and "darling" when he was being smug. His smugness had always been annoying. Now it just bothered her that he still thought it had some impact. But she was more bothered by the fact that he had the nerve to show up on her doorstep after all this time. What could he be after? Then she remembered the message her mother had left on her voice mail.

I spoke with Greg the other day. You really need to give him a call . . . He's not taking the break-up well. . . .

After six months, she'd hoped he'd moved on. Apparently this wasn't the case.

"You've seen me, now you can go tell my mother that I'm alive and well and haven't been committed to a mental hospital. By the way, you might also want to mention to her how manipulative, deceitful, and down-right vile you are."

"I don't deserve that, Katrice."

Staring at Greg in disbelief, she was absolutely speechless.

"You never gave me a chance to explain everything that happened."

"What's to explain, Greg? On top of everything else you had done, you decided to add infidelity to your list of infractions. You not only lost your job due to your inability to control your *urges*, you managed to destroy our relationship in the process."

"Sweetheart—"

She was beginning to hate that word. "Just stop it, Greg, okay? Whatever you have to say is going to be a complete waste of breath and will probably make my head explode just trying to figure out the difference between the big lies and the really, really big lies."

"Katrice, I came all this way. At the very least you can hear me out."

What could Greg have to say? She had heard it all before. What she hadn't heard, she'd found out for herself. Besides, there was no explaining away Greg's behavior or the pain and embarrassment he had caused her. She had moved on with her life and there was no place for Greg in it.

He moved closer, stroking her arm. He expected her to step back, but she didn't. Although his touch no longer made her feel special or evoked feelings of love or longing, deep down inside she remembered a different man she had once loved. How could someone have changed so drastically? Or had he been the one to that changed?

No! Greg is no longer the man I thought I loved, and I'm no longer the woman who too willingly gave her all to him. He's not to be trusted. She wanted so badly to tell Greg to go away and never bother her again. For some strange reason, she didn't. Was it that she needed to finish things between them once and for all so that she could move on to whatever her new life offered? If so, would it hurt to listen to what he had to say? He couldn't possibly hurt her anymore, could he?

She was doing it again, second-guessing herself. Why did she find it so difficult to stand up to this man and mean it? She had stood her ground with him before. This wouldn't be the first time. Although she had to admit, it hadn't happened very often. Unfortunately, when she had decided to take a stand and refuse to be Greg's enabler any longer, it felt like too little too late.

Maybe if she hadn't allowed herself to be so easily led early in their relationship. She had liked the attention Greg gave her and the way he naturally took control. Her mother had convinced her that having such a man would give her a sense of security that was necessary in any successful relationship. What she didn't know at the time was that his need for control would inevitably kill, not strengthen, their bond.

From day one Greg had taken his role of being the man in the relationship very seriously. He never asked her opinion about anything. He chose where they had dinner. The plays they attended. The movies they rented. He even went so far as to attempt to choose the clothes she wore, the people she saw socially. When she did try to make a decision or offer an alternative to anything he suggested, he always found a way to persuade her that his decision was the better one. Because of Greg's domineering ways and her inability to establish any degree of independence, she had never really felt like a partner in their relationship. It wasn't until she found out about Greg's problem that she fully understood the forces and everything that drove the behavior he exhibited.

Greg was a control freak, a workaholic, and extremely manipulative. He had a need to dominate and control everything and everyone around him. Just seeing him again brought back feelings of distrust, anger, and inadequacy, feelings that she had promised herself she would not allow to follow her into her new life. Now here Greg was, months after she walked out of his life, attempting to pull her back into a life that had done nothing but enable behavior that was both destructive to their relationship and devastating to her self-esteem.

Katrice knew she couldn't help Greg. She'd discovered that his problems were bigger than she had ever imagined. He needed to get help for himself. She had told him exactly that when she'd left, but he wasn't trying to hear it then. He had been more interested in covering his tracks and making excuses. At this point, she could only work on repairing the damage he had caused her.

Katrice looked at Greg, who seemed to be waiting for some sign that he was getting through to her. She knew the look all too well. She had seen it more times than she wanted to remember. It was the same look a parent gives to a confused child. But unlike before, this time would be different. She did not relent.

Looking past Greg, Katrice knew she needed to gather her thoughts and she had to do it quickly. She would have to be calm and confident as she spoke her mind, leaving no room for him to misunderstand what she meant. She trained her eyes on several objects on a nearby table until something grabbed her attention.

On the table where she kept her mail was a postcard from one of the local beauty salons. The front of the postcard read, "Ready for a change?" Change. She thought about all of the changes that had taken place in her life since moving to Benton Lake. A lot of what was old had been replaced by a new way of living, thinking, and dreaming. She liked who she had become and the direction her life was going. She drew courage from the knowledge that she alone could accomplish her dreams.

Greg was waiting impatiently for Katrice to offer him a seat. Apparently, she needed to get some things off her chest. He would listen as long as she eventually agreed to come back home and give up the silly notion of living in this dreary town and running her own business. He needed her. Somehow he would have to get her to understand that. The sooner she came to her senses, the better.

Katrice turned her attention to Greg. He looked uncomfortable and annoyed. Among her things and in her space, Greg seemed to be sorely out of place. Looking more closely, she also saw something she had not noticed before. She had always viewed Greg as strong-willed, almost forceful. Now something was different about him. The man she had once thought she knew so well appeared to be uneasy and a mere stranger in a place where she felt quite at home.

Katrice walked over to the front door. Opening it, she stepped aside so Greg could get by. "It's time for you to leave. I think anything we had to say to each other has already been said."

"That's not true," Greg protested. "There's a lot that I need to say to you and it's long overdue. I love you, Katrice, and I miss you like crazy. I've made mistakes in the past, but the biggest one was letting you go."

Katrice searched Greg's face. She heard what he was saying, but he couldn't possibly believe it any more than she did. "You didn't *let* me go, Greg. I left."

"That's only because I pushed you away. Guess it's just like the old adage, sometimes you don't know what you have until it's gone."

"Or until you betray the trust of someone who truly cared about you but who came to realize she is better off without you. And I am better off without you, Greg."

Greg wasn't getting anywhere with Katrice. He'd always been able to talk to her and persuade her to be reasonable, but not now. He saw a stubbornness in Katrice he had never seen before. His grandmother had always told him to pick his battles. The look in Katrice's eyes told him that this battle would best be waged another day.

Sitting in his car in front of Katrice's house, Greg plotted his next move. Getting her back in his life was going to take careful planning and a bit of finesse.

She had changed. In the time since she'd left and taken up residence in Hicktown, something or someone had caused this change. He had to get to the bottom of it or risk losing his hold on her and any chance of proving his innocence.

CHAPTER 19

The hour was late but Lee didn't feel much like sleeping. He'd been restless and unable to relax all evening.

Kyra was spending the night at a friend's house, and his father had taken Vonda to Cincinnati to dinner and a play. They wouldn't be home until late. Marshall had gone off to parts unknown and Lee couldn't even begin to speculate when he would find his way back home.

The house was quiet; in fact, too quiet, and Lee had too much on his mind to relax. Everything he had tried that evening to keep from thinking about Katrice had failed. Several times already he had picked up the phone to call her but had thought better of it. After all, she hadn't called to say why she hadn't bothered to show up at the picnic. That morning, she had given every indication she would be there. Well, not exactly, but she didn't say that she wouldn't come. Maybe something or someone had presented a more attractive offer, Lee thought sourly.

He grabbed the TV's remote control and began flipping channels. But nothing held his attention for very long. He clicked off the TV and picked up a magazine. When the magazine failed to hold his interest he went to the kitchen to make himself a cup of coffee. Looking in the cupboard for coffee he came up empty-handed. Perhaps it was for the best, he reasoned. It was much too late for a caffeine buzz.

Would it have been too hard to pick up the phone and say that she had other plans? Lee slammed the cabinet door closed. *She stood me up!* He couldn't understand why it bothered him so much that Katrice had rejected him, but it did. Just when it seemed as if they were making headway, she apparently deemed it okay to blow off his invitation.

After having a piece of Vonda's homemade cherry pie and a glass of milk, Lee decided to take a drive. A late evening drive and some good music usually helped clear his mind and relax him. Hopefully it would work tonight.

For most of the evening, his thoughts had centered on Katrice, but he also couldn't stop thinking about his brother's advice. *Was Katrice worth it?* If so, what plans did he have for them? He had given no thought to being in Benton Lake beyond the summer. After the Labor Day weekend, he and Kyra were heading back home. Back to their lives, their daily routine, and everything that had driven them to Benton Lake for the summer in the first place.

Would he and Katrice be able to maintain a long distance relationship? Would Katrice even want to have a relationship with him? After what had happened—or didn't happen—today, he didn't have much hope.

Why did women have to be so complicated?

Driving along the quiet streets of Benton Lake, Lee tuned the car's radio to the local R&B station. The late-night DJ announced that the next commercial-free set would feature old-school love songs. Not really in the mood to hear about lost loves and unrequited passion, Lee was ready to turn to another station when he heard the opening of one of his father's favorite songs, "At Last" by Etta James.

His father played that song so many times when they were growing up, Lee and his brothers would run to their rooms whenever the record started. However, as an adult, Lee had to admit that there was something about the song that seemed to pull him into another place. In recent years he had grown to appreciate the music and to understand the lyrics that unfolded a love story so vividly.

As the powerful words and the conviction with which Etta James brought them to life crept into his subconscious, Lee found himself caught up. He could hear the relief mixed with longing in the singer's voice as she shared her ups and downs. The listener knew that nothing else mattered to her at that moment except that love had finally been realized.

My lonely days are over. As the song continued to play in the background, he was reminded of the first time he saw Katrice. *The night I looked at you I found a dream that I could speak to, a dream that I could call my own.*

Their first kiss. Their dinner date. Holding her in his arms at the lake.

And then the spell was cast.

Had Katrice cast a spell? His logical and analytical self said no. But his heart told a different tale. He wanted Katrice in his life, but he couldn't clearly define what that meant. And it wasn't just *his* definition that mattered. What did *she* want?

At the song's end, Lee felt himself gently floating back to reality. He continued the drive, making a series of left and right turns, seemingly going nowhere in particular. But one question nagged him. *What did Katrice want?*

Then Lee slowed down and stopped.

And here we are in heaven, for you are mine at last!

It is a beautiful night, he thought, sitting in his car across the street from the old white house. Even though he felt silly just sitting there intermittently looking up at the stars and then at the house, Lee made no attempt to move.

Although surprised that his journey had brought him to Katrice's house, Lee was pleased to see that the downstairs lights were still on. Of course, he couldn't tell if she was still up or not, but he would find out soon enough. He cut the engine and sat in the car going over in his head what he would say if and when she answered the door.

"Hi, I was in the neighborhood and thought I would drop by."

No. Too corny.

"I was thinking about you and wanted to know if you were thinking about me."

Definitely no. He would sound every bit of twelve years old.

Was she still up? He kept looking for her silhouette to move past the window.

Make a move or go home.

The clock on the dashboard read nine forty-three. Maybe she was one of those people who always kept a light on to fool burglars into thinking someone was home and awake.

Make a move or go home.

Lee sighed. Even though he had a hard time admitting it, the fact that Katrice hadn't accepted his invitation to church or the picnic still bothered him, and the disappointment he had felt earlier in the day was still there. Yet, his eagerness to see her had dogged him all day. The idea for the nighttime drive hadn't stemmed from his desire to see Katrice, but if he had to be completely honest with himself, he knew he wouldn't be able to rest until he did.

Lee removed the key from the ignition and decided to take his chances. Hopefully, she wouldn't be upset with him for coming by so late and would just assume that he lacked good manners, or *home training,* as his father liked to call it.

Lee walked up the driveway and thought about how displeased he would be with any young man who showed up at his home to see Kyra at this hour. *Not the same thing.* He and Katrice were both adults. He checked his watch again. Nine fifty-two. It wasn't really that late.

Lee waited a second before knocking gently on the door. To his surprise, he saw a shadow move behind the living room curtain and then heard Katrice call out, "Who is it?"

"It's me. Lee," he answered in a voice that sounded almost too loud in the still of the night. Did he also hear relief?

Katrice turned on the porch light and unlocked the door. "Hi," she said, not appearing at all surprised to see him standing in her doorway. "Is everything all right?" she asked, noting his odd expression.

It is now.

At the mere sight of her, the disappointment that had plagued him just moments earlier melted like snowflakes on a warm surface. Now his only emotions were joy mixed with relief. He took in the view of her with one sweeping and appreciative glance.

Instead of inviting Lee inside, Katrice leaned against the doorjamb, waiting for a response.

Lee noticed that she wore her hair pinned up in a kind of bun that at some point had morphed into a ponytail. She had a pencil sticking out of the top, making him wonder if she had been working. Her attire had that working-at-home but still relaxed feel to it. Low-rise jean shorts hugged her hips and accentuated her sexy curves. They were paired with a bright yellow tank top that was just snug enough to give Lee a pretty good impression of what was beneath.

If he thought she looked sexy in the peach robe earlier in the day, this outfit took sexy to a whole other level. The yearning he'd felt all day to see her suddenly escalated to pure desire. His arms ached to reach out and pull her into his arms. And the need to kiss her nearly overwhelmed him.

Control! "Yeah, uh, everything is all right. I-I was just in the neighborhood." *Not what I wanted to say.* "I mean, out driving—around town—in my car."

And thinking about you.

Lee took a deep breath and exhaled slowly, needing to convey what he had on his mind—in his heart—without sounding like a complete idiot.

Katrice still hadn't invited him in.

"Let me start over. I've been in a really strange mood all evening. A little while ago, I decided to go for a drive, hoping that a change of scenery and some fresh air would relax me." *Talk about scenery.* Katrice stood just inches away from him looking better than he could have imagined. "I guess the bottom line is I needed to see you," he added.

Lee bit down on his bottom lip until it hurt. He'd said enough, actually more than enough. Forget about an invitation to come inside; now she would probably ask him to leave.

Katrice listened as Lee fumbled with his words, seeming to become more flustered with each completed thought. She tried not to enjoy his plight but couldn't help herself. Lee was good for her ego. For as long as she could remember, she'd always felt like an awkward and ugly duckling, but the way Lee looked at her made her feel beautiful.

"Your light was on," Lee said, hoping to redeem himself. "I hope you weren't busy." *Does this woman ever not look beautiful?*

"No." Katrice didn't quite know what to say, but was strangely pleased that Lee had ended up on her doorstep. She couldn't think of anyone else she would rather be talking to at that moment.

"I know it's late and normally I wouldn't have come by at this hour unexpectedly. I just, I hope I didn't interrupt anything."

"No, not at all. I was in the process of downloading some résumés for a job I posted for the bookstore. That's all." *Unless you count the effort in trying to get my mind off Greg's visit. And thinking about how I could have ever given myself to a man like him.*

Seeing Greg again had reminded her why she needed to be careful now. Katrice liked Lee more than she cared to admit and she enjoyed being around him. She wondered if he was what her Grandma Harry had referred to as a "good man." Since there didn't seem to be a guidebook, how could she tell? When it came to the opposite sex, she was a novice, a rookie, ill-equipped. Katrice's relationships with men had been limited at best. She had dated a little during and after college, but Greg had been her longest and most serious relationship, and it had ended in complete disaster.

Greg had been so undeserving of her love and she had been deserving of more. Would Lee be that careless with her heart? Could she trust him? Could she trust herself to know what she really wanted in a relationship and to go after it?

Would I have to give up who I am to be with you?

"Would you like to come in?" Finally Katrice moved to the side to allow Lee to enter.

He hesitated, trying to calm his intense need to lose himself in Katrice and experience everything that made her who she was. Lee wondered how any man would not want to make her his own. He knew he did.

His sensible side told him to get back in the car, drive home, and take a very cold shower. But Lee's emotional side teased him with memories of what it felt like to be held, touched, kissed, appreciated.

It was also this side that beckoned him to take Katrice into his arms and kiss her until she surrendered, letting her guard down for good. But, if he took that step, there would be no turning back.

"Maybe I should leave you alone so you can finish your work." He swallowed and fixed his gaze on the doorjamb. His mind raced. If he could keep his cool, maybe they could just sit and talk.

Riiiiight.

"No, really, it's all right," she said. "I didn't realize how long I had been sitting at the computer. I could use a break."

Lee finally stepped across the threshold into the bright light of the hallway. The faint scent of his after-shave trailed him and seemed to settle around Katrice like an embrace. She closed and locked the door, thinking that it ought to be a crime for someone to look *and* smell that good.

Lee followed Katrice down the short hallway and tried desperately to focus on anything except her. But his efforts were in vain; clearly, nothing else interested him.

Lee's heart thumped furiously. Katrice's short shorts and sexy walk were a dangerous combination, and he wanted nothing more than to experience that kind of danger. Her every move, sound, and even her scent, enchanted him. The short walk from the front door to living room further tested his resolve.

Right before entering the living room, Lee stopped dead in his tracks.

Bending down to pick up some papers from the floor, Katrice unknowingly gave Lee a most spectacular view of her backside.

She straightened up and turned around when she no longer heard Lee's footsteps. He stood in the doorway of her living room and for the second time that evening, she noticed an odd expression on his face. "Lee, are you sure everything is all right?"

Talk about a loaded question!

He took a series of deep breaths before trusting himself to answer. Katrice clearly had no idea of the kind of effect she had on him.

It was almost funny, he thought. She had to be one of the sexiest and most intriguing women he knew. She had a style that was all her own, one that exuded quiet sophistication, grace, spunk, and smoldering sensuality. She had no trouble speaking her mind, as he had witnessed on more than one occasion. And she possessed an independent streak that he both detested and admired.

From his limited observations, she ran her store with great savvy and an astute business sense. Her staff showed her the kind of respect and dedication that generally took years to earn.

There were many things that made her special. Lee even found her unpretentious nature both refreshing and alluring. In contrast, women he'd dated in the past had all been educated and classy, but boring as hell. None of them could hold a candle to Katrice.

Finally, Lee stepped out of the hallway and into the living room.

Katrice watched as he walked toward her, slowly and deliberately. With every step, her past with Greg and the memory of his visit faded deeper and deeper into her subconsciousness, tucked away in a place where she wouldn't have to deal with it if she didn't want to. And she didn't. Not right now. Not in this place. Not at this time.

Lee stopped within inches of Katrice.

She felt her body react as intense heat spread throughout her body, settling in places that yearned for Lee's touch.

He reached out and caressed her cheek. Leaning in just inches from her lips, he whispered, "If I don't kiss you right now I think I'm going to lose my mind."

Katrice closed her eyes and allowed her silence to give consent, for at that moment she wanted nothing more than to feel his lips on hers.

The kiss that ensued sent sparks through every nerve ending in Katrice's body. His mouth covered hers and his tongue teased her lips.

Lee deepened the kiss. She opened her mouth to allow him entry. Katrice felt his hands become entangled in her hair as he released a cascade of unruly curls. Her hair clip fell to the floor. She didn't care. It didn't matter to her what her hair looked like just then, only that it felt good to have Lee's strong hands entangled in it.

Feeling bold, Katrice pressed her body firmly against his. Lee's desire for her was evident, but it didn't frighten her, it gave her confidence. She allowed her hands to roam freely over his back, feeling taut muscles underneath the cotton barrier of his shirt.

Lee couldn't believe how hungry he was for Katrice. What he thought would be a simple kiss had turned into something more urgent.

Breaking the kiss, he turned Katrice around. Reaching under her top, his strong hands cupped her breasts. While nuzzling her neck, he whispered, "You are so beautiful."

Katrice's accompanying moan was deep and as sensuous. If she didn't know better, she would swear that her insides were turning to liquid. The man was driving her crazy and they were still fully clothed!

She moved her hips against his erection and he nearly came undone.

"Woman, you are driving me crazy."

Likewise! If only he knew what he was doing to her!

Turning to face Lee, she took his bottom lip between her teeth, nipping gently. She teased him with little kisses and traced his lips with her tongue. Then she wrapped her arms around his neck and kissed him with a fiery passion that she didn't know she possessed. She felt his hands cup her buttocks as he pressed her against his sturdy frame and the hard evidence of his desire for her.

No longer able to stand on legs that were growing weaker with each kiss and touch, Katrice broke away. "My bedroom," she said breathlessly. "It's upstairs."

Lee reached down and scooped Katrice into his arms.

"Oh!" she exclaimed, slightly startled by how quickly and effortlessly he carried her.

Not wanting to lose the intensity of the moment, Lee covered her mouth with his, taking what she so eagerly offered.

When he reached the top of the stairs, Lee pushed the bedroom door open with his foot, not releasing her until they had reached her bed. He gently put her down. She looked so beautiful. But as eager as he was to make love to her, he hesitated.

"What's wrong?" she asked, her voice laced with worry. Katrice looked around her bedroom. Was it messy? Did she do something wrong? Had he lost his desire for her that quickly?

Breathing hard, Lee wiped perspiration from his forehead.

What am I doing? His actions didn't suggest that of a man his age, but more closely resembled that of a sixteen-year-old who was about to experience his first sexual encounter. Lee wanted to have a relationship with Katrice, not a quick roll in the sack. When he arrived at her house he'd had every intention of taking things slowly, but his actions were belying those intentions. The last thing he wanted was to rush Katrice into something she may not be ready for or give her the impression that he was some sex-crazed animal needing to fulfill a primal need.

"I'm sorry, Katrice. We should probably slow down a minute. This isn't what I had planned. My reasons for coming here tonight had nothing to do with us ending up here, in your bed. I just really wanted to see you and to talk to you. That's all. I don't want you to get the idea that I'm something I'm not."

Relieved and pleased that Lee felt compelled to put her feelings before his desire she interrupted him. "How about if we don't talk right now. You started something that needs to be finished."

She smiled and looked so seductive that he was practically speechless.

Lee leaned down on the bed and supported his weight with one hand and caught Katrice under her shoulders with his other. He pulled her up so that her lips met his. Just one more taste from her sweet lips and he knew there was no turning back. This is what they both wanted, of that he was sure.

Taking advantage of his position, Katrice reached under Lee's shirt, stroking his back and intermittently running her nails up and down his spine. Judging by his moans, the action pleased and excited him. His skin felt good beneath her hands, smooth and warm. She imagined he tasted good, too. She needed to know, for sure.

Katrice was driving Lee crazy. He wanted, no, needed to feel her rich, warm skin next to his. In one quick motion he raised himself up and in the next second her yellow tank top lay in a heap on the floor.

How had he done that so quickly?

Her bra was next. Then she felt the snap on her shorts come undone, and so was she.

In no time, Katrice lay naked, vulnerable, and exposed beneath Lee's gaze. Did he like what he saw?

"Exquisite," he whispered breathlessly, answering her unasked question.

Capturing her lips in a kiss that stoked her internal furnace to higher intensity, Katrice felt dizzy with desire and anticipation. She was thankful she was already lying down, as she didn't trust her legs to support her.

She arched when Lee left her lips and took her breast in his mouth. Gripping the sheets, she moaned.

Lee used his tongue to trace designs around her nipples until each one hardened in response.

"Do you like that?" he asked with a seductive smile.

"Yes, very much," Katrice replied, "but I think we have a problem here."

"Not from where I'm standing."

Katrice blushed as Lee took in the full length of her body with one sweeping glance.

"I'm flattered," she said, "but I think one of us is overdressed."

Lee smiled mischievously. "And what do you plan to do about that?"

Not wasting another second, Katrice took hold of Lee's shirt and pulled it over his head. Taking time to admire his broad chest and the rich brown skin that appeared to have been poured over his delicious body, she ran her hands across his shoulders, over his chest, and down his flat stomach. Flicking her tongue over his hardened nipples, she heard him moan.

Continuing her exploration, she couldn't get enough of him. She stopped long enough to unfasten his belt buckle. Unsnapping his pants, she released the zipper with a sense of urgency that might have embarrassed her if she were with someone else. But with Lee, there were no awkward moments, only the discovery of something beautiful and new. She was as hungry for him as he seemed to be for her.

"Wow," she whispered. As he stood naked before her, there was no hiding his desire for her. Lee took very good care of his body. For that she was appreciative. Strong, broad shoulders topped a well-defined chest, leading down to a flat stomach and somewhat narrow hips sitting atop long, powerful legs.

"Satisfied?" Lee asked with a glint in his eyes.

"Not yet."

Lee joined Katrice on the bed and took her in his arms. He was completely intoxicated by her; feeling her body pressed to his, everything felt so right.

It had been so long since he'd allowed himself to be this close to anyone and to give of himself so freely. Making love to Katrice would be divine, exquisite, and—

"Oh no!"

"What's wrong?" Katrice asked, startled.

How could he have been so unprepared? This was just plain irresponsible. But he hadn't planned any of this, at least not consciously.

"What is it, Lee?"

"Protection. Katrice, baby, I don't have any. We can't—I can't—oh, baby, I'm sorry."

For the second time that evening, Katrice faced what threatened to be a disappointing end to her evening with Lee. Why hadn't she thought about protection herself?

But why would she? Until Lee came along, the possibility of sex was equivalent to a unicorn sighting. Some example of a modern woman, she thought.

Suddenly she said, "Wait here," and scurried off to the bathroom. Returning, she sat down on the side of the bed.

In the palm of her hand she held several condoms wrapped in the brightest and most festive packaging Lee had ever seen.

Before he could ask the question that she knew was on the tip of his tongue, she silenced him with a kiss him and said, "I have a perfectly good and innocent explanation, but I'll save it for later. Okay?"

He could trust her, couldn't he? He pushed his questions aside. For now. Taking one of the packages from her outstretched hand, Lee quickly applied the protective barrier.

No more delays. Lee had to struggle to take his time as he entered Katrice, allowing all five senses to benefit from the experience. Tasting her lips. Hearing her soft moans. Seeing the pleasure reflected on her face. Inhaling her scent. Feeling how perfectly they fit together, he plunged deep into her warm, wet core.

Katrice moaned and arched her back, taking everything Lee offered. Clutching his buttocks, she responded to his every stroke with one in kind. She moved her body to the rhythm he set and positioned her body to feel every inch of him.

She couldn't believe how her body responded to Lee. The fit of their bodies was perfect and any concerns she had about her inexperience were put to rest. Never before had she known such pleasure or been able to give so unselfishly. Lee touched her in places that she'd never been touched before and kissed her where she'd never been kissed, releasing a passion that she knew would never be matched or exceeded by another.

The experience of making love to Katrice was more than Lee could have imagined. He experienced sheer joy exploring her magnificent body, every dip and curve. He was delighted that she matched his fervor as she hungrily demanded what he willingly and satisfactorily delivered.

At the culmination of their lovemaking, their bodies moved in a synchronized rhythm as they soared to heights of pleasure neither anticipated nor would soon forget.

CHAPTER 20

Katrice slept soundly. Her long, lithe body stretched out along the length of Lee's frame. Each curve and contour found a complementary place to rest.

Breathing slow and steady, she rested her head against Lee's chest as he gently stroked her hair. She felt good in his arms, and his life, he thought as he pulled her closer.

She stirred and snuggled closer to him.

"Are you asleep?"

"No, but I thought you were," Lee replied, playing with a wayward curl and inhaling the fresh scent of her thick, shiny hair.

"No, I was just lying here wondering," she said lazily.

"About?"

"When you're going to ask me about the condoms."

Lee cleared his throat. "I-I'm sorry. That's really none of my business. Don't feel as if you need to explain anything to me. Your life is your life and I—"

"Stop, Lee. It's okay. One of ladies from the bookstore had a 'fun' party. Believe it or not, the condoms were party favors."

"I'm probably going to regret asking this, but what's a *fun* party?"

"Let's just say it's a place for grown-up girls to buy grown-up toys."

As understanding dawned, Lee was thankful Katrice couldn't see the embarrassment on his face.

"Wow. Do you have anything else you'd like to share with me?"

"I don't want to give away all my secrets," she answered, playfully running her fingers down his chest.

He thought about what he knew about Katrice, which wasn't very much. She had shared very little about herself and seemed almost uncomfortable whenever he asked about her family or her past.

"You haven't told me any secrets as far as I know." He no longer wore the playful expression that had softened his features just moments before. His voice now held concern.

Katrice could sense the change in his mood without looking at him. She certainly did not want to spoil the moment by being serious. Being in Lee's arms felt so good and so right. The only thing she wanted to do was to hang on to that feeling as long as possible and to not chase it away with real life drama or concerns. She opted instead to counter Lee's more serious mood with a lighter one. "Well, let's see. You want to know a few of my secrets, huh? How about likes and dislikes? Can we start there?"

"I'll accept whatever you're willing to share," he responded honestly.

"Okay. My favorite colors are fire engine red, royal blue, sea foam green, and sunshine yellow."

He chuckled. "Most people only have one favorite color. Not only do you have more than one, but I'd have to say that I don't think I've ever heard anyone be as descriptive."

"Maybe that's because you only know boring people. Now let me continue revealing my secrets, I mean, likes and dislikes. My favorite holiday is Thanksgiving; Christmas comes a really close second. Seems like it should be the other around, but that's just me. Now for dislikes. Bats and spiders give me the creeps. And even though I hate worms, I do like that wormy smell after a spring rain. It reminds me of being a kid and splashing around in mud puddles."

Lee chuckled again.

Katrice was growing fond of that sound. Feeling the rumbling in his chest before his laughter actually reached the surface, she snuggled closer to him, reveling in the lightness of the moment.

"Wormy smell? I don't know if I could actually say what worms smell like. That's a new one."

"I'm sure you know it; you just haven't really thought much about it."

"You're probably right. Why don't you enlighten me "

"Well, after a warm spring rain when the leaves are fresh and the first fragrant flowers have bloomed, the rain and the earth smells mix together and create what my sister and I always referred to as the wormy smell."

Once again Katrice felt the rumbling laughter in Lee's chest before she heard it. This time she laughed, too.

"Oh, yeah, I almost forgot one of my likes. I thoroughly enjoy slasher movies."

"Slasher movies? You mean those disgusting blood-and-gore movies where everybody at camp or in the house or in the insane asylum gets killed except for one person?"

"Yeah."

"Hmm, you like those types of movies, huh? I'll be sure and watch my back around you," he joked.

Satisfied that she had successfully steered the conversation back to less serious matters, she replied, "No, that's *my* job."

Lee and Katrice rested quietly in each other's arms for a while longer before Lee broke the silence. "I have to admit something to you."

"What's that?"

"I was disappointed that you didn't accept my invitation today."

Katrice stiffened. *The invitation to church and the picnic.* With Greg showing up out of the blue and sending her emotions into a tailspin, she had forgotten all about Lee's invitation. It was hard to believe that so much had happened in the span of just one day. She would have to explain to him why she stood him up, or at least offer a plausible excuse without blatantly lying.

Please don't ask what happened. "I, uh, something came up that I had to take care of."

Sensing Katrice's mood shift, Lee became concerned. "Was it something to do with the bookstore? Is everything all right?"

"It will be," she responded, more to herself than Lee.

"Is it something I can help with, Katrice?"

She sighed. She didn't want to think about Greg or anything connected to him. Not right now. And she really didn't want to involve Lee in any of her drama. "No, it's nothing I can't handle," she answered with as much conviction as she could muster.

She was doing it again, Lee thought. Why did she have to be so tough all the time? "You know, every time I offer to help you, no matter what the situation is, I get the 'I am woman, hear me roar' battle cry. I know you have strong, beautiful shoulders, Katrice. You don't always have to carry the weight of the world on them."

Pushing up on one elbow so that she could talk to Lee face-to-face, she said, "You don't understand."

"What?" he asked. "What is it that I don't understand? I'm a reasonably intelligent person. Talk to me. Do you think that people will think less of you if you occasionally ask for help?"

"I could care less what people think of me," Katrice responded defiantly, knowing she didn't fully believe what she was saying. She did care what people thought about her, although she really tried to appear unaffected by the outside world's opinions. "I told you before, Lee, I can take care of myself. The last thing I want is to be a woman who can't seem to stand on her own two feet and needs a man around to give her self-worth. I don't want to be in a constant state of needing to be rescued."

"I wasn't trying to imply that at all."

The atmosphere had just gone from relaxed to tense in a matter of seconds. This time Katrice was more annoyed with herself. She hadn't meant to sound so defensive, but everything she said was true. She wanted to be her own woman, with everything that came with it, no matter what. That meant that she couldn't treat her independence as something she would put on and take off whenever it suited her. This was how she had to live her life, each and every day.

Katrice stroked Lee's face. This wasn't how she wanted to spend their time together. "I'm sorry. I don't want to argue. Let's just enjoy this time right now. Okay?"

Lee reluctantly agreed. But he knew if they were going to have a relationship, Katrice would have to stop hiding behind her steel armor and reveal her true self. Was the real Katrice much different from the woman he held in his arms?

It was nearly three-thirty in the morning when Lee left to go home. Katrice hated that he had to leave but understood why he needed to. He had a family that cared about him and would want him home.

Katrice and Lee had made love two more times, and each time Lee's affection for her became more evident. Hours later Katrice was still reeling from the intensity of it all. She missed his touch, his smell, and his presence. But most of all she missed how wonderful it felt to be wrapped in his arms.

Katrice had not had many lovers, and by today's standards could be considered rather inexperienced. But with

Lee, none of that seemed to matter. He reacted to her every touch, kiss, and caress as if they were keys to his very survival. She especially enjoyed the freedom he gave her to explore his magnificent body. Katrice had never had those feelings with any other man, especially not with Greg. With him the act of lovemaking had been ritualistic and lacking in feeling. Simply put, there had been no passion or intimacy between them.

That wasn't the case with Lee. He loved exploring her most intimate and sensitive pleasure spots, and that he had! Even discovering some that she didn't know she had.

His mission was pleasure. Well, she had only one thing to say to that. *Mission accomplished!*

CHAPTER 21

Katrice checked her watch as she searched in vain for her other blue shoe, scolding herself for having hit the snooze button an unprecedented five times before getting out of bed. Now she had no time for a cup of coffee or even a quick breakfast. She would have to hurry to get to the bookstore in time to open.

She lost precious minutes on her way out the door when she had to stop and go back inside to get the résumés she had printed the night before. She wished she had scheduled Geneva to open instead of coming in later that afternoon. At least she would have had time to sit down and eat a bowl of cereal.

Arriving at the bookstore more frazzled than late, Katrice got, and ignored, a curious look from Millicent. She went straight to her office, tripping over a book display en route.

"Are you okay?" Millicent asked when she came back out.

"Yes, of course. Why do you ask?"

"No reason," Millicent replied, heading to Katrice's office to start the coffee. When she rejoined Katrice at the counter, she asked again, "Are you sure everything is okay?"

Katrice looked down at her clothes to make sure she hadn't forgotten to put on a key piece of clothing.

Satisfied that she was fully dressed, she ran her hand through her loose hair. "I'm fine, Millicent," she remarked as casually as she could. "I just overslept this morning, that's all."

"If you say so. There is something different about you today. Maybe it's just that you look so rested." Millicent yawned. "Glad somebody had a good weekend."

Katrice blushed. *If she only knew.*

Lee leisurely rolled over in bed and checked the clock on the nightstand. It was only seven-thirty. That explained why he hadn't heard any sounds outside his room. Apparently, no one was up yet. Kyra wouldn't be home until later that afternoon, and Lee was sure his father and Marshall would be sleeping in. Thankfully, neither had been home when Lee came in. Creeping back into the house and possibly having to explain his where-abouts that time of morning was not something he would have welcomed doing.

He could have stayed the night at Katrice's, but instead had made an excuse that he needed to get home. He wasn't sure why he had been less than truthful with her, but he was sure it had everything to do with his ever growing feelings for her.

Flipping the pillow over to the cool side, he laced his fingers and placed them behind his head. As he rested against the pillow's feathery softness, he wondered what Katrice was doing and if she was thinking about him or their night together. It had been a little over four hours since he'd left her house, but he missed her. The feel of her lying next to him. The perfect fit of their bodies. The softness and scent of her hair. The faint moans that escaped from her lips as his hands and mouth discovered uncharted areas of her body.

Everything, he thought, smiling. He missed everything about Katrice. How did he allow her to get under his skin so fast and so completely? Was it a case of extreme lust? Loneliness? Neither, he thought with certainty. It was more that drew him to her. She possessed something that compelled him to want to find out everything about her and to share everything he had with her.

Then there was the question that popped in and out of his mind: Did she feel the same about him? If he had to use last night as an indicator, he'd say yes. But he knew it wasn't fair to gauge her feelings based solely on one night. He needed her to give him more than her body; he needed her trust and friendship. He needed all she had to offer and even that which she didn't yet know she had to give. But there was one stipulation; it had to be given freely.

Whether she herself realized it or not, Lee sensed Katrice had much to give—to the right person. Unfortunately, she didn't trust him or herself enough to show it to him. *Was* he *the right person?* Could he be asking too much of her, more than she felt capable of giving? There were no fast or ready answers. Only time would tell. Unfortunately, time was something that was continuing to tick slowly away.

These days, Lee had been spending more time than usual thinking about what his life would be like when he and Kyra returned home to Columbus. The thought of returning to the house that he had shared with his wife and the job that no longer held the same excitement or satisfaction left him feeling strangely melancholy. Listening to a dog barking in the distance, he thought back to his first night back in Benton Lake and his father's suggestion that Lee might be ready to move on to a new phase in his life. *Could this be it?*

Getting out of bed, Lee embraced the beautiful day and decided to leave such serious thoughts for another time.

CHAPTER 22

Business had been brisk at the bookstore for most of the day. The local preschool had brought in a group of children for a field trip, which included a special story time just for them.

Geneva had readily volunteered to perform the reading honors; her three-year-old grandson was one of the preschoolers.

While Geneva read to the children, Katrice waited on customers and helped out in the coffee shop. It wasn't until Millicent returned from her break around three that Katrice had a chance to take a lunch break.

She badly needed a few moments to herself and decided to take her lunch away from the hustle and bustle of the bookstore. The sandwich shop down the street would provide exactly what she needed—a quick bite and a few minutes of alone time.

Waiting in line to place her lunch order, Katrice heard her stomach growling loudly. She self-consciously pressed a magazine against it. A man standing ahead of her turned around and smiled, amused by her stomach's declaration of hunger.

Katrice returned his smile but was too hungry to be seriously embarrassed. Tapping her foot against the tiled floor, she willed her stomach to be silent. But as soon as she caught a whiff of freshly baked bread, it was all she could do to keep the growling at bay.

After getting her food and weaving her way through the crowded restaurant, Katrice could finally relax, read her magazine, and satisfy her hunger. Sitting at a booth near the back with an overstuffed corned beef sandwich, a bag of potato chips, and a pickle wedge, she offered a quick prayer of thanks for her meal before diving in. She practically cooed as she bit into the fresh bread and the tender, succulent meat. Even the pickle wedge tasted divine. Who knew such a simple meal could be so satisfying?

While attempting to eat her sandwich like a lady, Katrice pulled out her ever-growing to-do list and pushed her magazine to the side. One side of the paper listed tasks that needed to be completed for the bookstore; the other side listed tasks she needed to complete at home. Both sides contained more tasks than she had the time or skills to finish. She sighed and began to doodle. Drawing a happy face beside one task that she had finished but had failed to mark off, she decided to reward herself with a scoop of ice cream before going back to the bookstore.

After doodling a flower next to "clean gutters", Katrice placed the pencil on the table and smiled to herself. She didn't feel much like focusing on leaf-filled gutters or anything else on her list. Instead, her thoughts shifted to the person whose name she had written beside the flower. *Lee.*

She had not stopped thinking about last night. As a result, more than once that morning, Millicent had caught her staring off into space with a silly grin plastered on her face. She couldn't help it. She felt giddy and excited. That morning, as she raced around getting ready for work, she had decided that today she would allow herself the luxury of being led by her feelings, throwing caution to the wind.

Although she and Lee hadn't made any plans for the evening, she hoped to see him. Maybe dinner and Lee for dessert, she thought with a wicked smile.

"I'm glad somebody is having a good day."

Startled, Katrice looked up. *Greg.*

"Imagine seeing you here. This really is a small town."

He loomed over her like a toxic cloud, and her light-hearted mood suddenly became dark. *Why didn't he just go away?*

"Mind if I join you?"

"Yes, I do mind," she said angrily.

Staring intently at Katrice, Greg placed his tray on the table and sat across from her. "Maybe I should have ordered what you have. It looks good, or what's left of it anyway. I see this country air has improved your appetite."

Katrice frowned. She quickly scribbled over Lee's name and her other drawings. Greg had killed her good vibe and her appetite.

"Go home, Greg. I have absolutely nothing to say to you."

"I think you said that the last time I saw you. Is it going to be like this every time we see each other?"

"No, not if you take my advice and go back home and come to terms once and for all with the fact that we're finished. I don't know how to make it any simpler than that."

Greg smiled. "I always loved your spunk, Katrice."

She winced. "You loved my spunk? I can't believe that just came out of your mouth. Is that why you never took me seriously about anything and squashed every bit of assertiveness I ever tried to exhibit? Somehow I don't buy that. Oh, wait. I think I might understand what you really mean. You weren't concerned about my spunk, more likely the lack thereof and how easy it was to manipulate me and everyone else around you."

Greg looked uncomfortable as Katrice continued without pausing. "Maybe that's why you felt that you needed to prove something to yourself by putting your secretary in a position where she had to sleep with you to keep her job. Did she have spunk, too? It wasn't enough that you tried to crush my spirit, you had to do the same with her? What real man doesn't love that kind of power? I'm sure you did." She'd had enough of Greg and needed to leave before she really lost her temper. When she tried to stand, he caught her firmly by the wrist, applying just enough pressure to prevent her from rising.

"Katrice, don't do this. At least hear me out. That's all I'm asking for right now. To just throw everything away that we had over some foolishness seems crazy."

"*Foolishness?* Everything about our relationship epitomized the word. And what's crazy is that you think I want to hear anything you have to say. Now let me go, Greg," she demanded, trying to pull away. Greg held her wrist firmly, causing her to wince in pain.

"Sooner or later we're going to talk."

"I believe the lady asked you to let her go."

Katrice and Greg looked up simultaneously in the direction of the ominous sounding voice. Lee was standing beside them.

Both relieved and surprised to see him, Katrice was startled by how lethal he looked. His jaw was clenched and his dark eyes blazed. With his mouth set in a straight line, his stance was firm and unyielding. She had never seen him that way, and hoped to never again. She was glad he was on her side.

"Now *I* am telling you to let go of Katrice, and I won't say it twice."

Greg looked at the angry stranger and felt dwarfed by his stature and intimidated by his presence. He definitely looked like someone he didn't want to tangle with.

Good sense prevailed and Greg let go of Katrice's wrist. As he stood to leave, he made an attempt to regain his composure. Before walking away, he leaned forward and whispered, "Looks like we'll have to resume this conversation later, sweetheart. Alone."

As Greg passed Lee on his way out, Katrice held her breath, fearful Lee might pummel him to the floor. He certainly looked as though he might.

Once Greg was out the door, she noticed curious stares from some of the restaurant's patrons. She closed her eyes and sighed, embarrassed that her private drama had now turned public. Her nerves were frazzled and she was upset. Once again she had allowed Greg to get the upper hand. He still felt as if he could intimidate her, and he had. As a result, she had let the situation get completely out of hand. If Lee hadn't shown up—*No!* As her breathing returned to normal, she grabbed her tray and dumped her half-eaten lunch into the trash receptacle.

"Are you all right?" Lee asked, still fuming.

"Yes," she answered through clenched teeth.

Katrice practically ran out of the sandwich shop, Lee trailing behind her.

"Katrice, wait," he called out, quickening his steps to catch up to her. "Slow down. What's the matter? What was going on back there? Who was that?"

Stopping and sucking in a sharp breath between clenched teeth, she angrily turned on Lee. "First of all, what happened back there was none of your business. I had the situation under control. Second, when I need to be rescued, I'll be sure and call you. Then you can ride up on your white horse and save the day. Third, stop following me. Just because we slept together doesn't mean that you now have total access to my life."

Stunned and speechless, Lee couldn't believe what he had just heard. Just minutes before he had witnessed what he thought was an angry confrontation between Katrice and another man, someone she seemed to know. He didn't like what he had seen or the look on her face when she spoke to the man. Lee felt he had done what any gentleman would have upon seeing someone he cared about in apparent distress.

This someone had been Katrice. His first and only instinct had been to protect her. Had he overreacted? He didn't think so. In fact, it had been sheer will that had kept him from putting his fist through that guy's face. His jaw tightened just thinking about it. The way he'd grabbed Katrice . . .

Who was that guy, and what had he said or done to make Katrice so angry?

Whether she liked it or not, Lee needed an explanation from Katrice. But no matter what it was, he had to be prepared to handle the fallout.

Greg sat in his hotel room nursing his hurt pride. Katrice had changed in the short time she'd been here. He couldn't quite put his finger on it, but she wasn't the same woman with whom he'd shared his life over the past two years.

There was a lot that seemed different about her, particularly the way she had stood up to him.

How much of that had to do with the man who had confronted him in the sandwich shop? He wasn't just a casual acquaintance. Judging by his threatening manner and his protective stance, he had to be someone with whom Katrice was involved. There was no mistaking the look that passed between the two of them. Recalling the scene, Greg knew he had been seconds away from something he physically wouldn't have been able to handle. Thankfully, cooler heads prevailed.

As Greg planned his next move he knew he first needed answers to important questions. Just how deeply were Katrice and this person involved, and would he get in the way of what he needed?

Greg remained thoughtful as he finished unpacking his clothes. He paced the length of the small hotel room and flipped through the business directory he had picked up from the front desk. He knew if he was going to get through to Katrice he would have to make it a point to find out just how much she had changed and who was reaping the benefits of those changes.

CHAPTER 23

Katrice stomped into her office. She stormed across the room to her desk, kicking a box on the way, scattering Styrofoam packing peanuts across her path.

Standing in the doorway, Geneva watched the scene with interest, completely undetected by Katrice. After a moment she cleared her throat.

Katrice whirled around with her hands on her hips, eyes blazing. "What?" she practically shouted.

Taken aback by her boss's sharp tone, Geneva stepped inside the office and closed the door behind her. She sensed that she needed to get something off her chest, and she was willing to listen if Katrice was willing to confide in her.

"What's going on? You practically ran a customer over just now."

Taking a deep breath and willing herself to calm down, Katrice replied through clenched teeth, "Men!"

"By men are you referring to Lee?" Geneva asked cautiously.

Katrice slumped down in her desk chair and blew out a long breath. "Yes. No. Yes."

"Okay, I'm confused."

"Join the club."

"This might be a moot point, but Lee came by a little while ago looking for you. I told him you had gone down the street to the sandwich shop for lunch." Geneva went over to the small refrigerator in the corner of the office and took out two bottles of water. Placing a bottle on the desk in front of Katrice, she took a seat across from her boss.

"I'm sorry," Katrice apologized. "I didn't mean to snap at you."

"I know. What I don't know is what set you off. When you left for lunch you were all smiles and had stars in your eyes. You come back a half hour later and daggers have replaced those stars."

Katrice waved her hand. "What is it with the men I meet, Geneva? Do I come across as some helpless, spineless creature who can't seem to make it through the day without some type of assistance? Or maybe I'm just a pushover. Do you think I'm a pushover?"

"I wouldn't say—"

"I'm not," Katrice cut in. "I know I haven't always made the best decisions or even stood up for myself when I should have, but those days are over. No more traveling through life with blinders on or being afraid to speak my mind."

"Well, that's how I—"

"Lee seems to think he has to be my protector. I never gave him the impression that I needed protection. Why would he think that? And what does he expect me to do when he shows up? Be grateful? Swoon?" Katrice placed the back of her hand against her forehead and pretended to swoon. "It ain't gonna happen!" she announced, sitting up sharply in her seat.

"Is that why you're—"

"We'll all be living on Mars and have two heads before that *ever* happens."

Geneva waited patiently for Katrice to finish ranting about bad relationships, overbearing men, and the benefits of staying single before tackling what was really wrong. Her expression said she understood what her young friend was going through.

"What?" Katrice asked when she concluded her speech.

Geneva sat quietly sipping her water and listening to Katrice, waiting patiently for her to finish. "Is that everything?"

Katrice leaned back in her chair and folded her arms. "Yes, I think so."

"Do you feel better now that you've vented?"

Katrice crossed her arms and asked cautiously, "Am I going to get a lecture?"

Geneva smiled. She liked and admired Katrice and had grown close to her in the short time they had spent together working side by side to build Book Wares into a profitable business. As far as Geneva was concerned, Katrice had to be one of the hardest working, determined, and kindest young woman she knew. However, it concerned her that she also tried so hard to prove herself to be confident and self-assured, almost to a fault. Somehow she didn't seem to see in herself what others saw—confidence and self-assuredness.

Maybe Katrice was the youngest child in her family, Geneva guessed. She had had a younger sister who had been a little like Katrice in her teens. When they were younger, her sister seemed to need constant reassurance. Thankfully, she grew out of that phase and blossomed into a poised and self-confident woman. Although it wasn't quite the same situation with Katrice, Geneva had to wonder if Katrice's family played a part in her deter-mined need to prove herself.

She often wondered about Katrice's family and why she rarely talked about them. In Geneva's mind, she couldn't imagine that they were terrible people. After all, Katrice was a wonderful person, whom Geneva felt couldn't be that much different.

"No, no lectures today, Katrice. But I have to admit that after your little tirade I am curious."

"That wasn't a tirade," she said defensively. "I just needed to get some things off my chest."

"There is absolutely nothing wrong with that. But something you said during the getting-things-off-your-chest rant puzzles me."

"What?"

"It's about this fierce sense of independence you have."

"What's wrong with that?" she asked, sounding even more defensive.

"Nothing, except that it's okay to be vulnerable some-times. Don't take this the wrong way, but to ask for or receive help is not a sign of weakness. Those are the things that make us human."

"I don't need help. I can take care of myself," she replied, slightly raising her voice.

"No one is saying that you can't."

"Lee thinks that, I bet," she said, beginning to calm down.

Still unsure of what happened between Lee and Katrice, Geneva continued, "Did it ever occur to you that he cares about you and wants to be there when you need him?"

"But I don't need him."

"Are you sure about that?"

"What are you getting at, Geneva?"

"I see the way that man looks at you."

"So?" she responded with as much indifference as she could muster.

"His face lights up the moment he walks into this store. He hangs on to your every word and seems to care about what you're saying, how you're feeling, and what interests you."

Katrice just shrugged.

Undeterred, Geneva continued. "Honey, the man notices every move you make, every time you blink, and even when you twitch your nose. There is no doubt in my mind that he would move heaven and earth for you. Let me tell you, that's something special. I can hardly get Harvey to move the couch from one side of the room to the other. And between the two of us, I think the only time he would pay attention to something I have to say is if I ran naked in front of the television with my hair on fire."

Katrice giggled when she thought about that image and Geneva's husband, Harvey, a quiet, burly man in his late fifties. Geneva often joked that her husband wasn't interested in much of anything unless it had to do with an outfield, goalpost, or basketball hoop. That wasn't what Katrice saw when she spent time with the couple. The few times she had spent with Geneva and Harvey, she had seen a very attentive and loving man who practically worshipped the ground his wife walked on.

Geneva was similarly affectionate toward for her husband. She knew that he loved her and she loved him. Katrice liked being around them, but she also secretly envied their relationship. What they shared was something Katrice wanted to experience herself, but not just for a moment, for a lifetime.

"So what you're trying to say is that I overreacted and that Lee does what he does because he cares about me?"

Geneva winked and stood up to leave. "Remember, I didn't say that. You did."

CHAPTER 24

The knocking at the front door was insistent. Having awakened from a fitful sleep, Katrice was in no mood for company, especially of the ex-boyfriend variety. She hoped to quickly get rid of whoever was at her front door.

Peering out the window, she was shocked to see a familiar figure standing on her front porch. She swung the door open, wondering if she was still dreaming.

"I was beginning to think you weren't home. I didn't dare go around to the back to look for your car. You might want to think about having a light put in back there."

"Mom?" Katrice stood in her doorway, robe askew, mouth agape, and wished she was still dreaming. "Wh-what are you doing here?"

"What a silly question. I'm here to see you, baby." Inviting herself in, Melinda pushed past her daughter and gave her a quick peck on the cheek. "Your father couldn't make it, but Taryn will be here tomorrow morning. She and the children couldn't get on the same flight, so they had to take one that will be leaving first thing in the morning. By the way, ask who is at the door before peering out. The world is filled with unsavory characters these days. You need to be more careful."

Taryn? And her children? Katrice tied her robe tightly and ran her hand through her hair. It had been a long day. First, she had to endure the run-in with Greg at the sandwich shop, followed by the confrontation with Lee after her run-in with Greg. Now here was her mother standing in her hallway for reasons that could not be good. If ever there was a time she needed her mother, it definitely wasn't now.

Watching her mother placing her car keys and purse on the table in the hallway and making herself at home, Katrice felt the faint yet unmistakable beginning of a headache. Suddenly, the image of Grandma Harry's old pressure cooker came to mind.

"I see you've made some changes to your grandmother's *décor*. God knows the place could have used it years ago."

Even if she wanted to, Katrice couldn't miss or ignore the blatant sarcasm that made her mother's words sting. Her face felt warm as her internal pressure cooker began building up steam.

"Why your grandmother kept this house looking like a museum is something I will never understand. Floral wallpaper, brown shag carpet, and that awful mouse-colored lumpy chair that used to sit in the living room. Ugh! Surely, there had to have been someone with a decorator's eye that she could have consulted. Well, that's all in the past. It's nice to see that you've added some color to the place and have gotten rid of that ugly wallpaper."

Katrice took a deep breath. "Yes, Mom, I did make some minor changes. You know what's funny, though? Even with all her little quirks and the odds-and-ends furniture she loved, I didn't have to work very hard to make

Grandma Harry's house mine. This is the one place that I've always felt at home. Even with Grandma gone, that hasn't changed one bit."

"I see."

There was an awkward silence as Melinda pretended that her daughter's remark hadn't struck a nerve.

"Tell me, what has been going on in your life? I can't believe you were asleep this early."

"It's been a long day and I'm tired, Mom."

"I see you're wearing your hair differently. I always liked it when you wore it straight and pulled back. It gave you a more polished look."

Unconsciously, Katrice smoothed her loose curls back, away from her face.

Taking a momentary break from scrutinizing her daughter's appearance, Melinda began to rattle on about people, things, and events that Katrice could care less about. One thing her mother hadn't lost was her gift for gab, she thought wryly.

As a dull pain settled in around her left temple, Katrice felt her stomach growl, a subtle reminder that she had skipped dinner. "Are you hungry, Mom? I've got some leftover spaghetti and salad and I think there might be a little bit of pot roast."

"You cook?"

"Normally, yes, but nothing as time-intensive as pot roast. I barely have time to shop for potatoes, carrots, and onions, let alone peel and chop them. One of the ladies at work made it and was kind enough to share her left-overs."

Melinda wrinkled her nose in distaste. "No, honey, I'm fine. I stopped on my way here and got something to eat. I wouldn't mind some coffee."

She could use a cup of coffee herself. With enough of a coffee buzz, maybe her mother's hateful attitude would be a mere annoyance instead of the hurtful experience it was fast becoming. Standing at the kitchen counter, she downed two aspirins with a large gulp of water.

While she waited for the coffee to brew, Katrice put a couple of pieces of bread in the toaster and took a jar of peanut butter from the cabinet. The last thing she needed was for the aspirin to irritate her empty stomach.

The aroma of coffee quickly filled the kitchen and Katrice yawned while she listened to her mother rattle on about everything and practically nothing. Katrice wished she had something stronger to dull her senses. Unfortunately, coffee was the only thing she had on hand.

When the coffee was ready, Katrice got mugs from the cupboard, and retrieved sugar and instant creamer from the pantry, and then poured a cup for herself and her mother, all the while half listening to Melinda's infernal jabbering.

"Pat and Lillian Brighton just returned from Maui. Pat had surprised Lillian for their blah, blah, blah . . ."

Katrice's mind wandered off to the paperwork she had left scattered over her bed. Some of it could be put off until later, but there were two or three things that she had to finish soon. While her to-do list was not in front of her, she could remember a few items that she could take care of on her lunch break the next day. She had to stop by the dry cleaners on her way to work tomorrow, and she needed to have the copier in her office serviced. The copies were coming out with black streaks across the top. It had been purchased secondhand and was no longer under warranty. Patrick had attempted to fix it, but the problem had been beyond his skill level. This needed to be taken care of soon. Image was everything, and sending out poor quality copies was unprofessional and simply would not do.

"Blah, blah, blah . . ." Melinda droned on.

Katrice took a few sips of coffee and sank her teeth into the hot toast she had slathered with crunchy peanut butter. A few years ago, she had switched to all-natural peanut butter. She liked it much better than the commercially processed brands that were loaded with preservatives and added sugar. *I wonder how many peanuts it takes to make one jar of peanut butter.* Enjoying her second piece of peanut butter toast, she made a mental note to set aside some time to pull weeds in the backyard before they completely overtook her flower garden.

"Katrice, honey, are you all right?"

Katrice licked peanut butter off her fingers and looked up blankly at her mother. "Huh?"

Melinda handed her a napkin. "I don't think you've heard anything I've said for the past five minutes. I asked you the same question twice, and you ignored me both times. Either it's none of my business or the answer is no."

"I'm sorry," she said, wiping her mouth with the napkin. "What were we talking about?"

"*We* weren't talking. *I* seem to be carrying on a one-sided conversation. If I didn't know better, I'd say you were ignoring me."

You think?

Katrice took another sip of coffee and replied blandly, "Why would I do that, Mother?"

Melinda added two spoonfuls of sugar to her coffee and sprinkled in creamer. "Never mind; it wasn't important."

Katrice wiped crumbs from the table onto a napkin and poured herself another cup of coffee. She would probably have to take a sleeping pill later to counter the effects of the caffeine, but she didn't care. The coffee calmed her nerves.

After her mother took a temporary vow of silence, the only sound she heard in the kitchen was the low hum of the refrigerator's motor. Neither mother nor daughter spoke, which suited Katrice just fine.

When the silence became uncomfortable, Katrice spoke up.

"Mom?"

"Yes, dear?"

"What are you doing here?"

"What do you mean? I can't visit my daughter?"

"Why now? I invited you to visit when I first moved here. You didn't come then. I invited you to come the weekend of the bookstore's grand opening. I was willing to set aside our differences because it was the one event I thought would be nice to share with my family, not to mention an accomplishment that I was excited about.

You didn't come then, either. So, again, I have to ask, why now?"

There was no mistaking the hurt in Katrice's voice, but Melinda appeared impervious to it.

"Katrice, I'm worried about you. You've changed so much over the past year. Your behavior has been nothing short of troubling. You leave everything and everyone you ever cared about and move to the middle of nowhere. There is no one here to look after you or who even cares about you. To make matters worse, we hardly talk anymore. I don't know what's going on in your life, who you've made friends with or even if you're happy. I spoke to Greg and he feels the same way. He's worried sick about you. He said that he hardly knows you anymore. He also said that you practically slammed the door in his face when he came to see you."

Greg. She should have known. Now they were getting to the real reason for her mother's visit. She could only imagine the lies he had told her parents.

Katrice walked over to the sink and poured the remainder of her coffee down the drain. Apparently, her failed relationship with Greg wasn't the only reason her mother had popped up out of the blue. Lack of communication, relocating to "the middle of nowhere," and her state of well-being were also hot topics. Where should she start?

Katrice sighed wearily. There was not enough time, patience, or energy for her to address everything her mother had just brought up. This was one conversation that definitely wouldn't happen tonight, she vowed, rubbing her aching temple.

Too tired to debate her mother and point out what should be obvious to her, Katrice decided it would be best if she just went back to bed. She wasn't even sure what her mother hoped to accomplish. As far back as she could remember, they had never had a heart-to-heart talk about anything. It wasn't that Katrice never wanted it, it simply never happened.

Well, nothing good would or could come out of trying to have that conversation tonight, that she was sure of.

Katrice turned to her mother, hoping for some sign she understood the bad timing and raw emotions. Disapproval was the only thing registered on Melinda's face.

Looking confused and worried, Melinda asked, "Can you at least explain to me what happened between you and Greg? I thought you were so happy."

"Why is everyone having a hard time with this?" she asked, making no effort to hide her exasperation. "The truth is for the past year or so we didn't have much of a relationship. How could you say that I seemed happy? Compared to what? Maybe I should explain the break-up this way: Ending the relationship with Greg could be called a mercy killing."

Melinda was shocked, but she tried to keep her voice calm. "How can you say that? Greg loved you."

And his secretary. One of her grad students. The lab tech that she later found out about from a friend. Katrice didn't know if Greg even knew how to love. One thing she did know, he had been an expert at hurting and disappointing her and destroying any respect she had for him.

Katrice had never confided in her parents or her sister everything that had gone on between her and Greg. She had wanted to and at times needed to, but now she didn't really see the point. Whatever she had told them up to this point would have to suffice. There was no real need to say anything more. What would it prove? She had been a poor judge of character? She had allowed herself to be tricked and manipulated into thinking he could be the man of her dreams, or at least the man her parents thought would be a suitable mate for her? Sharing this information with them now was the same as trying to put spilled milk back into a glass. It was just plain useless.

Melinda had thought the world of Greg. In her eyes, he could do no wrong and seemed to be everything she thought her daughter needed in a man. Maybe that was why it seemed she was more upset over the breakup than Katrice.

Katrice again looked to her mother for understanding but saw none. Well, if her mother loved Greg so much, *she* could date him.

There was no need to go into the details of Greg's infidelity or why she would be perfectly all right if she never saw him again. As long as *she* had reconciled the reasons, that was all that really mattered.

"It's late, Mom. Let's get your things upstairs so you can get ready for bed and I can get some sleep. I've got to be up early in the morning to open up the store."

For the first time since her arrival, Melinda's face reflected what looked like disappointment.

"I thought we might spend some time together tomorrow. Maybe go to Cincinnati to shop and have lunch."

Katrice fought to keep her anger in check. "Mom, I have a business to run. I can't just decide on a whim that I'm going to take the day off and go shopping. The bookstore is how I earn my living now. Not only that, my employees and customers count on me to be there, too."

Melinda threw her hands up and pretended to be indifferent. "That's fine. I'm sure I can find something to do in this dreadful town while you're gone."

After Katrice helped her mother get settled in, she couldn't help feeling that her mother's visit somehow signaled a turning point in their relationship. It remained to be seen what the final outcome would be and if their relationship would survive.

CHAPTER 25

Business had been brisk ever since Book Wares opened its doors that morning, and was related to a new promotion that each day offered customers a different opportunity to save. Today's special was a buy one, get a second item at half price deal.

A small retirement community in a nearby town regularly organized day trips for its residents. Today, they were going to Amish country, stopping in Benton Lake for breakfast and a side trip to Book Wares.

From the beginning, Katrice had made a point of advertising her large selection of recorded and large print books. It was something she was especially mindful of, since her grandmother had often complained about the small print used in newspapers and books. Her advertising efforts were now paying off. The customers from the retirement community bought a number of recorded books, and a recent shipment of large print mysteries and inspirational books were almost sold out.

"Wow. Who knew old people were that much into reading."

Katrice reminded Millicent that once a reader, always a reader.

"I'm going back to my office for a little while. I need to place some orders and confirm some upcoming event dates."

"No problem. It's slowed down a lot; I think I can handle things by myself for a while. If I need you, I'll yell."

Katrice stared at the flashing cursor on her computer screen and sipped herbal tea, waiting for its relaxing effect kick in. Although there wasn't a great deal of work getting done, she hadn't actually lied to Millicent. There was work to do; she just didn't feel up to doing it. She simply could not get her mind to focus on the needs of the bookstore right now. Her needs, not the bookstore's, were more pressing.

All she could think about was how crazy her life had become. According to her plan, life in Benton Lake was supposed to be carefree and unencumbered. There weren't supposed to be any complications. When did things take such a crazy turn?

To set her life back on a sane path she knew she would have to clear up a few pressing matters. For one, she would have to get Greg to understand that there was nothing left for them. He couldn't possibly expect her to come back to a man who had repaid love and affection with lies and deceit. Then again, she was talking about Greg, a man who had perfected the art of playing emotional games. And he thrived on control. Maybe once she explained things to Greg rationally, he would go home and leave her alone. Wishful thinking?

Her next daunting task would be getting her mother to understand that she was perfectly capable of making her own decisions and dealing with the consequences of those decisions. Experience had taught her that trying to take control away from a control freak, specifically her mother, was not an easy task.

And then there was the matter of her growing feelings for Lee. Feelings that she had a tough time figuring out the *whys, whats, whens,* and *hows. Why* was she straying from the course she had set for herself? *What* could Lee offer her that she didn't already have? *When* did she get to a point that she spent time more time daydreaming about him instead of getting her work done? *How* was she going to make everything right?

What a mess!

Trying to rationalize her feelings for Lee in an attempt to make herself feel better, she blamed her attraction to him on her unresolved issues with her family. Perhaps there was some deep-seated psychological need to belong. Even to her own ears, that excuse sounded contrived.

Katrice slumped in her chair and groaned. Lee had done more than get under her skin. He lived in her daydreams and invaded her thoughts. The memory of his fingers exploring her body and the taste of his lips were ever in her mind. Those memories weren't confined to kisses or touches; lately it seemed as if everything evoked memories of him. A song on the radio. A book she thought he might enjoy. A couple strolling past the bookstore. Even the aroma of cookies baking in the café.

On two occasions she had called Lee arrogant. Both times she had been irritated with him. But once she settled down, she accepted that he wasn't arrogant at all. Self-assured, yes; arrogant, far from it.

The night he threatened to carry her over his shoulder when she had refused his offer to walk her to his car, she had thought he was pushy. Again, when she calmed down, she realized he was simply being a gentleman.

Lee had other qualities that were easy to identify and hard to mistake. She called them "good-guy characteristics." And Lee possessed them in bunches.

First, he had strong family ties. She adored that about him, especially since she barely spoke to her family at all. Next, he seemed to appreciate and value the time they spent together. He listened and seemed to care about the things she cared about. That earned him big points, but more importantly, it made her feel valued and appreciated. Just as importantly, Lee made her laugh, and laughter was something she needed in huge doses these days.

And there was something else about Lee that she could easily grow fond of—the way he made her feel when they made love. No man had ever made her feel so special and cherished. In just one night the man had turned her world upside down and set it right again leaving her feeling connected, appreciated, satisfied, and loved. But that one night was enough for her to conclude that never again would she settle for what appeared to be right according to the standards of others. And never again would she look at another man without thinking about Lee Oliver, the man had put his brand on her. There was no turning back.

235

The breakfast rush had all but ended when the waitress came by to top off Lee's coffee. Serving a group on a bus tour to Amish country had kept her busier than usual. She hoped that she hadn't neglected the lone diner sitting by the window who'd barely touched his breakfast.

"Didn't you like your food?" she asked, looking down at the half-eaten hungry man's special. "I can get you something else."

Lee had been staring out the window, oblivious to the hustle and bustle of the diner. He turned to face the petite redhead, who looked barely older than Kyra. Folding his unread newspaper, he smiled. "No, the food is fine. I guess I'm not that hungry."

As soon as the waitress left, Lee rested his head against the seat's cool vinyl upholstery and absently stirred his coffee. He wondered how Katrice's morning was going and if she'd had trouble sleeping, too.

He replayed the scene outside the sandwich shop for the hundredth time. It had been almost a week since he'd last seen or talked to Katrice. He wanted to remain angry with her, but found the emotion too difficult to sustain. The effort left him feeling drained, both physically and emotionally. But most troubling was the knowledge that the eggshells he routinely walked on around her had now been smashed to smithereens. He needed to make things right again, but he didn't know how. He didn't even know what had happened in the first place to change everything so radically.

He took a sip of coffee and gave up trying to push thoughts of Katrice out of his head, allowing them instead to flood his consciousness. His confusion over their relationship, or the lack thereof, frustrated him. As images of her exquisite body and beautiful face tortured him, despite everything, he could think of nothing more pleasurable than spending the rest of the day making love to her, satisfying the hunger within he had ignored for so long. He now knew that he had not been the only one who had buried unfulfilled hunger.

Lee thought about the night he and Katrice had made love. He hadn't planed for it to happen, at least not that soon, but he had no regrets. Even now, thinking about Katrice's soft, supple body and the way she had responded to him brought heat to his loins, a quickening to his heart, and butterflies to his stomach.

Katrice hadn't held back, responding to his touch as much as he had responded to hers. They had connected and if he let that connection be broken, the emotional penalty would be high. Knowing he couldn't just walk into Book Wares right now and take her in his arms, kissing her senseless, drove him crazy.

He was falling in love with Katrice. He knew it before he ever touched her. Each time he spoke to her, kissed her, or saw her, he came closer to the point of no return.

Realizing he was falling in love with Katrice was easy enough to deal with. Knowing that she might not have the same feelings for him would be hard to accept. At this point in his life, there were many things Lee could accept. Katrice's rejection would truly break his heart.

CHAPTER 26

"Welcome to Benton Lake, Taryn," Katrice muttered under her breath. "Never mind that you weren't invited."

Carefully maneuvering her car past the oversized luxury SUV taking up most of her driveway, Katrice was thankful it could accommodate both vehicles, only if barely. While forced to suffer her family's intrusion, at least she wouldn't have to park on the street.

Turning off the engine, she waited a few minutes before going into the house. The certainty that her mother and sister were waiting inside to ambush her the moment she walked through the door was reason enough to stay in her seat and wish that her meddling relatives would go back home.

Why did they think they knew better than she how best to live her life? Who made them the experts? If she had a nickel for every piece of unsolicited financial, fashion, or career advice she had received from them over the years, she would have enough money for her dream car. Then there was the relationship advice. This was an area in which her mother truly believed she had a divine anointing. Sure, by most accounts her parents had a good marriage, but Katrice knew it was due to her father's uncanny ability to tolerate her mother at levels beyond mortal comprehension. It also helped that he never stood up to her about anything. Unfortunately, her mother expected that exact behavior from everyone. Well, Katrice no longer felt a need to accommodate her.

"This is nuts. I shouldn't be afraid to go into my own house. These people are in *my* space, not the other way around."

Grabbing her purse off the seat with a little more force than she had intended, Katrice managed to scatter most its contents in the driveway. Sighing angrily, she picked up the items and made the short walk from the driveway to the house, summoning as much strength as she could with every step.

As soon as she crossed the threshold, Katrice's niece and nephew came running. Wearing remnants of peanut butter and jelly sandwiches on their excited faces, they seemed genuinely delighted to see their aunt.

"Auntie Kat!" exclaimed six-year-old Jewel and eight-year-old Kalil.

Katrice's sour mood mellowed the moment she saw her niece and nephew. The sight of their sweet little faces quickly changed her frown into a wide smile. Marveling at how much they'd grown since she'd last seen them, she forgot for a moment how quickly time passes.

She knelt down and wiped a sticky smudge from her nephew's cheek and planted a kiss in its place. "I see your mom found the peanut butter. You know, if I knew you were coming I'd have baked a cake," she joked, remembering something her grandmother used to say.

Kalil looked puzzled then asked, "Cake? You were going to make us a cake? That would have been good because you don't have a lot of food, Auntie Kat. But that's okay, we like peanut butter."

It was true. Her cupboards were pretty bare. Except for coffee, bread, a couple cans of soup, and a few measly leftovers, she didn't have much that could be put together to make up a meal, and even less that would appeal to a child. She made a mental note to pick up some items from the grocery store later that evening. Even if her mother and sister were uninvited, the kids shouldn't have to suffer.

"Grandma found some jelly to go with the peanut butter and it was really good," Jewel said excitedly. "The jelly had big chunks of strawberries in it."

"That's because it was *strawberry* jam, dummy."

"Don't call your sister a dummy, Kalil. Not only is it not nice, but it also isn't true," Katrice chastised her nephew. "From what I've been told, she's the smartest kid in the first grade. Won the spelling bee, too."

Kalil rolled his eyes.

Jewel beamed. "I made the Principal's List, too."

"So what, I got perfect attendance," Kalil added.

"That's because I had *chickenpops* and had to stay home for a whole week," Jewel retorted.

Katrice was still kneeling when down talking to the children when Taryn came into the hallway.

"If you two aren't good, I'm going to put you in a box and mail you back home. Remember what I told you on the plane—Auntie Katrice is not going to stand for arguing and fighting. Okay?"

Katrice stood to greet her sister and was taken aback by her appearance. Instead of being annoyed with her for showing up to be their mother's ally, Katrice felt concern. Several months had passed since they last saw each other, but in that short time Taryn had gotten considerably thinner. Dark circles framing her eyes made her look tired and sad. Katrice even thought she detected a few streaks of grey in her perfectly coiffed hair. While wondering about the dark circles, Katrice hoped the weight loss was intentional—although a little excessive in her opinion—and not due to health issues.

Taryn had never been either overweight or skinny. By most standards, she had always been just right. Standing a little shorter than her younger sister, Taryn had always had the more curvaceous figure. When they were younger, Katrice had secretly envied her sister's curves and the way her clothes seemed to fit her to a T. In contrast, Katrice always felt gangly and awkward in anything other than jeans and sweatshirts. It didn't help matters that boys typically paid more attention to Taryn and would put a lot more effort into asking her out. Katrice, with her long legs and slender figure, was virtually ignored.

Katrice hugged her sister and the brief embrace confirmed her initial observation: Taryn had lost quite a bit of weight. Again, she hoped her sister was not ill. They would have time to talk later, away from their mother. Hopefully, Taryn would feel she could confide in her.

The light summer sweater Taryn wore appeared to be at least one size too big. She self-consciously adjusted it on her shoulders while ushering her children back into the kitchen to finish their sandwiches.

"I see you all managed to find something to eat. I'll try to run out later and get something from the grocery store, at least some eggs, milk, and cereal for the kids. Make a list of things you'd like."

Katrice took a bottle of juice from the refrigerator. "Where's Mom?"

"Upstairs resting. When the kids and I got here this afternoon, she was in the backyard pulling weeds. Guess all that yard work tired her out."

Katrice bit her tongue. Weeding was on her to-do list. She just hadn't gotten around to it. Leave it to her mother to zoom in on that. "If she's looking for things to do, tell her the deck needs to be power washed."

"You've done a lot of nice things with this house," Taryn remarked, ignoring her sister's snide comment. "I hardly recognized the living room and hallway."

Katrice glanced sideways at her sister to see if she was being sarcastic or sincere. "Thanks," she replied dryly.

"What did you do with that big stuffed chair Grandma Harry used to have in the living room? Remember how she would curl up in that beat-up old thing on rainy afternoons and lose herself in a book?"

Katrice smiled and nodded. "I remember. That's why I kept it and had it reupholstered. It's still in the living room but that weird fabric had to go. Still makes a good place to curl up in on rainy afternoons."

"Auntie Kat, are there any kids to play with around here?"

Jewel had eaten all that she was going to eat and was now ready to explore her new surroundings. The familiar glint was in her eye. It was the look of an adventurer, and the same look Katrice had worn whenever she arrived at Grandma Harry's for the summer. The big backyard had been the ideal place for a kid to play and let her imagination run wild. The same held true today.

"No, Jewel, I don't think there are very many kids around here. But if your mom doesn't mind, you can go in the backyard and play with your brother. I think I saw an old wagon in the shed."

Kalil and Jewel looked at their mother with pleading eyes.

"It's safe," Katrice assured her sister, noting her hesitation.

Taryn nodded and the kids were out of the kitchen in a flash. "Make sure you stay in the backyard. Don't wander off. And leave the flowers alone," Taryn called after them.

After they left, Taryn sat down at the table and motioned for her sister to join her. Maybe they could have a few minutes to themselves before their mother got up from her nap.

"My girls, together again," Melinda exclaimed from the doorway.

Too late.

"I feel so much better after my nap. What time is it? I didn't mean to sleep so long. Katrice, could you get me a bottle of water from the refrigerator?" Melinda sat beside Taryn. "Honey, you might want to see about hiring a gardener. I think you had more weeds than flowers in your garden. Also, the hedges around back could stand some work. If I were you, I'd put up a privacy fence. Your neighbor, Mrs. Jenkins or Pinkins, or whatever her name is, seems just a bit too friendly if you ask me."

After getting a bottle of water from the refrigerator, Katrice reluctantly joined her mother and sister. "Mrs. Parkins," she remarked dryly.

"You look good, Kat," Taryn said, hoping to redirect the conversation.

"Really? What did you think you'd find when you got here?" The question was posed to Taryn, but Katrice was looking at their mother. "Sackcloth and ashes?"

"Not exactly. It's just that when Greg—"

"Greg again? Okay, you can stop right there," Katrice interrupted angrily. "I have had it up to here with you and Mom campaigning for that man."

"Wait, Kat."

"No, Taryn, you wait. Greg is not who you think he is and he never really was. If you knew what I know, then you would agree that I am better off without him in my life. Can we just leave it at that? Please!"

Upset that her daughter was being less than forth-coming, Melinda pressed on. "Katrice, that's the second time you've alluded to the possibility that Greg has been anything other than what he appears to be. What is it that you're not saying? I think you owe us some kind of explanation."

"See, that's where you're wrong, Mom. I don't owe anything to anyone, other than myself. Would it really make a difference if I laid out all the dirty details of the relationship? Isn't it enough that *I* say things are over and that *I* made the decision that Greg was not the man for me?"

"We just want to understand what's going on, Katrice, that's all. Most sane people don't quit their jobs, end their relationships, and become hermits," Taryn added.

Not bothering to hide her disappointment in her sister's lack of support, Katrice refused to buckle. "Again, you're only choosing to see things from your perspective. Did it ever once occur to either of you that my old life didn't make me happy or that I needed a change?"

"So every time you're unhappy or feel a need to make changes in your life you pull up stakes and move?"

Katrice looked at her mother and sighed. *It's like talking to a wall with her!*

Katrice leaned forward and fixed her eyes on her mother. She tried to keep her anger in check, but failed. "Who am I hurting? No one. Who is responsible for my actions and who has to deal with the consequences? Me. Whose business is it what I do with my life? Mine and mine alone. If Greg has a problem with any of that, I think he needs to be a big boy and handle it all by himself. This business of running to my family so he can try to weasel his way back into my life is exhausting and is becoming extremely annoying."

Katrice was interrupted by a knock at the front door. "Don't move. This conversation isn't over. We need to settle this once and for all," she said as she left to answer the door. Her mother and sister had decided to invade her life, and now they were going to have to deal with the consequences. She would no longer be the compliant daughter and sister that they were accustomed to.

Without checking to see who was at the door, she flung it open, prepared to bark her displeasure at being interrupted. But before she could utter a single word, strong arms pulled her forward and a warm mouth covered hers with a familiar urgency that made resistance nearly impossible.

Once contact was broken, she stood on her porch feeling lightheaded but longing for the closeness that had abruptly ended. Slowly, she opened her eyes. *Lee.* Pride kept her planted and unwilling to move, but need beckoned her to give in as she slowly exhaled.

"You are the most pigheaded, exasperating, obstinate woman I have ever known. Any sane person would have run screaming for the hills by now. But what do I do? I spend countless hours trying to figure you out and even more hours missing how good you feel in my arms and remembering the sweetness of your kisses."

Katrice stared at Lee, listening to his rant but unsure what to say or do.

He didn't wait for her a response. "You know what's funny? You're still a mystery to me, Katrice. Call me crazy, but instead of wanting to run away from you, I find myself needing to run to you. Girl, you make a man wanna holler, punch a wall, and spit nails. But I can't stay away from you."

Katrice remained speechless. She searched for the right thing to say, but came up empty. Apparently, he was as conflicted as she was.

Without putting it into words, Lee showed how much he had missed her and why he had just taken her into his arms and kissed her so passionately.

She wanted to let him know that it was all right. She wanted to see him as badly as he wanted to see her. But she wouldn't let herself say the words. He had no idea how good he looked to her at that moment and how much her body ached to be close to his. He was the calm center she missed and now needed so badly. She looked down at the floorboards, willing her feet to stay planted. With a little self-control she might be able to keep her hands from running along the contours of his chest or pressing her body against his and kissing those sexy lips. She desperately wanted to forget how wonderful and safe it felt to be in his embrace, but practically every part of her being fought to hold on to that memory.

CHAPTER 27

Lee was now pacing from one side of Katrice's porch to the other. He was upset. That was painfully obvious. Had he been pushed too far?

Suddenly, he stopped directly in front of Katrice, waiting patiently for her to say something. She said nothing. The dimple in his cheek disappeared and reappeared as he struggled to keep his emotions in check.

Katrice searched his face for a sign, any sign, that she hadn't completely messed things up between them. While not quite sure what they had together, she still didn't want whatever it was to end. She needed time, time to sort out her feelings. Until then, she couldn't make any promises to Lee or herself.

She tried to think of something appropriate to say, but was at a loss for words. When she finally opened her mouth to speak, nothing came out. Here she was standing on her front porch staring up at him, completely unable to utter a coherent thought. All she could do was stare and wonder why just one look from this man made her knees tremble and turned her insides into molten lava. Given her continuing silence and erratic behavior, she wouldn't blame him if he turned on his heels and left and never came back.

"I'm sure you want to say something. Go right ahead. I'm ready." Lee cocked his head to the side and waited for what he thought would be a verbal assault. He was unsmiling, but his attempt to appear stern failed when his cheek dimpled and softened his features, melting her heart all at the same time.

His eyes softened and Katrice saw something that she couldn't quite define, but the anger and frustration had vanished. Unexpectedly, she found herself willing to give in to him. With that realization came no warning bells or anxious thoughts, no fear of regret. She didn't quite know what she would be giving in to, but there was one thing of which she was sure: She could give Lee her trust.

"Well? I can't continue to be the only one talking."

"I-I'm not angry with you," she said in a voice that didn't sound nearly as strong as she tried to make it. "Not anymore."

Lee relaxed and breathed a sigh of relief. The fear felt just minutes before gave way to hope. Maybe things between them weren't so bad after all. "Then why haven't I heard from you? The last time we saw each other, you nearly took my head off, for reasons I'm still trying to comprehend. I know I may have overreacted when I saw you in the sandwich shop with that . . . that other man, but you can't blame me for that, can you? Things seemed tense and I did what any man would've done."

"I-I'm sorry about that," she said. "I know you probably think I overreacted, too, but I just needed to clear some things up between me and that other person. That's what you saw. Nothing more. Nothing less."

"What things, Katrice? What I saw appeared to be more than a simple misunderstanding. What is it that you don't want to tell me?" he asked earnestly.

There it was, the million-dollar question. Katrice avoided Lee's gaze, looking down at the floorboards. Any ground she had gained in the willing-to-trust department seemed to be rapidly dissolving. How was she going to explain who Greg was and what he had meant to her? There would be no way she would be able to leave out all of the ugly details, the main one being how much of a fool she had been.

As she wrestled with what and how much she should tell Lee, she felt a gentle touch on her arm. She looked up at him and the understanding she saw touched her heart. Maybe he would understand. Maybe she could explain that she had tried to be everything that Greg wanted, but in the end it hadn't been enough nor had any of it even mattered. Would he think that she had been foolish or just in love?

Lee gently stroked her cheek. "You don't have to be strong all the time, sweetheart. I'm not looking for a superwoman, just a pretty lady whose eyes can't hide that she is willing to be open and honest with me."

Katrice fought to maintain some semblance of composure, but Lee was making it exceedingly difficult.

"You know what else I see in those beautiful brown eyes right now? I see pain that runs deep and needs to be soothed. I see mistrust that undoubtedly came from someone who didn't hold you near and dear to his heart.

But even with all of that, I see something stronger. I see hope. Just a glimmer, but it's there."

"Hope?" she asked quietly.

Lee lifted Katrice's chin and kissed her tenderly. "Yes, hope that I can make you forget the hurt and pain from your past and concentrate on all the wonderful things that we can make happen right now, together."

At that moment the only thing Katrice wanted was to have Lee pull her into his arms, shower her with love and affection, and make all her troubles go away. She could forget Greg, forget her family, and not have to worry about anything—if only for a little while. If Lee knew of such a magical place, she would go there in a heartbeat. That's just how much she trusted Lee at that moment.

"Auntie Kat, there's a rabbit in the backyard and Kalil is chasing him away!"

Startled by her niece's intrusion, Katrice quickly returned to reality and was left with moist eyes, a dry throat, and a yearning body. The magical moment with Lee had ended as quickly as it had begun.

She took a step back. *What was she doing?* She needed to put some distance between him and the security and affection that he offered. There was no magical place that she could run to. She had to be a big girl and face reality like an adult. No matter how much she wanted to believe that he could make her world right, there was just too much uncertainty to believe that right now. She had trusted her heart before and had been betrayed. Now was the time to listen to reason without being swayed by emotion.

Jewel came rushing up the steps, but stopped when she caught sight of Lee.

Seeing her niece hesitate, Katrice moved to the porch steps, beckoning Jewel to sit with her.

Stealing glances at the massive stranger, Jewel sat next to her aunt and returned to her original tattle-tale mission, exclaiming, "Auntie Kat, the rabbit. I think Kalil scared him away. I was being really quiet, trying to get close enough to pet him, and Kalil made this loud noise and started chasing him."

"*Auntie Kat*, aren't you going to introduce us?" Lee came down from the porch and sat beside Katrice, his thigh grazed hers slightly.

"Uh, Lee, this is my niece Jewel. Jewel, honey, this is my . . . my friend, Mr. Oliver." Katrice tried to ignore how close Lee was to her. She moved over slightly, but couldn't sit any closer to the edge without ending up in the flower bed. She needed to maintain some space between herself and Lee. *Why was he sitting so close?*

Katrice's emotions lurched from one extreme to another. One minute she wanted to be lost in Lee's embrace, the next she wanted to push him away and shut herself off from any further hurt or disappointment. Right now she wanted to do the former.

Jewel, remembering her manners, extended her hand. "Hi," she said shyly.

"It's very nice to meet you, Jewel. Your aunt never mentioned that she had such a pretty little girl living here, or any other family."

Katrice ignored Lee's mention of her family. Now was not the time for introductions. She was having a hard enough time dealing with Lee one-on-one. Dealing with her mother's scrutiny of him would prove to be too much.

"We don't live here. We're only here for a visit. My brother is in the backyard and my grandma and my mom are in the house. Do you want to help me find the rabbit?"

Having decided Lee was okay, Jewel grabbed his hand and began pulling him toward the backyard.

Katrice followed reluctantly. Any hope of whisking Lee away from the house before her mother and sister saw him died the moment he took Jewel's hand. Now she would be forced to introduce him to her family, something she had wanted to avoid at all costs.

Jewel chatted incessantly on the short walk to the backyard, barely giving Lee a chance to answer any of the questions she threw at him.

"Do you have kids that me and my brother can play with? Mommy let me bring some of my dolls. I have a new one and you can make her hair different colors. Do you live around here? It took us a long time to drive here from the airport. Mommy said that's because Auntie Kat lives in the sticks." Getting closer to the backyard, she lowered her voice. "Do you think we can find the rabbit? Are you Auntie Kat's boyfriend?"

The question caught Lee and Katrice off guard. They stopped and wondered the same thing. *Had Jewel seen them kissing?*

"Let's look for that rabbit," Katrice offered, hoping to get her niece's mind off her personal business and back on the business of being a child.

Kalil ran up to his aunt, practically out of breath. He pushed his sister. "I wasn't trying to scare the rabbit. I was only trying to catch him. Jewel scared him when she tried to get close and pet him."

"No, you scared him away!" Jewel retorted, pushing him back.

"No fighting or I'll send you both inside and you'll have to go straight to bed," Katrice warned.

"But I want to play with the rabbit," Jewel said, on the verge of tears.

"Only if you're good *and* quiet. Then, maybe he'll come back. He almost always shows up early in the mornings and late in the evenings, usually with the rest of his friends," Katrice said, softening her tone. Later she would have to explain that the rabbits in her yard were wild and extremely timid and there would be very little chance that the children could get close enough to play with them.

Just then Melinda and Taryn emerged from the house to see what the excitement was all about.

"Mommy, Grandma, we saw a rabbit. It was gray and had a white tail. I was going to pick him up and show him to you, but Kalil scared him away. Auntie Kat said there's more than one and that they come around a lot."

"I didn't scare him. You did!" Kalil lunged forward as if to hit his sister but remembered his aunt's warning and thought better of his actions.

"Okay, enough, you two. Regardless of what happened, the rabbit is gone. But I bet he'll come back just as I said," Katrice offered, trying to calm the children.

During the discussion around the rabbit, Lee stood to the side observing Katrice's mother and sister and waited for an opportune time to introduce himself—or for Katrice to make the introductions. While he waited he quietly observed Katrice's mother.

Sharing the same flawless complexion as her mother and sister, Katrice stood apart from the other two women with her slender figure, deep-brown skin, and curly hair. It was easy to see the resemblance between the mother and daughters, but Lee could tell that they were different from Katrice.

Katrice's mother was a model of polish and sophistication, but something seemed to be missing. She appeared slightly out of place in the inviting and laid-back atmosphere Katrice had created in her backyard.

Satisfied that the rabbit would return if they were quiet, Kalil and his sister found a spot toward the back of the yard where they decided to wait him out.

Once the children had settled down, Katrice tried to think of a believable and tactful excuse to get Lee out of there.

But Taryn was the first to speak, "I'm sorry. We must seem so rude. I'm Katrice's sister, Taryn, and this is our mother, Melinda Ware. And you are?"

Too late.

Extending his right hand and placing his other arm around Katrice's shoulder, Lee responded with, "I'm a *friend* of Katrice's. Lee Oliver."

What was he doing? Katrice wondered as she pulled away. The simple gesture had been enough to cause her mother to raise a perfectly waxed eyebrow. Katrice sighed. Yippee. More probing questions from her mother would be forthcoming.

"Katrice didn't tell me she had family visiting." Lee pulled her closer.

"Oh really? Well, she is quite busy and seems to have a lot on her mind lately," Melinda remarked sarcastically. "I just put on a pot of coffee, Lee. Would you like to come inside and join us?"

No! Katrice screamed silently. She did not want Lee to be subjected to her mother and sister. She did not want to put Lee through an interrogation over coffee. She could only imagine what her mother's reaction would be when she found out that he worked for legal aid. And when Melinda found out that Lee had a child . . . Katrice winced just thinking about it. *No, not tonight.*

Not giving him chance to answer, Katrice answered for him. "No, Lee was just about to leave. Don't you have an appointment or something that you need to attend to?" She grabbed Lee's arm, and hustled him out of the yard and back to the path that led to the front of the house. "Maybe he can come over and have coffee another time," she said over her shoulder. *Preferably, when the two of you are gone.*

When they reached his car, Katrice apologized before he had a chance to ask questions. "I'm sorry. Now is not the time for a quaint family get-together. My mother and sister are uninvited guests, and I didn't want to subject you to them for any length of time. The results could be life-altering," she said, attempting to make light of the situation.

"They seemed nice." Lee was confused. Why wouldn't Katrice want him to meet her family?

"Don't be fooled by outward appearances."

"I don't understand."

"I'll explain later."

"When? I'm not just talking about your family, but our earlier conversation, too."

Katrice shook her head. "I don't know, Lee. Just not now, okay?"

Moving in closer and barely speaking above a whisper, he said, "I meant what I said. You can talk to me about anything. Don't feel as if you have to be a rock all the time."

Katrice watched as Lee pulled away from the curb and drove off. She touched her cheek where he had kissed her before leaving. Walking back into the house to join her mother and sister, she wished she could simplify her life with a blink of the eye. Instead she knew it was going to take quite a lot more than magic to accomplish that.

CHAPTER 28

Jasmine and vanilla lent its scent to help create the room's ambiance, which was further enhanced by the faint glow of candles placed throughout the room.

It had been a divine evening of lovemaking. Lee had thought of everything to set the perfect mood—candles, soft music, even champagne. Katrice had asked what special occasion had called for champagne. Lee's reply, "Any time spent with you is special."

With her back to him, Katrice snuggled in close to Lee. She never grew tired of feeling his strong arms around her or the way his magnificent body felt next to hers. He awakened a passion in her that was new and exciting. Each time they made love it was a wonderful experience that brought her closer to him. She never had to be reserved with Lee, and she wasn't.

Katrice stirred when Lee began to place feathery kisses on her neck. Instinctively, her body reacted to the feel of his lips and touch of his hands as he cupped her bare breasts.

He loved to touch Katrice, not just her breasts, but all over. This time was no different. He continued stroking and touching her until he heard her soft moans. Straddling her body, he leaned down to kiss her. At first, his kisses were slow and deliberate. But as she reached out to pull him closer he deepened the kiss, letting his tongue glide in and out of her mouth, teasing her tongue and lips with his.

He ended the kiss and whispered, "I want to take my time loving you."

Katrice closed her eyes and prepared to allow Lee to do just that.

Lee placed a kiss on her forehead and entangled his fingers in her thick fragrant hair. Using his tongue, he then traced tiny circles over her eyelids, down the bridge of her nose, and paused to gently nip the top of her lip.

She moved beneath him, heat coursing through her body.

Releasing her hair, Lee continued his trail of kisses down to her stomach, his fingers stroking every inch of her body along the way. He stopped. He needed to position her body just right to give him full access to her most sensitive areas.

"Don't stop," she whispered.

"No, baby, I won't."

Lee stroked the inside of Katrice's smooth thighs with his tongue. Inhaling deeply, he drank in her scent, a heady combination of femininity and passion.

He continued to tease her, each stroke and caress of his tongue taking her to a deeper level of pleasure.

She tried to maintain some control, but the man was driving her crazy.

Lee knew what she wanted, and she would have everything she desired. He stopped teasing and plunged his tongue deep inside her. Her sharp intake of breath followed by a low moan fueled his desire to pleasure her in ways that only he was privy to.

Hot and sweet, he couldn't get enough of her.

"Lee," she cried weakly. Her body on fire, she widened her legs, to give him complete access and her intense pleasure.

She was ready. And it was torture for him to make her wait any longer. Reaching beneath her, Lee lifted her buttocks to position her at the exact angle to expertly give her the release her body begged for.

Again she called his name, "Oh . . . Lee . . . baby." Her heartbeat quickened as white-hot heat erupted from the base of her stomach and exploded throughout her entire body. Losing all control, she gave in and the release came with a force that threatened to lift her off the bed.

She heard Lee call her name.

Katrice.

He called again, but his voice sounded strange.

Katrice . . . Katrice!

"Katrice!"

Katrice sprang upright. Panting, she looked around the darkened room and wondered where Lee had gone. As her eyes adjusted to the darkness, she recognized her surroundings and realized that she hadn't been in Lee's bedroom, or his arms.

It had all been a dream.

Katrice's breathing had returned to normal by the time she heard her bedroom door being pushed opened. Taryn stuck her head in, and the bright light from the hallway further distanced herself from the sensuous dream.

"I'm sorry to wake you, but Jewel had an accident. Where do you keep the clean sheets?"

Katrice swallowed. Even though her breathing had returned to normal, her body still tingled from the passionate lovemaking she had shared with Lee in her dream.

Confused, Katrice asked, "Sheets?"

"Where do you keep the clean sheets?" Taryn repeated, feeling awful that she had to wake her sister in the middle of the night.

What her sister was asking finally registered and Katrice replied, "There are twin-sized sheets in the linen closet on the second shelf. Don't worry about the mattress. There's a waterproof cover on it."

"What do you have that I can use to wipe it off?"

"Hold on. I'll show you where I keep the sponges and spray cleaner."

Once she had helped her sister change the bed and her niece had drifted back to sleep, Karice returned to her room. Lying in the darkness, she wondered if she would be able to go back to sleep without help. Not wanting to take a sleeping pill, she instead turned on her side and closed her eyes, attempting to calm her frazzled mind. But after tossing and turning for what seemed like an eternity, she gave up trying to repress thoughts of Lee and the dream.

What was she going to do about him? She couldn't just push him out of her life and ignore him until he went back to his home and life in Columbus. Their connection wouldn't allow it; nor would he, she suspected.

Lee was someone who had impacted her life. She could no longer hide or deny her feelings for him. He had left his imprint on both her mind and body and now he had invaded her dreams. No other man would be able to make her feel the way he had. She knew that as surely as she knew the sky was blue. She had to admit Lee was not someone who could be ignored, and ignoring her feelings for him was now no longer an option.

CHAPTER 29

The sun had barely peeked over the horizon. Song birds were noisily announcing the emergence of a new day. Wanting to take advantage of the early morning solitude to collect her thoughts, Katrice had risen early. Her backyard was the perfect place for getting some quiet time to herself, something she was in dire need of this morning.

Katrice did not have the chance to finish her conversation with Taryn and her mother. After playing a while longer in the backyard and chasing rabbits with the kids, she was worn out, as were her mother and sister. Even though it was very obvious that Kalil and Jewel were tired, they had done everything within their power to persuade their mother to let them stay up late. But Taryn had prevailed. After their baths, she read them a bedtime story and got them settled into bed. She went to her room soon after.

Katrice had noticed an improvement in the children's behavior since her last visit. While still prone to rowdiness, Taryn wasn't constantly scolding them or threatening to report their bad behavior to their father. Finally, it seemed as if her sister had control of her kids.

After the house had settled down, Melinda went out to buy groceries. She had remarked to Katrice that there wasn't enough food in the house to make a decent breakfast. Katrice had intended to go shopping later that evening but was just as happy to give her mother directions and send her on her way. At least she wouldn't have to listen to complaints about the grocery selections.

Not having to deal with her mother or sister the rest of the night was a mixed blessing, but Katrice still had unresolved issues that prevented a decent night's rest. After helping Taryn with Jewel, Katrice had tossed and turned the remainder of the night, her thoughts tumbling from one thing to the next. But no matter where her thoughts roamed, somehow they always drifted back to Lee.

The analytical part of her brain that she relied on when everything else landed her in hot water needed to be brought out of storage. She needed clarity, and the emotional part of her brain wasn't offering that.

Katrice mentally prepared for a detailed internal analysis. Lee Oliver had gone from a stranger whom she ran into at odd times to someone who now affected her sleep, invaded her dreams, and forced her to reevaluate her idea of the ideal life. She had only known him a few short months, but in that span of time he had managed to upset her well-ordered life. Although she had reacted to their first few encounters rather irrationally, they had gotten past all of that. He still had the rather irritating habit of trying to be her knight in shining armor, but it really wasn't as irritating as she tried to make herself believe. Love it or hate it, that was just one of Lee's quirks that she would have to deal with. She probably couldn't change that about him if she wanted to. In fact, most women would love to have a man with whom they felt safe.

Speaking of most women, Katrice wondered if Lee had been serious with anyone since his wife died. How long did most people in similar situations wait before they moved on? Her uncle, her mother's brother-in-law, had waited all of six months after his wife died before remarrying. Of course, Melinda had openly speculated that the woman he married had been his mistress all along. *Totally different situation.*

When they'd had the picnic out at the lake Lee had mentioned that Paulette had been a wonderful wife and loving mother. If it ever came to that, could she also be a wonderful wife and loving mother? Did she even want to?

Too serious. Subject change.

Retrieving her coffee mug and munching on one of Mrs. Parkins's homemade muffins, Katrice closed her eyes and allowed herself to relax and clear her mind of anything that was negative, stressful, or that would require serious thought. However, it wasn't that easy. As soon as she closed her eyes and felt the sun warming her face the scene on her front porch when Jewel interrupted her conversation with Lee began to replay in her mind. *What would have happened if her niece hadn't come along when she did?*

She had been so close to allowing herself to be swept up in the moment. Just one tiny step and she would have been in Lee's arms and deeper in his life. She knew that step would have been a turning point, one that she suspected would have changed them irrevocably.

Last night's dream had tormented and delighted her but was clear evidence of how Lee's presence in her orderly life was wreaking havoc. She had never experienced such eroticism in a dream. In fact, when Taryn had awakened her, she had been on the brink of a climax! *What kind of man stirred up that type of response in a dream?*

Thank goodness Taryn hadn't suspected a thing. She didn't know what she would have said to explain herself.

She couldn't understand her attraction to Lee or the equally strong urge to push him away whenever it appeared he got too close. Why did she do that? Had Greg hurt her that deeply or could she simply be using her failed relationship with him as an excuse to hide from the realities of life?

"Good morning, beautiful."

Startled, Katrice dropped her mug, spilling coffee on her robe.

Greg. "What are you doing here?"

Checking the time on the watch Katrice had bought for his last birthday, he smugly remarked, "I remembered what an early bird you were and decided to try and catch you before you left for work. By the way, your little bookstore is—*cute.* Pretty busy, too. But my timing must be terrible, because I've had a hell of a time catching you there."

Pulling the sash on her robe tightly around her waist, Katrice shoved her feet into her slippers and grabbed a napkin to clean up the spilled coffee.

"Here, let me," Greg offered. He came up on the deck and handed Katrice the empty coffee cup and leaned casually against the railing.

Snatching it out of his hand, she turned and glared. "I asked you a question, Greg. What are you doing here? This is my house and I don't remember inviting you here."

Greg rubbed his hand over the back of his closely cropped hair and sighed. "Katrice, let's cut to the chase. We never finished our conversation from the other day. There are some issues that we need to work through and frankly, my patience is wearing thin."

"*Your* patience?" Katrice asked, her voice rising. "You have got to be kidding." Moments from exploding, she counted to ten and took a deep breath, trying with all her might to regain her composure. "You want to talk about *issues*. Then let's talk. For starters, I cannot believe that you have the nerve to show up in Benton Lake uninvited. You damn near accosted me in public. Then you come to my house where you're clearly not welcome, not once but twice, mind you. My family has invaded my life because you called them whining about how I've mistreated you. On top of all of that, you have the gall to stand there and say that *your* patience is wearing thin. What makes you think I care one bit about your patience, or you, for that matter?"

"What do you expect, Katrice? Exactly how should I have handled this? There is no easy or polite way to approach you right now, especially after everything we've been through. I'm here trying to talk to you and apologize for all the drama I caused. All I'm asking for is a chance to explain my side of things and maybe, just maybe, convince you to give me another chance."

Katrice drew in a sharp breath and gripped her coffee cup. "So you want a chance to explain yourself? Well, go right ahead. Tell me something I haven't heard before. Please."

Greg took a moment to think about what he was going to say. He was treading on thin ice and knew it. He needed to choose his words carefully.

"I was wrong, Katrice. Is that what you want to hear? I'll happily say it again. *I was wrong.* My saying it doesn't change a thing. But if that is what you want to hear, fine, I'll say it. Hell, I'll shout it from the rooftops if that's what you want."

Katrice shook her head and said, "I don't want you to tell me what you think I want to hear. I want you to realize just how much you hurt me. I want you to know and understand that you not only destroyed my trust in you and our relationship, you also violated the trust of someone who looked up to you."

Greg clenched his jaw. "I'm sorry about what I did to destroy our relationship, but you need to stop blaming me for Marilyn. She didn't mean anything to me; you know that."

Katrice was incredulous. She had to cross her arms to keep from hurling the coffee mug at Greg's head. "She didn't mean anything to you? Well, you meant something to her. Some people don't have the world handed to them on a silver platter. They have to work for a living. Marilyn was one of those people. You were her boss and you put her in a position where she felt she had to sleep with you to keep her job. You know, the job she needed to feed her children and keep a roof over their heads."

"That's a lie, Katrice, and you know it," Greg said angrily. "I didn't force her to do anything."

Katrice held her hand up to stop Greg from telling any more lies. She had heard enough. "What I know is that you seem to be in denial."

Regaining his composure, Greg continued, "Look, I'm not here to talk about Marilyn. I'm here to talk about us and when you're coming back home."

She looked at Greg in disbelief. "How can I get you to understand? None of that is going to happen."

"You're going to let that indiscretion with Marilyn come between us? I find that a little hard to believe."

"What?"

"I think it's something, or *someone,* else. Maybe this has to do with your new man."

"Greg, stop it. You're either being very stubborn or incredibly stupid. Either one, I've had enough. Until now, I thought you would eventually be man enough to admit what you've done, but I see that I couldn't have been more wrong."

"What? I told you about Marilyn. What more do you want?"

Katrice exploded. "Greg! This is not just about your secretary, which by the way wasn't a *thing*; the correct term is sexual harassment. I believe that was the write-up placed in your personnel file when you were fired, if I'm not mistaken."

Greg looked surprised.

"Oh, yes, I know you were fired. I also know that the university severed ties with your research lab because of your bad behavior. Don't even bother to deny it. In fact, now is a good time to clue you in on everything else I know.

"This, all of this," she said derisively, "is about your inability to see women as anything other than playthings who were put on this earth to give you pleasure. It's about you being spoiled and selfish and never having to atone for your bad behavior. And last, but certainly not least, this is about your putting my life at risk because you decided it was all right to sleep around behind my back. I'm sure you were too stupid and selfish to protect yourself, which in turn put my life at risk. That is proof positive that you don't care about anyone other than yourself."

Greg looked uncomfortable, wondering how Katrice knew all this.

Reading his expression, she continued, "Yes, Greg, your dirty little secrets are not secrets to me anymore. I know about the waitress at the coffeehouse and the dean's assistant. I even know about Tanya, my grad student. During one of her academic counseling sessions, she made sure to mention the wildly passionate time she'd spent with you. According to little Miss Tanya, you're quite the lover. Coming from someone who didn't have sense enough to keep your little secret, I wouldn't exactly take that as a compliment. You know, she was even brazen enough to show me the jewelry you'd bought for her. I would have thought she was lying, except that you were foolish enough to hold on to the receipt and leave it in open view in your apartment. If I didn't know better, I would think you left it for me to find."

Beads of perspiration dotted Greg's forehead, and he nervously ran his hand over the back of his neck. The confident stance he had assumed just moments before vanished and he slumped against the deck's railing looking as if he needed to sit down.

Katrice walked over and leaned against the deck's railing, just inches from him. "Uncomfortable, *sweetie*? Maybe that's how Rachel Jamison felt. You remember Rachel, don't you? The lab tech who also filed sexual harassment charges against you when you made her life at work a living hell. It's a wonder she didn't take a gun and blow your head off. Or, better yet, other overly active parts of your anatomy. What did you do to that poor woman to make her drop the charges? Unfortunately for you, it seems as if management at the research lab wasn't as forgiving as Rachel. I guess talent, good looks, and charm aren't everything. Imagine that."

Katrice pretended to brush a piece of lint off Greg's shirt. "It's amazing what information you can gather from people who despise you. And let me tell you, that's quite a large group."

Greg stood mute, increasingly uncomfortable and utterly speechless.

Looking him squarely in the eye, she said, "So you see, Greg, with all your dirty little secrets exposed, plus the contempt I have for you that seems to grow stronger by the day, there is no us. Get it? No more Greg and Katrice. Our relationship was killed, eulogized, and buried so far underground there is *no* hope for resurrection. You did that with my consent because I ignored clues that I shouldn't have, clues that could have saved some of those women a lot of heartache. So do us both a favor and stop trying to resurrect something that can't be restored." Turning to leave, she added, "By the way, this town and this house are home to me now. It's where my heart is and where my soul is at peace. But most of all, it's far away from you."

Katrice left Greg on the deck looking shamefaced, dejected, and lost. Her hands shook slightly and her breathing was rapid, but she kept looking straight ahead, never turning back. Not one time in her life had she ever spoken to anyone the way she had just spoken to Greg. And she didn't feel one iota of regret; he deserved that and a lot more.

What nerve. How could he possibly be so dense? What had he taken her for all those years? A doormat? Someone he could walk all over, not once or twice, but more times than she cared to admit. Well, no more being a doormat or walking through life wearing blinders.

"No more drama," she sang aloud, mimicking Mary J. Blige as she began to relax.

"I'm so sorry."

Startled, Katrice turned to see her sister standing in the doorway of the kitchen.

"Katrice, I am so sorry," she repeated. "I had no idea what was going on."

"How long have you been standing there?"

"A while."

"Did you hear everything?"

Taryn nodded.

"All of the pathetic details?"

"Yeah. All this time I thought Greg was the perfect man for you and that you were crazy for not appreciating what you had. I guess he wasn't anything more than a dog parading as a real man."

Katrice sat down at the table and breathed a sigh of relief. She had finally told Greg everything that she had been keeping bottled up inside. It didn't just feel good, it felt liberating. Now Taryn knew, too.

"Why didn't you say something before?"

Katrice shrugged and leaned back in her chair. "Would it have made a difference? I shouldn't have had to explain. It should have been enough that I said the relationship between us was over. There didn't need to be a detailed explanation."

Katrice got up and placed her cup in the sink. "You and Mom were so busy judging me that you never considered that I knew what I was doing when I left him. You refused to accept that there were good reasons I needed to put as much distance between us as possible."

"But, Katrice, seriously, I think if you had explained things to us, we would have stood behind you."

"Taryn, I tried to explain. Do you remember when I told you that I was going to surprise Greg in Orlando at the conference he was attending?"

"Yeah, it was around the first of the year."

"Well, the surprise was on me. That was when I found out about Greg and his secretary. He tried to make the whole thing appear as if it were an affair, but I found out later that he had threatened her with losing her job and her scholarships if she didn't sleep with him. Both of which she needed to provide a better life for her family."

Taryn nodded. "And that was when you came for a visit right before you moved here. I guess I wasn't very in tune to what was going on with you then. You said you'd quit your job and left Greg. That was all I heard."

"Exactly."

"Now I understand why you quit your job and pulled up stakes. I guess if I were in the same situation, I would have done what you did, too."

Katrice looked over at her sister. "What do you mean?"

"I would have probably run away and tried to lose myself in a place like this, too."

Katrice shook her head. Her sister still didn't get it. "I didn't come here to run away or hide."

Taryn smiled knowingly. "Come on, Kat. Why else would you move to this backwater town and into Grandma Harry's musty old house? I would have sold this place seconds after the will was read."

"How can you ask me that, Taryn? We spent some of the best years of our lives in this town. In this house!"

"*You* spent the best years of your life here. I spent my time counting down the days until it was time to leave. I still don't see any other reason to come here, of all places."

"Where else would I have gone?"

"Why do you do that, Katrice?"

"Do what?"

"Isolate yourself from us. Sometimes you act as if you don't even have a family."

"I don't have to act, Taryn."

"What's that supposed to mean?"

"Please, don't pretend you have no idea what I'm talking about. I swear if you and Mom would spend just a little bit of time looking at things from my perspective, life would be a whole lot easier on all of us. I'm not your clone, Taryn, and I don't need to be in order to be happy. Mom has tried to guilt me into being something I'm not for most of my adult life."

"All any of us want is for you to be happy, safe, and secure."

"Guess what? I have all of that right here, even though it may not be all that obvious to you. I'm happy here, Taryn. I love the fact that I've created something with the bookstore. I know you don't know this, but having a place like Book Wares is something that I've wanted for a long time. I have friends and a wonderful home that I'm transforming into my very own space with all of the special touches that are uniquely me. I have good neighbors who look out for me and check to make sure I'm okay. Mrs. Parkins brings me homemade muffins. The Rendlemans, who live two houses down, invited me to their twins' first birthday party. Mr. Ackerman, the widower who lives at the end of the block, cut down the maple tree in his backyard and offered me the wood for my fireplace. He even stacked it behind the deck for me. And you know what? He wouldn't take a dime for his trouble, but you should have seen his eyes light up when I brought him cookies and a package of freshly ground coffee from the bookstore. I've never lived anywhere that was even remotely like Benton Lake. Do you even know your neighbors, Taryn?" Not waiting for an answer, she continued. "This is a good place to be. It's quiet, peaceful, beautiful, safe, and secure. So let me ask you again, when all hell broke loose in my life and I needed a place where I could be at peace and try to find some direction, where else should I have gone?"

"You could have come home, Katrice."

"That's exactly what I did."

CHAPTER 30

After locking up the shop, Katrice dreaded going home, feeling a need to be alone, at least for a little while. She was still struggling to make sense of the events of the past few days, and she knew the only way she could sort through it all would be in a nice, quiet place—away from the bookstore, away from home and her visiting mother and sister.

Thankfully, Greg had made no further uninvited visits to her house or to the bookstore. Presumably he had left town, but she didn't care if he had or not. As long as she didn't have to see him, talk to him, or occupy the same space with him, she would be fine. Maybe he had finally gotten the message that they had nothing left to build upon, not even friendship. He had destroyed everything they had built together, and their relationship was beyond repair. But even more a matter of concern was the fact that Greg needed help. Confronting his obsessive need to be in control and recognizing his resultant destructive behavior were steps he would have to take. Otherwise, he would be doomed to repeat behavior that had already cost him and others so much. He needed help. Professional help. There was nothing she could do for him.

Still parked at the bookstore, she sat in her car and reflected on her tumultuous relationship with Greg. Yes, he had hurt her and betrayed her trust, but she also felt compassion for the other women he had wronged. At some point Greg needed to face those women and acknowledge what he had done to them. Facing him might be part of the healing process for those women. It had been for her.

After she had faced Greg and told him unrestrainedly what she knew and felt, she was finally been able to let go of the anger that she had held on to for months. That single act had been more freeing than anything else she could have done. Some remnants of her anger and resentment still lingered, but she had reached a point of healing. For a long time she hadn't realized that she needed healing; denial had been a much easier path to take. An unwillingness to trust and a tendency to keep people at arm's length were two of the most definable symptoms of the fallout from her failed relationship.

Her self-esteem had also taken a major hit. It still amazed and sickened her to think how much control she had given Greg over her life. The residual effects of their years together still lingered, a painful reminder of what could happen when giving your heart to someone clearly not worthy of your trust.

"It's a new day, Kat," she declared. She had wallowed in the past long enough. To move on and be open to all life had to offer, she would have to remember her no-more-drama mantra.

Katrice drove around town with no particular destination in mind. She was just driving and taking in the scenery. Waiting for a traffic light to change, she cued up one of her favorite CDs and found the song best suited to her mood. She briefly considered biting the bullet and going home. At least she could spend time playing with her niece and nephew. Sooner or later she would have to go home and face her family. She was pretty sure that Taryn had told her mother about Greg, but no one was talking about it. Instead, they all walked around as if tiptoeing on eggshells. If it weren't for the children, the house would be as quiet and somber as a tomb.

The sense of triumph that would have come with throwing Greg's deceit in her mother's face held no appeal for Katrice. And she certainly didn't feel much like gloating. Actually, she wasn't sure what she felt, but being under the same roof as her mother and barely speaking to her, evoked feelings that were new to her. Yes, there had been times when there had been tension, even anger. This was different. She couldn't quite explain it but her heart felt heavy, weighed down by a sense of loss that she just couldn't shake.

For years she had pretended that it was okay that she didn't have a close relationship with her mother. She used to shrug indifferently when her girlfriends talked about chatting regularly with their mothers and seeking their advice about important life issues. Katrice would pretend that she didn't need any of that and would make a point of stressing that she could make her own decisions. She even made excuses to Geneva and Millicent when they asked about her family visiting the shop. She said they were busy and didn't have time to stop by. That excuse was wearing thin.

Yeah, she had almost convinced herself that she could live without her mother's love and acceptance. *Almost.*

Katrice drove a while longer, becoming lost in the drive and the scenic beauty of Benton Lake. For a little while she could pretend that all was right and just in her world. When the CD she had been listening to started again at the first selection she switched to another CD. Slowing the car to get her bearings, she turned the music's volume down. Until now she had been driving on autopilot, making random turns here and there. She peered out the window, taking in the unspoiled beauty of the brick houses along the tree-lined street. Not much had changed in this section of town, or in Benton Lake in general over the years. Yes, there were a few new stores and some new homes, but the town's overall charm remained intact. She continued to enjoy the view until one house in particular caught her attention.

How did I end up here?

With its vibrant pink and yellow rose bushes occupying one entire wall of the brick structure and the meticulously trimmed hedges along the driveway, there was very little that distinguished it from the other houses, excepting the stuccoed front. This wasn't a familiar area, but it wasn't entirely unfamiliar. She had given Kyra a ride home once but hadn't gone inside.

The car behind her sounded its horn. Katrice pulled over to the curb, allowing the impatient driver to pass.

Throwing the driver a cursory wave and flashing a phony smile as he passed, she hoped her momentary day-dreaming hadn't landed her in the crazy-driver category.

What am I doing? Katrice asked herself as she sat in front of the Oliver house. Of all places, this is where her aimless driving had landed her.

Lee's car was parked in the driveway next to a late-model sedan that she assumed belonged to his father. Would she be intruding if she just showed up on their doorstep unannounced?

It had been a few days since she'd spoken to Lee. He hadn't called or even stopped by the shop. He probably assumed she would be enjoying the company of her family while they were in town. If the whole situation wasn't such a mess, such a thought might have actually been heartwarming.

Katrice checked the time and wondered if there was a proper way or time to barge in on someone unexpectedly. She wistfully noted that this normally would be the time of the day moms and dads came home from work, picked up their children from daycare, the pool, or from wher-ever. While dinner was being prepared, the kids would play outside until they were called in to supper. Then the whole family would be sitting around the table laughing and talking about everything and nothing in particular.

Katrice sighed. Okay, maybe she didn't know anyone whose family life was really that whimsical, but it sounded good.

She sat through two more selections on the CD and debated the wisdom of leaving the safety zone of her car and knocking on Lee's front door. It was either that or going home to face her mother and sister. She cut off the engine. Before releasing the seatbelt and stepping outside, she listened to one more song to give her a boost of confidence.

When the song ended, Katrice checked her reflection in the rear-view mirror. A man across the street who had been mowing his lawn seemed unusually interested in what she was doing. Slightly embarrassed that she might have aroused his suspicion by lingering in her car and staring at the Olivers' house like a prowler casing the joint, she took a deep breath and finally stepped out onto the street. She flashed the man her best I'm-really-not-strange smile.

Kudos to the neighborhood watch program.

The closer Katrice came to the house, the slower her steps became. She looked back at her car and considered getting back inside and driving away. But the neighbor/crime stopper had kept her in his sight. He had stopped mowing and was now leaning against the machine's handgrip. If she turned around now to make a hasty retreat, he would probably be on the phone reporting her to the police in two seconds flat.

Okay, really, what am I doing here?

If Lee asked her that question, she should have a clever response; right now she didn't have one.

The neighbor had cut the mower's engine and was now walking toward his house, looking over his shoulder once or twice. Katrice's imagination went into overdrive, and she speculated that he was going inside to report her to the police.

That possibility was incentive enough for her to quicken her steps, and she made it to the front door in record time. She knocked timidly and anxiously listened for footsteps. No one came. She counted to ten before knocking again, not wanting to seem impatient or desperate. Keeping an eye out for the lawn-cutting neighbor—and the police—she knocked again, a little more vigorously this time.

Finally, she heard a man's voice on the other side of the door and she stepped to the side as it was flung open.

Sam broke into a wide grin when he saw Katrice standing on the front porch.

"What a pleasant surprise," he exclaimed, reaching out to hug her.

Sam's warm greeting made her feel better about dropping in unannounced, although she still felt the need to apologize. "I-I don't want to barge in. I was in the neighborhood. I saw the cars in the driveway and thought you and Vonda might be here. I, uh, just wanted to stop in and say hi," she explained, hoping her words did not sound as scattered as her thoughts.

"Come on in. You're welcome here anytime, no invitation needed." Sam opened the door wider and grabbed Katrice by the elbow leading her inside. "Have you eaten? We were just sitting down to dinner."

"Dinner?" She couldn't even remember if she had eaten lunch. "Uh, no, I haven't eaten yet." Realizing that she had practically invited herself to dinner, she quickly backtracked. "I'm sorry, I don't mean to impose. I can come back after you've eaten."

Sam smiled and said, "Nonsense. There's more than enough."

As if on cue, her stomach growled. After that it didn't take much arm-twisting for Katrice to follow Sam to the kitchen.

"Look who showed up for dinner," Sam announced.

Everyone at the table stopped talking and turned to see Katrice standing in the kitchen's doorway looking like an orphaned child who had just been brought in from the cold.

Now she really felt awkward. She wondered what she must have looked like, showing up out of the blue with no particular reason for being there other than having nowhere else to go.

The silence was fleeting and was quickly broken when Vonda rose to greet her. Following Vonda's lead, Kyra got another place setting from the cabinet and Lee stood and pulled out the chair beside him. This all happened in a matter of seconds, leaving her no time to bolt and run.

"As soon as I finish mixing the lemonade, we can eat," Vonda announced.

Remembering her manners, Katrice asked, "Can I do something to help?"

"Come on over here and sit down. Vonda has everything under control," Sam assured her.

Just as quickly as the conversation had stopped when she entered the room, it resumed without missing a beat. Drawn in as much by the hospitality as by the lively atmosphere and the prospect of a delicious meal, Katrice took a seat beside Lee, trying to be unmindful of how close he had placed her chair next to his. The two of them exchanged glances but nothing else.

As she settled at the table and listened to the easy conversation between Sam and Vonda, she found herself smiling, not so much at what they were saying, but the way they were with each other. They seemed so right together. It was evident in their every move, and in their glances and touches.

"Sam, ask the blessing so we can eat."

After a chorus of "amen," Vonda and Kyra drew Sam into their previous discussion. Lee ate his food in silence.

"Not hungry?" Lee asked Katrice when he noticed she wasn't eating.

"I wasn't when I first got here, but I am now."

"So dig in before you hurt Vonda's feelings," he whispered.

"I don't know if I can eat all of this," she replied, eying the lumberjack-sized helpings of potato salad, baked beans, cornbread, and the enormous pieces of grilled chicken. She was hungry, but not that hungry. However, her stomach growled in protest.

The bantering between Kyra, Vonda, Sam, and Lee continued through dinner. At times Katrice was in stitches listening to Vonda's stories about the characters she encountered at the beauty salon where she worked. Katrice was practically in tears listening to a story about a lady who had let her husband perm and color her hair only to be left with a bright-orange head of hair that resembled a rusty scouring pad.

After everyone had finished eating, Sam helped Vonda load the dishwasher and put the food away. Katrice's offer to help was rejected and she was ordered to stay seated until Vonda served dessert. Her compliance was rewarded when Vonda placed an enormous slice of cake with a scoop of vanilla ice cream in front of her.

"Lee tells us that your family is here visiting," Vonda remarked.

Katrice's fork stopped midway between the dessert plate and her mouth. *Her family.* She had been having so much fun with Lee and his family that she had successfully managed to put her own family out of her mind for a while. *Why did Vonda have to bring them up?*

"You should invite them over," Sam suggested to Vonda.

"That's a good idea. We could grill out," Vonda added.

Panicking, Katrice knew she would have to decline the invitation and do it quickly. She couldn't imagine her snooty mother sitting down with Vonda and Sam over a plate of barbecued ribs and cornbread. Melinda's taste ran more to prime rib, bitter greens, and goose liver pâté. As much as Katrice enjoyed being around Lee and his family, throwing her mother into the mix wasn't something she welcomed.

"Uh, I-I don't think they're going to be here much longer. My sister needs to get back to her husband."

Her excuse sounded flimsy, and Katrice knew it the second it came out of her mouth. Regardless, she hoped they bought it.

Vonda and Sam exchanged glances. Sam didn't know Katrice well enough to know when she was being evasive, but he did sense her uneasiness.

Vonda ignored the hesitation she saw and heard. "Nonsense. We can put together a finger-licking-wanna-slap-somebody meal in little or no time at all."

Sam nodded agreement. "If anybody can do it, Vonda can."

"How about Saturday? It'll be our almost-end-of-summer bash."

"Saturday? Uh, I—" Katrice stammered.

"Wait, Vonda, we're supposed to be in Cincinnati that day."

"Saturday it is," Vonda said with finality. "Don't worry, honey. We'll invite some of the neighbors and grill up a feast. It'll be a time to be remembered."

That's exactly what Katrice feared most.

CHAPTER 31

After dinner, Sam offered to treat everyone to a night out at the movies. Vonda and Kyra took him up on his offer. Katrice reluctantly declined, although she knew she would likely have a good time and be able to delay going home a little while longer.

Lee declined as well. Sensing that Katrice wanted to talk, he invited her to stay.

"It's a nice evening. Want to sit outside on the patio?" Lee asked after they had put the dishes away.

She nodded and followed him outside.

It was a pleasant evening, typical of the southern region of Ohio that boasted rolling hills and heavily wooded landscapes. A gentle breeze carried the fragrant scent of hydrangeas, honeysuckle, and roses. Crickets chirped noisily and fireflies skittered about. The clear sky revealed thousands of stars twinkling in the heavens. For both the casual and the dedicated observer, this was one of those rare summer nights that was meant to be enjoyed and not taken for granted.

Katrice sat beside Lee on the park-style bench, fully aware it was getting late. With very little effort she had convinced herself it would be all right to stay a little while longer. Being with Lee and his family had been once again, a lot of fun. She could easily get caught up in their lives and forget all about hers. There was always plenty of laughter, good-natured kidding around, and a feeling of belonging that she hadn't experienced since her summers with Grandma Harry.

Sitting quietly listening to the night sounds and completely lost in thought, Katrice was unaware that Lee was secretly studying her.

Lee didn't mean to stare, and he absolutely didn't want to be caught gawking at Katrice like a lovesick little boy, but he couldn't help himself. He could very easily spend the rest of his life gazing at her. He noticed the way the moonlight lent an ethereal glow to her skin and accentuated the highlights in her hair. His fingers ached to run through her soft, fragrant tresses. But before he got carried away, he needed to know why her eyes reflected such sadness.

"A penny for your thoughts," he said, winding a silky curl around his finger.

Katrice pulled herself away from her thoughts and turned to face Lee, cleverly masking the tumultuous thoughts swirling around inside her head. "Only a penny? Even in Benton Lake I don't think a penny will buy very much."

"Well, if you refuse my offering of money, how about this?" He leaned in and kissed her tenderly, taking time to savor her sweet taste and luscious lips.

She smiled and allowed him to pull her closer. There wouldn't be any harm in permitting the reassuring sense of closeness and security that Lee gave her, and she secretly desired, even if it would only last for a little while. For now, she gave herself permission to get lost in the moment.

Lee felt her relax and pulled her closer.

"What's wrong, Katrice? You've been quiet all evening. Considering the chaos you were subjected to at the dinner table, that's a little strange."

"Is that the only thing that seemed strange to you?" *What about my showing up tonight out of the blue? What about the lame excuse I gave for not wanting to accept Vonda and Sam's invitation to bring my family over for dinner? Even stranger, why is my body reacting to your touch and kisses in a way that confuses the heck out of me?*

"Well, since you asked, I was wondering what brought you here tonight. Don't get me wrong. It's not that I don't enjoy seeing you. I was just a bit surprised, that's all."

Katrice remained silent. Instinct told her she didn't have to hide things from Lee. Deep down inside, she knew he would listen to whatever she had to tell him and wouldn't judge her for past mistakes. She could trust him, couldn't she? He hadn't done anything to hurt her and he seemed to genuinely care about her feelings and opinions. He hadn't lied or been deceitful. In fact, being mean or sneaky seemed as out of character for him as being reckless was for her. And as far as she could tell, he didn't seem to have any ulterior motives. By any measure, he had proven himself trustworthy. But so had Greg. He not only hurt her but had left her feeling humiliated and ashamed although she felt part of the blame was hers. Being naïve and too quick to trust had been her downfall. Now it was more important than ever to learn from her mistakes or she'd be doomed to repeat them.

She again reminded herself that Lee wasn't Greg. Sooner or later she would have to stop punishing him for Greg's mistakes. *Easier said than done?* Could she simply move on and accept whatever a relationship with Lee had to offer? She had made a vow to let go of the past but it wasn't as easy as she thought it would be.

Her heart wanted to be carefree and open to love but her mind warned her to be careful. Past experiences aren't easily forgotten, nor are the wounds from those experiences easily healed.

Katrice rested her head against Lee's chest, drinking in his scent and enjoying the smooth softness of his shirt against her cheek. A protective arm rested easily on her shoulders and seemed to be sending a message that she had absolutely nothing to fear. Lee's breathing was easy and relaxed, and as his chest rose and fell she was lulled into a sense of security that was unfamiliar but certainly not unwelcome.

She wished she had a crystal ball that could predict the future and tell her what lay ahead for her. Would Lee be in her life? If so could they maintain a long-distance relationship? Would she even be the kind of women he needed and wanted in his life?

Could he make the ache in her heart go away and make her feel loved and cherished?

Lee heard her sigh. She sounded so tired. He wanted to comfort her, but he didn't know what to do. Every time he reached out to her, she pulled back, never fully giving him her trust.

He stroked her hair. "Talk to me, baby. What's wrong?"

She took a deep breath and decided to take a chance. "How does a person go about erasing mistakes from her past?" she asked sadly.

Lee was silent. He didn't know what to say. Had Katrice done something in her past that would cause his feelings for her to change? It was possible. Just how well did he know her? Not quite sure what to say, he searched for the right words. Then he looked into his heart.

"That's a tough question to answer, especially since we've all made mistakes. I've always thought that what happens in the past shapes us into who and what we are now. You know the saying, what doesn't kill you makes you stronger."

Lee cringed inwardly. That wasn't exactly what he'd wanted to say. Finally, Katrice had felt comfortable enough to open up to him and all he could offer were clichés.

"My grandmother used to say things like that. Sometimes when I would complain about my life—usually stupid, teenage drama—she would come up with one of her famous sayings from out of nowhere at exactly the right time. Back then, I didn't understand what she meant when she offered those words of wisdom, but as I got older, more and more of what she used to say began to make sense to me."

Lee continued to listen. He didn't want to say anything for fear that Katrice would again put on her armor of steel and shut him out.

"I miss her. My grandmother. She would encourage me by telling me I could do anything, as long as I was willing to work for it. She always had the right answer and knew exactly what to say and when to say it."

The sadness in Katrice's voice bothered Lee. He wanted her to know that she could share her secrets with him and he would guard them as if they were his own.

"Are you afraid that I would judge or ridicule you?"

She shrugged without answering.

"If that's what you truly feel, then I think you need to give me a chance to prove myself," Lee said firmly. "When people care about each other, I'd say that's the only fair and natural thing to do."

Katrice was a little surprised by his tone; it almost sounded as if he was scolding her. She tilted her head upward, but his face didn't reflect the sternness she expected.

This is it. Now, Lee thought, was his chance to tell Katrice what was in his heart. If he didn't say it now, he may not have the nerve or the occasion to say it later.

"Katrice, it's no secret that I care about you, and without being too presumptuous, I think you feel the same about me."

Not giving her a chance to interrupt, he continued, "Do you know what I see when I look at you? I see a beautiful, vibrant, sexy, caring, intelligent, and troubled woman. It kills me to see you struggling to overcome whatever or whoever hurt you in the past. Whether you're ready to admit it to me or not I know that this need you have to be a one-woman army has something to

293

do with the man from the sandwich shop. But you can't let what happened between the two of you serve as a death sentence to any other relationship that you're entitled to have."

Katrice was awestruck. How could he know so much about the things she hid in her heart?

"Yes, Katrice, that's right. No matter what happened to you in the past, you're entitled to some happiness."

She tensed. "Thanks for the advice, Lee, but why don't we have this conversation after your heart has been broken and you're left alone to rebuild your life after it has been smashed into a million little pieces. Better yet, let's see what advice you have when you've spent years trying to be something and someone you're not just to please your family *and* your man. Then you realize it's not enough and will never be enough. More importantly, you realize what a fool you've been. So, you see, there are a few good reasons why I choose to live by my own rules now."

"Katrice, I understand and my heart has been broken. When my wife died, I was angry, hurting, and lonely. I thought if I didn't allow myself to feel, I couldn't be hurt. That was the rule I lived by for a long time. But that's no way to live. I made myself even more miserable, and everyone else around me."

"I'm sorry. I didn't mean to be callous."

"As for your family, you can't live your life trying to please them. I would think they would be very proud of your accomplishments. If they are, that's good, if they aren't, oh well."

Katrice shook her head. "My family isn't like yours. No matter what's going on, whether it's dinner or fishing or just hanging out, your father and Vonda always make me feel welcome and a part of the family."

"That's because you are."

"Your family has opened their arms to me and welcomed me, with no strings attached. Why can't my family be that way, too? You have to damn near walk on water for them to even acknowledge that you're a worthwhile human being."

"Honey, I can't make excuses for your family or even explain why they do the things they do. All I can do is listen to you and be there when you need me, without any preconceived notions or judgments."

Katrice sighed. "I'm sorry."

"For what?"

"You didn't ask me to stay tonight so you could listen to me whine about my problems. I should never have dumped this on you." She stood to leave.

Just like that the closeness they'd shared just minutes before vanished In its place was a void that unmistakably bought sadness and emptiness to both Lee and Katrice.

"Tell your father and Vonda that I said thanks for dinner. I really did have a good time."

Lee reached out to stop her, but Katrice had already started walking back inside. Catching up to her in three quick strides, he caught her by the shoulder.

She stopped and turned to face him. She was hurting inside. Her eyes reflected a sadness that Lee wanted to wipe away, but he just didn't know how.

"Why do you do that?"

"What?"

"One minute you're being open and honest with me and not a split second later, you clam up."

"I told you that I was sorry about that."

"Well, stop it. Stop apologizing for allowing yourself to trust me. Stop hiding what I know you feel when you're with me."

She looked at him disbelievingly.

He didn't dare stop now. She needed to hear what he had to say and he needed to say it.

"I want to be with you, Katrice. I'm having the hardest time getting you to see that, and I don't know why. When we're together, I can't imagine another place I'd rather be. It just feels so right. I don't know any other way to describe this *thing* between us. You can't tell me that you don't feel it, too."

Katrice tried to mask her feelings. However, Lee was right; she did feel what he felt. But she couldn't let him know that. Not right now.

He wouldn't let her go. "Baby, I want to hold you, kiss you, and wrap you in my arms and protect you from everything that threatens to harm what we have together. I want to drive every trace of sadness from your life. Making you happy and seeing that beautiful smile of yours makes my heart melt. I want to have that feeling all the time. Do you know that when you walked in with my father tonight, I was so excited to see you that I wanted to jump out of my chair and sweep you off your feet? I didn't because I didn't want to overwhelm you.

Believe me when I say that it took every ounce of self-control for me to sit so close to you at the table and not touch you."

Katrice listened to Lee, afraid of what he was going to say next but needing to hear it nonetheless.

"You want to hear something else crazy?" he asked, his voice raw with emotion. "Lately, when I'm supposed to be working, I find myself daydreaming about you. I wonder what you're doing, wearing, how you're feeling, and hoping you're thinking about me even if it's just a little bit. When I'm alone, I close my eyes and without even trying I can almost detect the faintest scent of your perfume and feel the softness of your hair between my fingers." He reached out and stroked her hair tenderly. "At the oddest times I swear I can hear your sweet voice whispering my name the way you did the first time we made love. I'm not the same man that I was when I came here at the beginning of the summer, Katrice. Do you know why?"

"Why?" she whispered, trying to keep from shivering as his knuckles brushed her cheek.

Leaning closer, he softly answered, "It's you, sweetheart. You've changed me. You have reminded me what it's like to care for someone and to have those feelings returned. And, baby, it feels so good. I laugh more than I have in years. I pay attention to the stars and whether or not there's a full moon. I notice little things I probably wouldn't have noticed before you came into my life." Lee straightened up just enough to see Katrice's expression, but he remained close. "Katrice, you've got a hold on me, and I have never experienced anything like this. I don't want to lose this feeling."

"What are you saying, Lee?"

He threw his head back and laughed. The puzzled look on her face told him that she clearly had no idea of the spell she had cast on him or how she had unwittingly wrapped his heart around her little finger.

Stepping closer, Lee stroked Katrice's face. His heart beat wildly and his legs felt like rubber, but he felt compelled to let his feelings be known once and for all. No more pretenses and no more walking on egg shells.

"What I'm trying to say, baby, is that I—"

Before he could finish, Katrice pressed two fingers against his lips.

"I can't trust my feelings for you right now, and the last thing I want to do is to hurt you. So please, don't say anything that we may both regret later. And please, don't make promises that are too hard to keep," she said sadly.

CHAPTER 32

Katrice had purposely stayed late at the bookstore, hoping everyone would be asleep by the time she arrived home. It had been a long, busy day and she was physically, mentally, and emotionally exhausted. Sleep had eluded her the previous night; all she had been able to think about was Lee and what she had prevented him from declaring last night. Well, she refused to have another sleepless, fretful night. If need be she would take a sleeping pill and quickly fall into a dreamless sleep. Sooner or later she would have to deal with Lee, but it wouldn't be tonight.

Pulling into her driveway, she groaned when from the back of the house she saw the faint glow of the kitchen light. Maybe, she hoped, Taryn and her mother were asleep and had just forgotten to turn off the light. The three of them were barely speaking these days, and Katrice didn't much feel like putting an end to that arrangement tonight. It was time they went back home and left her alone.

Vonda had stopped by the bookstore all excited about the upcoming cookout and Katrice didn't have the heart to tell her that she hadn't mentioned it to her family. And didn't plan to. Time was running out. She needed to make sure her mother and Taryn were on their way back home before the cookout. Then she wouldn't need an excuse and her life could return to normal.

"No, that's not what I want and I don't think you do either. Why can't we just talk through this and work it out?"

Katrice stopped in the darkened hallway when she heard Taryn's voice. After placing her keys on the hall table and removing her shoes, she tiptoed down the hall, hoping to slip by unnoticed. Thankfully, the hallway was dark and had just enough light from the kitchen to make her furtive ascent to her room successful. Each careful step brought her closer to the sanctuary of her room. There she could hide from the outside world, which at the moment consisted of her sister and their mother.

As she neared the staircase, she could almost feel the soothing comfort of her sheets. Her body practically sagged with fatigue and longed for rest. Her scattered thoughts needed to be stilled, at least for a little while. The sleeping pills in her purse assured her that sleep would come quickly.

The last few steps to the staircase brought her near the kitchen. Just as she placed her foot on the bottom step, something her sister said made her stop cold.

"I just want us to be a family again. Is that asking too much?"

Was she talking to Robert?

Katrice stepped back and hid in the shadows. As she listened she could hear the anxiety in Taryn's voice. Suddenly, she forgot all about her own tiredness and problems.

300

What was going on between Taryn and Robert? It had seemed odd that he hadn't joined his family in Benton Lake, but Katrice simply assumed he was busy with work. When he called the house, he mainly talked with the children.

Katrice also thought it odd that Taryn seemed distracted and was particularly clingy with the children. Once, when Jewel asked if she could talk to her daddy, Taryn told her that he was too busy working and couldn't talk to her. Katrice could have sworn that Taryn looked tearful right after that.

Even though Taryn had lowered her voice, Katrice could still hear bits and pieces of her conversation. When she heard her sister placing the receiver back on its cradle, Katrice scrambled to get to her room. As she placed her foot on the first step, she lost hold of her shoes and they dropped on the uncarpeted steps, causing a magnified thud in the quiet house.

Taryn came from the kitchen expecting to find one of the children wandering about. Instead she saw her sister barefooted and lurking in the shadows. She wondered how long she had been in the hallway.

"I didn't hear you come in," Taryn said, trying to sound casual.

Katrice stood with her back to her sister and sighed. "I, uh, I just got in. Long day. I probably should get ready for bed now."

"Oh, okay," Taryn replied quietly.

Although Katrice stood with her back to Taryn and could not see her face, there was no mistaking her tearful voice. She turned around and saw her red, puffy eyes. Her heart went out to her sister. "Wanna talk?"

Taryn nodded, not trusting her voice.

Katrice followed her sister to the kitchen and sat down at the table.

"I've really made a mess of things," Taryn began.

"What do you mean?"

"My marriage. My life. My kids' lives. Everything."

"What happened, Taryn?"

"Robert and I are separated. We have been for the past several weeks."

Shocked, Katrice asked, "What? When? What happened? Do Mom and Dad know?"

Taryn shook her head. "I haven't told them. Whenever they ask about him, I just say that he's busy at work or he's traveling on business."

"Taryn, I can't believe you've been keeping this a secret. After ten years of marriage what could have possibly happened?"

Tears streamed down Taryn's face as she began to recount how her marriage had begun to crumble.

"I guess I would say this all started about a year ago, but according to my husband, he has been unhappy for much longer than that." Taryn dabbed her eyes and laughed bitterly. "We had just moved into the new house and Robert had received a promotion. I didn't really think too much about it at first, but he began spending more and more time at the office. I figured he had to because added responsibilities."

"Did you ask him about it?" Katrice asked, handing Taryn a napkin.

"Not at first, but when I did, he just said that he had a lot to do at work. It seemed like a reasonable explanation. Besides, I knew he had at least one or two contracts with West Coast firms and sometimes had to have meetings with them that ran into the evening to accommodate the time difference."

Taryn took a deep breath and her bottom lip trembled. She dabbed at her eyes with the crumpled napkin. "One night I tried to reach Robert. Kalil had been impossible all day. I needed Robert to come home and help me deal with him. I called him at his office, on his cell, and left messages with his answering service. I didn't hear from him. Before he left for work that morning, he had told me that he would be home late because he had a dinner meeting with a client. Nothing unusual. Well, there's late and then there's *late*. I started to worry. Then around midnight he came strolling in and he had been drinking."

"You said he had a meeting with a client. He more than likely had a drink or two," Katrice said, offering what seemed like a reasonable explanation.

But Taryn quickly rejected her sister's theory. "Kat, Robert can barely finish a glass of wine or a bottle of beer, and he never drinks when he's with a client. He says for him to keep his edge, he has to have a clear head."

"So you think he might have lied about where he was?"

Taryn nodded. "Even though he denied it, I'm pretty sure the whole dinner meeting was a big fat lie. That wasn't his first lie, either. Over time, he started to become more and more distant." Taryn dropped her head and tried unsuccessfully to blink back tears. "One night I was out with some girlfriends. One of them asked how I liked the flowers Robert had sent me. As it turned out, she had seen him at the downtown florist near his office buying roses and had assumed they were for me."

"What did you do?"

"That night when Robert came home I asked him about the flowers. More important, I asked him if he had someone else. You want to know what he said? He denied having an affair, but said it wouldn't matter if he was being unfaithful or not because I didn't care anything about him, only what he could give me. Kat, he said he felt as if he was only a means to an end for me. According to him, he didn't know how to make me happy anymore. I always had to have a bigger house, flashier clothes, a newer car, more exotic vacations, and he had grown tired of it. He even had the nerve to accuse me of being pushy and manipulative."

"Why did he say that?" Katrice asked, beginning to understand what had driven her sister and brother-in-law apart.

"Supposedly, he only accepted his new position because I pressured him into it. Isn't that just crazy?" Taryn seemed entirely focused on convincing herself than Robert was the culprit.

Katrice tried to digest everything she heard her sister say and even what she'd left unsaid. She wanted to sympathize with her and she did, to a point. Katrice could also see her brother-in-law's side. She knew he loved Taryn and knew that her sister loved him. She also knew how important social status and wealth were to Taryn, but she couldn't say she understood it. She would probably never admit it, but Taryn had grown more and more like their mother as she'd gotten older.

"I don't know, Taryn. Have you and Robert really sat down and talked about this? How about seeing a counselor?"

"He won't. I try to talk to him when he comes by the house to see the kids, but he doesn't have anything to say to me." Taryn rested her forehead in her hands and sighed. "Robert said he didn't cheat, but he did admit to thinking about it. He sent the flowers to someone who he said paid attention to him and cared about what he needed." Taryn lifted her head, her bottom lip trembling. "This is tearing me apart, Kat. I can't eat. I hardly sleep. I'm sick of pretending my fairytale life is still intact. I don't know what to do. My husband won't touch me or even talk to me. I want to be the one to give him what he needs. Not some stranger. It's like he's become this person who has me wondering how I could have ever loved him."

"You did love him and he loved you," Katrice said. "You don't just fall out of love that easily, Taryn."

"I know," she said, her voice breaking. "I remember the way things were when we first got married. We were both so young and in love. We had so many good times together, Kat. I can't just forget about that. What went wrong?"

"You still love him, Taryn. I know you do."

Taryn nodded. "Yeah, I still love him. I just don't know how to get him to love me back."

That night Katrice lay awake staring into the darkness. She thought about her sister and Robert and the love she knew they both still felt for each other. She thought about her strained relationship with her mother and wondered if their relationship would always be so tumultuous. She thought about Lee. Despite the turmoil that seemed to have taken over her life, he seemed to be the only one offering the possibility of peace.

CHAPTER 33

Katrice had just put on a pot of coffee when Taryn walked in.

"It's early. I can't believe the kids are up and about already. Did they eat?"

"Yeah. Mom is still sleeping, so I made them oatmeal and toast. They're outside playing. Here." She handed Taryn a piece of buttered toast and joined her at the table. "I told them we're going to a picnic today, and they were really excited."

"A picnic? Where?"

"Lee's family invited us over. I didn't feel much like going, but I didn't decline the invitation. We don't have to stay long."

Taryn just nodded. She seemed a million miles away.

"You look as bad as I feel."

"Lack of sleep and a ruined marriage will do that to you," Taryn said, slathering more butter on her toast.

"Coffee?"

"Sure."

Katrice placed a mug of steaming coffee in front of her sister and sat down heavily in her chair. "Taryn, you can't keep going on like this."

"I know. I've been thinking about that a lot lately."

"What have you decided?"

"That my husband was right in leaving me. Actually, I've known that for a long time. I've just had a hard time facing the ugly truth. I'm surprised he didn't leave sooner."

"Robert left you?"

Hearing their mother's voice, Katrice and Taryn turned sharply.

Melinda marched in, glaring at her eldest child. "What in the name of God happened?" she demanded. "Did he cheat on you?"

Taryn gripped her mug with both hands and stared down at the dark liquid. "No, Mother, he did not cheat on me."

"Why didn't you mention this to me before?"

Katrice felt a sudden need to defend her sister, but she was at a loss for as to what to say or do. She had been subjected to Melinda's disappointment and anger before. Taryn had not.

"I didn't mention it because I knew you would over-react, just as you're doing right now."

"*Overreact?* You're damned right!"

"Stop it!" Taryn snapped, jumping up to face her mother. "Please, just stop. Yes, Robert left me and the kids. I have been trying to handle this on my own, but I have to admit I'm failing miserably."

"Well, do you have a lawyer? Is he still supporting you and the children?"

"No and yes."

Caught off her game, Melinda sat down and looked to her daughter for some reasonable explanation. "You're going to have to help me understand this. Right now none of this makes any sense to me."

"Well, let me help clarify some things for you," Taryn began. "For years I've listened to you tell me how to treat my husband, raise my children, decorate my house, and make the right friends. I listened to your sage advice and did all of those things. I even listened when you told me that it was my job to push my husband to be successful. You said to never let him get too comfortable in a position. Always encourage him, you said, to aim higher and higher up the corporate ladder and I would reap the benefits. Fine clothes, fancy cars, country club memberships, more jewelry than I could ever wear. I pushed him to get all those things for me, because I thought that meant I was shaping him into the man he was meant to be. Besides, all *good* husbands did those things. Right?"

"Taryn, you've been a good wife and mother. You deserved all of that and more."

"No, Mother, I didn't. I pushed Robert and pushed him. The more he gave me, the more I thought I should have. If it seemed like he was getting too settled in a position, I took that as a sign that he needed to put in for a promotion. Enough was never enough. Except for him."

"I don't understand. If it hadn't been for you, Robert might still be in the mailroom and you all would be living in a two-bedroom apartment."

"At least we would have been happy and I would still have my husband."

Melinda waved her hand as if to dismiss her daughter's words. "This is crazy. You can't possibly be thinking clearly."

"Oh, but I think I am . . . for the first time in a long time," Taryn said, turning to her sister. "And I have my little sister to thank."

Katrice had been listening intently to the exchange between her bewildered mother and a determined Taryn, so she was caught unaware when her sister turned to her.

Taryn sat down and further surprised her. "Kat, I know I haven't said this to you since I've been here, but I'm proud of you, proud of the way you've made a wonderful home and a new life for yourself. I'm especially proud of the business you've started. Book Wares is beautiful!"

Surprised, Katrice asked, "You've been there?"

Taryn nodded. "The kids and I dropped by one day, but you were out running errands. I didn't tell anyone that I knew the owner," she added, winking.

"Kat, I now understand why you left Greg and appreciate the strength it took to start all over again in a new place. At first it hurt that you didn't come to me. But why would you after the way I acted toward you? Also, you probably suspected before I did that my life was a big fat mess, so I wouldn't have been very much help. I haven't been much of a big sister to you for a long time."

Katrice smiled and touched her sister's hand. "We haven't been much of a family for a long time."

Taryn nodded. "True. At a time when you needed us most, we abandoned you. Mom, Katrice never told you, or any of us, but Greg cheated on her multiple times. He even lost his job for sexual harassment."

"What? Katrice, why didn't you tell me?"

"Honestly, Mom, I didn't see the point. The bottom line is that you should have trusted me and you didn't."

"That has to change," Taryn added. "Right, Mom?"

Still reeling from the news of her daughter's broken marriage and Greg's cunning lies and deceit, Melinda stared blankly at Taryn, truly at a loss for words. "Wh- what do you mean?"

This time Katrice spoke up. "She means you have to let us live our own lives—not according to your rules, but ours."

"But I want you both to be happy."

"No, you want to manipulate us. That has to end. I love you, Mom, but I can't keep trying to live up to some impossible expectation you've set for me. I've allowed you to influence where I live, where I work, and whom I love for so long that when I had to make life decisions on my own, I couldn't even trust my own instincts," Katrice said.

Melinda was near tears. "Are you asking me to stop caring?"

"No," Taryn said softly. "We're asking you to love us for who and what we are and trust us to make our own decisions, good or bad."

"But I've done tha—"

Katrice stopped her. "No you haven't, but it's time you do."

"What do you want me to do?" Melinda asked, sounding more defeated than Katrice had ever heard her sound.

Katrice collected the coffee cups and took them to the sink. Then she turned and addressed her mother. "I want

311

you to get dressed and put your best face forward. There's something I need to show you."

Confused, Melinda asked, "Why? Where are we going?"

"We're going to a picnic."

Lee hadn't heard from or seen Katrice since her dinnertime visit. That had been a week ago. She had been so close to opening up to him but something had caused her to clam up. Sooner or later she had to make a decision to trust him and take a chance on love. Or . . . walk away and break his heart.

Vonda had come over early to begin preparations for the barbecue later that day. "Where's Kyra this morning?" Vonda asked, throwing a handful of chopped onions and celery into the potato salad she was preparing.

"Upstairs watching a movie. Amber slept over last night. The two of them were up all night giggling and talking. At least Ky's home for a change. She's been gone so much lately I was beginning to forget what she looked like."

"It's summer. Surely, you remember being a carefree kid with no responsibilities or worries. Let her have her fun. Before you know it, you'll be heading back home and your carefree summer will be over."

"Yeah," Lee replied soberly. "Back to reality, or something resembling it."

Vonda handed Lee a forkful of potato salad to sample.

"It's good," he declared.

"Just *good*? Not *divine* or *delicious*? Do you think you could muster up a little more enthusiasm?"

"I'm sorry. I've got a lot on my mind, that's all."

Vonda sprinkled paprika on top of the potato salad and placed it in the refrigerator next to the macaroni salad and pasta salad. "Wash your hands and sit down and help me shape the ground beef into patties," she ordered, carrying a bowl of the seasoned meat over to the table.

Moving robotically, Lee did as he was told.

"What's wrong, Lee? You've been moping around for the last few days like you lost your best friend."

He took a portion of ground beef from the bowl and began shaping it into a patty. "That's because I feel like I have."

"Katrice?"

He nodded.

"When are you going to tell that girl how you feel about her?"

"I've tried."

"Then what's the problem?"

Lee shrugged and placed a puny ground beef patty atop one of Vonda's super-sized stack. "She doesn't want to hear it."

Vonda removed Lee's patty from the stack and put it back in the bowl. "I find that hard to believe. That girl is crazy about you, and I know you adore her."

"Apparently, that's not enough," Lee responded, scooping out another mound of ground beef.

"When is love not enough?"

"When someone has been hurt to such an extent she is too afraid to give love another try. Katrice has been hurt, and I don't know how to get her to understand that I don't want to add to that hurt. To further complicate matters, she's fiercely independent, and, for some strange reason, she thinks I'm a threat to that independence."

Vonda plucked Lee's second patty from her stack and put it back in the bowl. "Looks like you've got your work cut out for you and not a whole lot of time to spare. Summer is almost over and you'll be heading back home."

"I know," Lee said solemnly. "Any advice?"

"Yes," Vonda replied, moving the bowl of ground beef out of Lee's reach. "I suggest you decide whether or not you want Katrice in your life. Once that's decided, all you have to do is follow your heart."

"That's it? That's your advice? No offense, Miss Vonda, but I already know that I want Katrice in my life. The problem is that I can't get *her* to see that."

Vonda finished shaping the last two patties and began clearing off the table to start her pies. "It's obvious to me that you're in love with Katrice. From what I've seen, I'm pretty sure she is in love with you."

Lee looked up, hopeful. "You think so?"

She nodded. "I know so. That's why I think it's time you make her an offer she can't refuse." Vonda winked and then shooed Lee out of the kitchen.

CHAPTER 34

Her mother, sister, and kids in tow, Katrice stepped into the Olivers' backyard and thought she had happened upon a block party. *A few neighbors?* The whole neighborhood seemed to have shown up for Sam and Vonda's barbecue.

Katrice ushered her family over to an empty table near the patio and immediately started scanning the crowd for the one person she really needed to see. Wondering where he could be, she felt apprehensive and this time, didn't bother to pretend his absence didn't affect her. Realizing Lee could be anywhere, she tried to relax and get her family settled.

"Can I go over there and play?" Jewel asked, pointing at a group of girls surrounded by an array of Barbie dolls and every conceivable accessory.

Kalil had already found another little boy to play with and hadn't bothered asking for permission to leave.

"Go ahead," Taryn replied. "Play nice and remember to share."

"I thought you said this was going to be a family event. Just how big is this family?" Melinda asked.

Just then Vonda walked by carrying a plate of roasted corn. She kissed Katrice on the cheek but kept walking. "Let me set this down, and I'll be right back to meet your family," she said.

"Do you need any help?" Katrice called after her.

"Nope. Got it all under control."

As Vonda hurried away, Sam walked up. "Hi, honey!" he greeted Katrice, giving her a big hug and kissing her on the cheek. "I'm so glad you came. We were beginning to wonder." Turning to Melinda, he extended his hand, saying, "You must be Katrice's mother. I'm Sam Oliver and this," he said, reaching out to grab Vonda as she passed, "is my best girl, Vonda Griggs."

Just being around Sam and Vonda had a calming effect on Katrice. Losing some of her earlier apprehension, Katrice continued the introductions. "Sam, this is my mother, Melinda Ware, and my sister, Taryn. There's also two little rugrats running around somewhere who belong to us. As soon as I find them, I'll introduce them, too."

"Nice to meet you both," Sam said.

"I need to tend to the grill," Vonda said. "Katrice, would you go inside and bring me a container of bar-becue sauce from the refrigerator? It's in an orange bowl, and I think it might be on the top shelf."

"Sure," she replied. "Taryn, Mom, I'll be right back."

Taryn stood up. "I'll be right back, too. I need to see what Kalil is up to."

Sam took a seat beside Melinda. "I want to you to know, Mrs. Ware—"

"Call me Melinda."

"Melinda, I just want to say what a wonderful daughter you have. Vonda and I have sort of adopted her. I know it's not easy being in a place where you don't have any family, but we've been more than happy to fill in."

Melinda sniffed. "That was Katrice's choice to move so far away. She could have come home if she wanted to."

Sam looked puzzled. "Pardon me for saying so, but it seems as if your daughter came here because she wanted to."

Melinda couldn't forget what Katrice and Taryn had said to her that morning. She still hadn't absorbed it all. "I'm afraid that's because I've pushed her away for so long that she felt moving here was her only choice."

In conversation with his father a few days ago, Lee had explained why Katrice had kept her family away. Lee had revealed that Katrice and her mother were not close and that she had never felt she could live up to her mother's impossible expectations. Listening to Melinda, Sam understood why Katrice felt that way.

"Melinda, Katrice is a smart, kind, and wonderful young lady, someone I'd be proud to call my daughter. She has taken that little bookstore of hers and turned it into something special. Everyone—her customers, neighbors, me and Vonda—think the world of her. And my son, Lee, he's so much in love with that girl he can hardly see straight."

"He is?" Katrice hadn't mentioned that.

"Yes, and if you want my opinion, she loves him, too. I just don't think she's ready to admit it yet."

Melinda stared past Sam in the direction Katrice had gone. *Katrice was in love.* How could she have missed that? How could these *strangers* know more about the events of her daughter's life than she did? Then it struck her. Sam and his family weren't strangers to Katrice; they were the only family she'd had over the past several months.

Melinda sank back in her chair, suddenly ashamed of the way she had behaved over the years and for the way she had practically pushed her daughter out of her life.

"My baby is in love," she said quietly. "And your son . . . Lee . . . he loves her?"

"Very much."

"She's been hurt, you know. I don't know if she trusts herself to venture into another relationship."

"I know."

"I guess it's too late for motherly advice at this stage in her life," she said sadly.

"Sometimes we make mistakes as parents, but our kids still love us and give us another chance to do what's right." Sam patted Melinda's hand and smiled reassuringly. "It's not too late for you to tell Katrice how much you love her and that you want to stand by her." Sam paused briefly. "You know, it's a rare and beautiful thing to find the kind of love that lasts a lifetime. Let's hope Lee and Katrice have done just that."

Katrice opened the refrigerator door and groaned. Practically every bowl in there was orange. Vonda and Sam must have purchased the fifty-piece set.

Opening and then closing the lids of several bowls on the top shelf, she came up empty-handed. *Vonda had missed her calling. She should have been in the catering business.*

Why had his father been so insistent that he get more ice from the freezer? There was plenty outside already. Lee was in a bad mood, which he attributed to the fact that he missed Katrice and was disappointed that she hadn't shown up to the picnic. Hell, he didn't just miss her, he longed for her.

A few times he had set out to go to her house or the bookstore but had thought better of it. She needed her space and he needed to respect that. But ever since his talk with Vonda that morning, he had been to pondering her advice: Make Katrice an offer she couldn't refuse.

Coming from the sunbathed backyard and entering the more subdued lighting inside the kitchen, Lee stopped in his tracks, relieved and downright thrilled by the sight in front of him. Removing his sunglasses for a better view, he felt his heart begin to race.

Bent over low and rummaging through the refrigerator, Katrice was reaching something in the back, giving Lee an unobstructed view of her beautiful long legs. He had no idea what kind of fabric her skirt was made of; all he knew was that it clung to every single curve.

He bit his bottom lip and sucked in his breath.

Hearing someone come in and assuming it was Vonda, Katrice turned slightly, still bent over, and exclaimed, "Vonda, I don't see the barbeque—"

Katrice's V-neck top was cut low in the front and clung seductively to her breast, giving Lee a generous view of cleavage. *Damn if that woman isn't about to give me a heart attack!*

319

"Oh, hi," she said, quickly straightening up and closing the refrigerator door.

"Hi."

He looked good, Katrice thought. She put her hands behind her and leaned against the refrigerator door for support. Every fiber in her body yearned for his touch, yet she remained still.

She had missed him and did need him, but pride had kept her away. One night on her way home from work, she had driven by the house to see if his car was in the driveway. The only car she had seen had been Sam's. She briefly feared that he'd gone back home to Columbus but then remembered his plans were to stay until the week before Labor Day. *Just three more weeks.*

Lee tried to think of something to say but could think of nothing. In contrast to the laughter and chatter coming from the backyard, the silence in the kitchen seemed almost unnatural. He shoved his hands into his pockets and pressed his body against the kitchen counter. What he really wanted to do was to press his body against Katrice and feel her luscious curves. He wanted to kiss her until she was breathless. He wanted to hear her soft moans as he made love to her. But above all else, he wanted to spend the rest of his life loving her.

He'd missed her. A lot.

"I was just—" they started and stopped in unison.

"I didn't think you were coming."

"I had to take a detour. Sorry I didn't get here sooner."

Lee pushed away from the counter and walked toward her. "I'm not," he said. "I've never prided myself on being a patient man, but I'd wait a lifetime for you."

Katrice remained still, afraid any movement would expose her most secret desires.

He stopped within inches of her, short of kissing distance. He could smell her perfume and feel her breath on his skin. "I've missed you," he said softly.

Katrice let her hands drop to her sides. She needed to be close to him. "Good, because I've missed you, too."

"I can't believe you're admitting that."

"Me either."

"So what are we going to do about this?" he asked, coming even closer.

Katrice looked into his eyes and experienced an emotion so strong it gripped her and rocked her to her very soul. "Can you start by holding me?"

Lee took her into his arms. A thousand emotions flowed through him all at once, the most prominent being love.

He held Katrice at arm's length and looked into her eyes. She loved him. She couldn't hide her feelings from him any longer. She had to say it. She had to allow herself to love him or this wouldn't work.

"The first time we met you made it abundantly clear that you didn't need me or my help. After my bruised ego healed, I accepted that and the fact that you are fiercely independent. I know you don't have a need for a knight in shining armor, but if you ever did, I'd be there in a heartbeat. But that's not all I have to offer. If you'll let me, I want to be the man who knows just the right thing to say or do to make you smile. I want to be the one who holds you on moonlit nights. I want to be there with you late at night eating popcorn in bed and watching scary movies. Katrice, I want to be the man who loves you for the rest of your life."

"What are you saying, Lee?"

"Do you love me, Katrice?"

I do! Say it. "I-I . . ."

He brought her closer and stroked her cheek. "Just say it," he urged gently. "Say what your heart already knows."

Katrice's gaze locked with his. She could say it, she thought. She did love Lee and he loved her. Her mind and heart were in agreement. "I do. I do love you, Lee."

Relief swept over him and he wrapped his arms tightly around her, not wanting to ever let her go. "That's all I needed to hear."

She, too, felt relief. But admitting that she loved him was only their first hurdle. "Lee, I don't know how we're going to make this work. I don't want to give up my life here, and I can't ask you to uproot Kyra and move to Benton Lake. Long distance relationships don't always survive."

Lee cocked his head and smiled. "That's already taken care of."

"What do you mean?"

Just then Kyra burst into the kitchen. Oblivious to the moment being shared by her father and Katrice, she ran up to Lee and exclaimed, "Dad, did you know that if

I cut through the back of our new house and down that one street by the church, I can be at Amber's house in like five minutes?"

"No, Ky, I didn't."

"I think I'm going to like living here," she announced and then left in a flash.

"New house? You're moving here?"

Lee nodded.

"But your job—"

"I'm opening my own practice in Benton Lake."

Stunned, Katrice didn't know what to say. This all seemed to be happening so fast.

"Katrice, I know we've both taken some pretty big steps here today, but can you do one more thing for me?"

Lee held her in his arms and she felt safe, secure, and loved. For so long she had denied herself what she now knew she was entitled to, and it felt better than she could have ever imagined. She had overcome a lot since she'd moved to Benton Lake and she refused to lose any of the ground she had gained.

She looked into Lee's eyes and the love she saw assured her that she would be safe with him. That was all she needed.

"Yes, Lee. Anything. Just ask."

"Be my wife."

CHAPTER 35

"Yes, I received the flowers. They're gorgeous. I put them on the counter, and I'm looking at them right now." Katrice looked up when a couple with two children walked in carrying one of her sales fliers. "Look, Taryn, I've got to run. Give the kids a kiss for me and tell Robert that Lee managed to get tickets for the Reds game next week."

Katrice hung up and checked her watch. *One more hour to closing.* Opening day business had been better than she had expected. But after running around and being on her feet all day she was tired and ready to go back to the hotel.

Katrice looked around for the store manager she'd hired to run her newest store and spotted her coming from the café. "Selena, can you take over for me for a few minutes? I need to check the tracking on a shipment that's supposed to be here tomorrow morning."

"Take your time. I can handle things for a few minutes. I'll call if I need you."

Katrice sat down heavily in her overstuffed office chair and slid her shoes off. The quiet serenity of her office provided a brief moment to catch her breath and regroup. Before she checked on the book order, she noticed she had an e-mail. It was from Lee.

Hi, baby. I just wanted to let you know that the judge dismissed the case. The research you found helped us tremendously and it paid off.

I owe you (smile).

Hope to see you soon. Home just isn't the same when you're not here.

We miss you . . . but I miss you more.

Your loving and lonely husband,

Lee

Katrice smiled. *I love that man.* In the three and a half years since they'd been married she had seen first-hand the love and patience it took to be a real family. And she wouldn't trade the experience for anything in the world.

Over and over again she marveled at how fortunate she had been to have found a man who had promised to love her unconditionally and had never failed on his promise.

She looked down at her wedding ring, recalling the day Lee asked her to be his wife. It had started out as such a crazy day. First, there was the heart-to-heart she and Taryn had with their mother. They needed to convey to her once and for all that while they loved her, they could no longer live the life she wanted for them but had to make their own choices and mistakes.

Later that day Katrice had driven her mother around Benton Lake, to share with her the things, people, and places that gave her a sense of home. She introduced her mother to her neighbors. She took her to the lake and talked about the time spent there with Grandma Harry and more recently with Lee and his family. They drove past the small church that Katrice occasionally attended. The turning point, however, had been their last stop before going to the Olivers' cookout, Book Wares.

Melinda seemed amazed by the business her daughter had started from scratch and equally ashamed that she hadn't acknowledged her accomplishment sooner. She had been especially impressed by Katrice's interaction with her staff and was moved by their loyalty and dedication to her.

That day for the first time since she could remember in her adult life, Katrice heard her mother utter words she had longed to hear: *I'm proud of you.*

By the time they had arrived at Sam's for the cookout, Katrice's need to see Lee had made her realize and fully accept that she could open her heart to love and happiness. Telling Lee she loved him proved to be the beginning of that happiness.

"Katrice, there's a customer out here who asked to see the owner."

Logging out of her e-mail account, Katrice hoped she wouldn't have to face a disgruntled customer. Hopefully, it would turn out to be someone who wanted to book an event at Book Wares.

"They're in the café," Selena said.

Even though it was almost closing time, quite a few patrons lingered at the small café tables. She looked over the group, hoping to catch the eye of the person looking for her, but then she heard a small voice squeal, "Mommy!"

Reaching down to scoop up her bright-eyed, dimpled angel, her heart swelled with love for her son.

He wrapped his chubby little arms around her neck and planted sloppy kisses on her cheek. "I missed you," he said.

Hugging his little body tightly and drinking in his little boy smell she said, "I missed you, too, sweetie, and I am *soooo* happy to see you." She placed him down gently and asked, "Where's Daddy?"

"Right here, baby."

After all this time, Lee's presence still made her heart flutter. It was something she never grew weary of.

Lee kissed his wife. "I couldn't wait until Sunday."

Katrice leaned her head to the side. "And you drove all the way to Cambridge because you couldn't wait two more days?"

"It was two hours well spent."

Leading her back to her office, Lee made eye contact with Selena and nodded as she whisked Taj off to the children's book area.

When they were alone, he said, "Woman, I would have walked here barefooted if I had to."

Katrice laughed but didn't doubt him for one minute.

"Can Selena and the crew close up without your help tonight?"

Katrice started to protest but stopped when she realized that her husband wasn't asking so much as telling her.

"Dr. Roland said that you're to start taking it easy," he reminded her.

Katrice sat down heavily in her chair and pushed off her shoes.

He knelt beside her and patted her protruding belly. "If this little one is as feisty as her mother, I predict she'll be making her presence known much sooner than expected."

Shifting her weight, she felt a sharp kick to her ribs. "I don't doubt that. With all of the kicking, poking, and prodding that she has been doing today I'm beginning to wonder if we're going to make it four more weeks."

Lee spun her chair around to face him and began massaging her feet. "Kyra and Vonda finished the curtains for the baby's room and made a matching cushion for the rocker."

"Angels," she said, trying to hide the tiredness in her voice.

"Oh, yeah, your mother called. She said to let her know if she's needed when the baby is born. I told her we'd keep in touch."

Katrice's relationship with her mother had changed a lot over the years. While old habits died hard, Melinda had finally understood that she had to let her daughters live their own lives or risk losing them.

"Come on, baby," Lee said, helping to put her shoes back on. "Let's go to the hotel. I'll run a hot bath for you and order room service. Taj and I will even go out and get some of those little donuts that you like. How does that sound?"

"Like heaven," she replied, extending her arms for help getting out of her chair. "By the way, have I told you lately how much I love you and how happy I am to have you in my life?"

Pulling her gently to her feet, Lee replied, "Even if you said it a million times a day, I would never get tired of hearing it. Sweetheart, you have brought more joy to my life than I ever thought possible, and I didn't know I could love anyone as much as I love you." He kissed her tenderly.

When the kiss ended, she looked up at Lee and smiled. "I'm glad you were impatient and couldn't wait to see *us*," she said, resting her hand on her tummy.

Returning her smile and flashing his dimple, he took Katrice by the hand and said, "Come on, Mrs. Oliver, let's go."

"Home?"

"Yes, baby, home."

The End

ABOUT THE AUTHOR

Alicia Wiggins began her wring career more than ten years ago. She has had a lot of fun creating characters that she hopes readers fall in love with.

Alicia is a graduate of Central State University and Franklin University. She spends her days wonderfully entwined in the world of insurance and her nights caught up in drama and romance. When she's not writing, Alicia enjoys reading, critiquing horror movies, and baking.

An Ohio native, Alicia lives with her three children and beloved cat. She also loves to travel, but finds there's no place like home.

2009 Reprint Mass Market Titles
January

I'm Gonna Make You Love Me
Gwyneth Bolton
ISBN-13: 978-1-58571-294-6
$6.99

Shades of Desire
Monica White
ISBN-13: 978-1-58571-292-2
$6.99

February

A Love of Her Own
Cheris Hodges
ISBN-13: 978-1-58571-293-9
$6.99

Color of Trouble
Dyanne Davis
ISBN-13: 978-1-58571-294-6
$6.99

March

Twist of Fate
Beverly Clark
ISBN-13: 978-1-58571-295-3
$6.99

Chances
Pamela Leigh Starr
ISBN-13: 978-1-58571-296-0
$6.99

April

Sinful Intentions
Crystal Rhodes
ISBN-13: 978-1-585712-297-7
$6.99

Rock Star
Roslyn Hardy Holcomb
ISBN-13: 978-1-58571-298-4
$6.99

May

Paths of Fire
T.T. Henderson
ISBN-13: 978-1-58571-343-1
$6.99

Caught Up in the Rapture
Lisa Riley
ISBN-13: 978-1-58571-344-8
$6.99

June

Reckless Surrender
Rochelle Alers
ISBN-13: 978-1-58571-345-5
$6.99

No Ordinary Love
Angela Weaver
ISBN-13: 978-1-58571-346-2
$6.99

A PLACE LIKE HOME

2009 Reprint Mass Market Titles (continued)

July

Intentional Mistakes
Michele Sudler
ISBN-13: 978-1-58571-347-9
$6.99

It's In His Kiss
Reon Carter
ISBN-13: 978-1-58571-348-6
$6.99

August

Unfinished Love Affair
Barbara Keaton
ISBN-13: 978-1-58571-349-3
$6.99

A Perfect Place to Pray
I.L Goodwin
ISBN-13: 978-1-58571-299-1
$6.99

September

Love in High Gear
Charlotte Roy
ISBN-13: 978-1-58571-355-4
$6.99

Ebony Eyes
Kei Swanson
ISBN-13: 978-1-58571-356-1
$6.99

October

Midnight Clear, Part I
Leslie Esdale/Carmen Green
ISBN-13: 978-1-58571-357-8
$6.99

Midnight Clear, Part II
Gwynne Forster/Monica
   Jackson
ISBN-13: 978-1-58571-358-5
$6.99

November

Midnight Peril
Vicki Andrews
ISBN-13: 978-1-58571-359-2
$6.99

One Day At A Time
Bella McFarland
ISBN-13: 978-1-58571-360-8
$6.99

December

Just An Affair
Eugenia O'Neal
ISBN-13: 978-1-58571-361-5
$6.99

Shades of Brown
Denise Becker
ISBN-13: 978-1-58571-362-2
$6.99

2009 New Mass Market Titles

January

Singing A Song…
Crystal Rhodes
ISBN-13: 978-1-58571-283-0
$6.99

Look Both Ways
Joan Early
ISBN-13: 978-1-58571-284-7
$6.99

February

Six O'Clock
Katrina Spencer
ISBN-13: 978-1-58571-285-4
$6.99

Red Sky
Renee Alexis
ISBN-13: 978-1-58571-286-1
$6.99

March

Anything But Love
Celya Bowers
ISBN-13: 978-1-58571-287-8
$6.99

Tempting Faith
Crystal Hubbard
ISBN-13: 978-1-58571-288-5
$6.99

April

If I Were Your Woman
La Connie Taylor-Jones
ISBN-13: 978-1-58571-289-2
$6.99

Best Of Luck Elsewhere
Trisha Haddad
ISBN-13: 978-1-58571-290-8
$6.99

May

All I'll Ever Need
Mildred Riley
ISBN-13: 978-1-58571-335-6
$6.99

A Place Like Home
Alicia Wiggins
ISBN-13: 978-1-58571-336-3
$6.99

June

Best Foot Forward
Michele Sudler
ISBN-13: 978-1-58571-337-0
$6.99

It's In the Rhythm
Sammie Ward
ISBN-13: 978-1-58571-338-7
$6.99

A PLACE LIKE HOME

2009 New Mass Market Titles (continued)
July

Checks and Balances
Elaine Sims
ISBN-13: 978-1-58571-339-4
$6.99

Save Me
Africa Fine
ISBN-13: 978-1-58571-340-0
$6.99

August

When Lightening Strikes
Michele Cameron
ISBN-13: 978-1-58571-369-1
$6.99

Blindsided
Tammy Williams
ISBN-13: 978-1-58571-342-4
$6.99

September

2 Good
Celya Bowers
ISBN-13: 978-1-58571-350-9
$6.99

Waiting for Mr. Darcy
Chamein Canton
ISBN-13: 978-1-58571-351-6
$6.99

October

Fireflies
Joan Early
ISBN-13: 978-1-58571-352-3
$6.99

Frost On My Window
Angela Weaver
ISBN-13: 978-1-58571-353-0
$6.99

November

Waiting in the Shadows
Michele Sudler
ISBN-13: 978-1-58571-364-6
$6.99

Fixin' Tyrone
Keith Walker
ISBN-13: 978-1-58571-365-3
$6.99

December

Dream Keeper
Gail McFarland
ISBN-13: 978-1-58571-366-0
$6.99

Another Memory
Pamela Ridley
ISBN-13: 978-1-58571-367-7
$6.99

Other Genesis Press, Inc. Titles

Other Genesis Press, Inc. Titles (continued)

Other Genesis Press, Inc. Titles (continued)

Ebony Angel	Deatri King-Bey	$9.95
Ebony Butterfly II	Delilah Dawson	$14.95
Echoes of Yesterday	Beverly Clark	$9.95
Eden's Garden	Elizabeth Rose	$8.95
Eve's Prescription	Edwina Martin Arnold	$8.95
Everlastin' Love	Gay G. Gunn	$8.95
Everlasting Moments	Dorothy Elizabeth Love	$8.95
Everything and More	Sinclair Lebeau	$8.95
Everything but Love	Natalie Dunbar	$8.95
Falling	Natalie Dunbar	$9.95
Fate	Pamela Leigh Starr	$8.95
Finding Isabella	A.J. Garrotto	$8.95
Forbidden Quest	Dar Tomlinson	$10.95
Forever Love	Wanda Y. Thomas	$8.95
From the Ashes	Kathleen Suzanne	$8.95
	Jeanne Sumerix	
Gentle Yearning	Rochelle Alers	$10.95
Glory of Love	Sinclair LeBeau	$10.95
Go Gentle into that Good Night	Malcom Boyd	$12.95
Goldengroove	Mary Beth Craft	$16.95
Groove, Bang, and Jive	Steve Cannon	$8.99
Hand in Glove	Andrea Jackson	$9.95
Hard to Love	Kimberley White	$9.95
Hart & Soul	Angie Daniels	$8.95
Heart of the Phoenix	A.C. Arthur	$9.95
Heartbeat	Stephanie Bedwell-Grime	$8.95
Hearts Remember	M. Loui Quezada	$8.95
Hidden Memories	Robin Allen	$10.95
Higher Ground	Leah Latimer	$19.95
Hitler, the War, and the Pope	Ronald Rychiak	$26.95
How to Write a Romance	Kathryn Falk	$18.95
I Married a Reclining Chair	Lisa M. Fuhs	$8.95
I'll Be Your Shelter	Giselle Carmichael	$8.95
I'll Paint a Sun	A.J. Garrotto	$9.95

Other Genesis Press, Inc. Titles (continued)

Icie	Pamela Leigh Starr	$8.95
Illusions	Pamela Leigh Starr	$8.95
Indigo After Dark Vol. I	Nia Dixon/Angelique	$10.95
Indigo After Dark Vol. II	Dolores Bundy/ Cole Riley	$10.95
Indigo After Dark Vol. III	Montana Blue/ Coco Morena	$10.95
Indigo After Dark Vol. IV	Cassandra Colt/	$14.95
Indigo After Dark Vol. V	Delilah Dawson	$14.95
Indiscretions	Donna Hill	$8.95
Intentional Mistakes	Michele Sudler	$9.95
Interlude	Donna Hill	$8.95
Intimate Intentions	Angie Daniels	$8.95
It's Not Over Yet	J.J. Michael	$9.95
Jolie's Surrender	Edwina Martin-Arnold	$8.95
Kiss or Keep	Debra Phillips	$8.95
Lace	Giselle Carmichael	$9.95
Lady Preacher	K.T. Richey	$6.99
Last Train to Memphis	Elsa Cook	$12.95
Lasting Valor	Ken Olsen	$24.95
Let Us Prey	Hunter Lundy	$25.95
Lies Too Long	Pamela Ridley	$13.95
Life Is Never As It Seems	J.J. Michael	$12.95
Lighter Shade of Brown	Vicki Andrews	$8.95
Looking for Lily	Africa Fine	$6.99
Love Always	Mildred E. Riley	$10.95
Love Doesn't Come Easy	Charlyne Dickerson	$8.95
Love Unveiled	Gloria Greene	$10.95
Love's Deception	Charlene Berry	$10.95
Love's Destiny	M. Loui Quezada	$8.95
Love's Secrets	Yolanda McVey	$6.99
Mae's Promise	Melody Walcott	$8.95
Magnolia Sunset	Giselle Carmichael	$8.95
Many Shades of Gray	Dyanne Davis	$6.99
Matters of Life and Death	Lesego Malepe, Ph.D.	$15.95

Other Genesis Press, Inc. Titles (continued)

Meant to Be	Jeanne Sumerix	$8.95
Midnight Clear (Anthology)	Leslie Esdaile Gwynne Forster Carmen Green Monica Jackson	$10.95
Midnight Magic	Gwynne Forster	$8.95
Midnight Peril	Vicki Andrews	$10.95
Misconceptions	Pamela Leigh Starr	$9.95
Moments of Clarity	Michele Cameron	$6.99
Montgomery's Children	Richard Perry	$14.95
Mr Fix-It	Crystal Hubbard	$6.99
My Buffalo Soldier	Barbara B. K. Reeves	$8.95
Naked Soul	Gwynne Forster	$8.95
Never Say Never	Michele Cameron	$6.99
Next to Last Chance	Louisa Dixon	$24.95
No Apologies	Seressia Glass	$8.95
No Commitment Required	Seressia Glass	$8.95
No Regrets	Mildred E. Riley	$8.95
Not His Type	Chamein Canton	$6.99
Nowhere to Run	Gay G. Gunn	$10.95
O Bed! O Breakfast!	Rob Kuehnle	$14.95
Object of His Desire	A. C. Arthur	$8.95
Office Policy	A. C. Arthur	$9.95
Once in a Blue Moon	Dorianne Cole	$9.95
One Day at a Time	Bella McFarland	$8.95
One in A Million	Barbara Keaton	$6.99
One of These Days	Michele Sudler	$9.95
Outside Chance	Louisa Dixon	$24.95
Passion	T.T. Henderson	$10.95
Passion's Blood	Cherif Fortin	$22.95
Passion's Furies	AlTonya Washington	$6.99
Passion's Journey	Wanda Y. Thomas	$8.95
Past Promises	Jahmel West	$8.95
Path of Fire	T.T. Henderson	$8.95
Path of Thorns	Annetta P. Lee	$9.95

Other Genesis Press, Inc. Titles (continued)

Peace Be Still	Colette Haywood	$12.95
Picture Perfect	Reon Carter	$8.95
Playing for Keeps	Stephanie Salinas	$8.95
Pride & Joi	Gay G. Gunn	$8.95
Promises Made	Bernice Layton	$6.99
Promises to Keep	Alicia Wiggins	$8.95
Quiet Storm	Donna Hill	$10.95
Reckless Surrender	Rochelle Alers	$6.95
Red Polka Dot in a World of Plaid	Varian Johnson	$12.95
Reluctant Captive	Joyce Jackson	$8.95
Rendezvous with Fate	Jeanne Sumerix	$8.95
Revelations	Cheris F. Hodges	$8.95
Rivers of the Soul	Leslie Esdaile	$8.95
Rocky Mountain Romance	Kathleen Suzanne	$8.95
Rooms of the Heart	Donna Hill	$8.95
Rough on Rats and Tough on Cats	Chris Parker	$12.95
Secret Library Vol. 1	Nina Sheridan	$18.95
Secret Library Vol. 2	Cassandra Colt	$8.95
Secret Thunder	Annetta P. Lee	$9.95
Shades of Brown	Denise Becker	$8.95
Shades of Desire	Monica White	$8.95
Shadows in the Moonlight	Jeanne Sumerix	$8.95
Sin	Crystal Rhodes	$8.95
Small Whispers	Annetta P. Lee	$6.99
So Amazing	Sinclair LeBeau	$8.95
Somebody's Someone	Sinclair LeBeau	$8.95
Someone to Love	Alicia Wiggins	$8.95
Song in the Park	Martin Brant	$15.95
Soul Eyes	Wayne L. Wilson	$12.95
Soul to Soul	Donna Hill	$8.95
Southern Comfort	J.M. Jeffries	$8.95
Southern Fried Standards	S.R. Maddox	$6.99
Still the Storm	Sharon Robinson	$8.95

Other Genesis Press, Inc. Titles (continued)

Other Genesis Press, Inc. Titles (continued)

Tiger Woods	Libby Hughes	$5.95
Time is of the Essence	Angie Daniels	$9.95
Timeless Devotion	Bella McFarland	$9.95
Tomorrow's Promise	Leslie Esdaile	$8.95
Truly Inseparable	Wanda Y. Thomas	$8.95
Two Sides to Every Story	Dyanne Davis	$9.95
Unbreak My Heart	Dar Tomlinson	$8.95
Uncommon Prayer	Kenneth Swanson	$9.95
Unconditional Love	Alicia Wiggins	$8.95
Unconditional	A.C. Arthur	$9.95
Undying Love	Renee Alexis	$6.99
Until Death Do Us Part	Susan Paul	$8.95
Vows of Passion	Bella McFarland	$9.95
Wedding Gown	Dyanne Davis	$8.95
What's Under Benjamin's Bed	Sandra Schaffer	$8.95
When A Man Loves A Woman	La Connie Taylor-Jones	$6.99
When Dreams Float	Dorothy Elizabeth Love	$8.95
When I'm With You	LaConnie Taylor-Jones	$6.99
Where I Want To Be	Maryam Diaab	$6.99
Whispers in the Night	Dorothy Elizabeth Love	$8.95
Whispers in the Sand	LaFlorya Gauthier	$10.95
Who's That Lady?	Andrea Jackson	$9.95
Wild Ravens	Altonya Washington	$9.95
Yesterday Is Gone	Beverly Clark	$10.95
Yesterday's Dreams, Tomorrow's Promises	Reon Laudat	$8.95
Your Precious Love	Sinclair LeBeau	$8.95

Order Form

Mail to: Genesis Press, Inc.
P.O. Box 101
Columbus, MS 39703

Name _____

Address _____

City/State _____ Zip _____

Telephone _____

Ship to (if different from above)

Name _____

Address _____

City/State _____ Zip _____

Telephone _____

Credit Card Information

Credit Card # _____ ☐ Visa ☐ Mastercard

Expiration Date (mm/yy) _____ ☐ AmEx ☐ Discover

Qty.	Author	Title	Price	Total

Use this order form, or call

1-888-INDIGO-1

Total for books	_____
Shipping and handling:	
$5 first two books,	
$1 each additional book	_____
Total S & H	_____
Total amount enclosed	_____

Mississippi residents add 7% sales tax